I0818185

The GIRLIE Playhouse

The GIRLIE Playhouse

a novel

V. N. Alexander

Heresy Press books may be purchased in bulk at special discounts for sales promotion, corporate gifts, fund-raising, or educational purposes. Special editions can also be created to specifications. For details, contact the Special Sales Department, Heresy Press, 307 5th Avenue, 4th Floor, New York, NY 10016 or info@skyhorsepublishing.com.

Skyhorse Publishing® is a registered trademark of Skyhorse Publishing, Inc.®, a Delaware corporation.

Visit our website at skyhorsepublishing.com.

HERESY PRESS LLC
P.O. Box 425201
Cambridge, MA 02142
heresy-press.com

10 9 8 7 6 5 4 3 2 1

Library of Congress Cataloging-in-Publication Data is available on file.

Cover design by David Ter-Avanesyan

Print ISBN: 978-1-949846-80-5
Ebook ISBN: 978-1-949846-81-2

Printed in the United States of America

To Tricia, my mother

The GIRLIE *Playhouse*

1

Inside the Girlie Playhouse, white afternoons are still discreetly extinguished in candlelit rooms, while outside the demonstrators have begun their second week. The street is lined with sleeping bags and coolers. Activists hoot and holler muddled slogans. Misguided, albeit well-meaning, City University students from the Oppression Studies Department show their support, passive, by sitting on the curb eating avocado wraps. Matrons and old ladies wag banners and jerk pickets, respectively.

I have to go under the police department's clumsy blue sawhorses just to get into work. As I do so, one of the Gideon Angels in a provocative red cap, worn stylishly askew, shows me her poster: "A Woman Is Not a Plaything."

I suppose she means Trixie. She was once my partner: pale, waifish, with long limp black hair and navy eyes. Trixie still skips through my sphincter-clenching dreams. Onstage, her skin reflected blue light; mine reflects pink. She liked sequins; I like feathers, and we danced sometimes in sync.

I loved the girl, so I can understand why just the idea of her keeps the Gideon Angels up at night, keeps their confusion tickly and keen. She was attractive, absolutely, but with a trace of tawdriness about her that—irritatingly, unreasonably—made her all the more fascinating. The Angels formed a loose circle around the Playhouse and made their demands. Our boss invited them in to have a look for themselves, but they declined.

Then came the cameras. Unfortunately, the outline of Trixie's story is, I confess, perfect for the tabloids: chock-full of sex and controversy. But there's more, if one cares to look. I'm still waiting for public television to arrive, set up, and start filming a proper documentary. Anything would be better than *Inside Story*.

Everyone, no doubt, has heard about the married man who won seven million dollars in the lottery and squandered it on seven strippers? Well, I was one of the seven, and Trixie was the favorite. (We actually received less than seven million, but the alliteration was too much for the press to resist.)

The story hit when the wife filed for divorce. Her husband—whom we knew as "Max"—was portrayed as a toothy libertine, though he was actually too preoccupied to smile much. He had a silverback gorilla build and slow, thoughtful speech, which made him a natural target for an impatient press.

The dancers fared no better. During the televised proceedings, an "expert witness"—one of our own, redheaded Audrey—provided some pretty damaging testimony. She disclosed all the details about how and why the "prodigal playboy" had taken us to a beachside "motel" (actually, it was an *inn*), and how we had each been paid for our trouble with a red sports car. In the wake of all this negative news coverage, the Girlie Playhouse became the neighborhood hot spot for about one week, and we really "raked in the dough," as reporters were quick to point out. But now that the initial excitement has died down, only the dregs remain. Most of my regulars have been scared away. Gadfly-ish rumors are going around that we will soon be closed down, boarded up, condemned.

Max's wife won her suit. When she came out of the courtroom, she looked in the cameras and sobbed, "Max, I still love you. Come home." I, like everyone else no doubt, pitied Max's attractive, humiliated little wife. Her lot was truly sad, however common.

Trixie's story, on the other hand, is gorgeously uncommon. My aim in telling it is to be kind, but above all, thorough; to be truthful, but more than that, poetic—after that farce on TV. I'd always thought Trixie was inexplicable, not easily reduced to a type. But they managed it. Yes, indeed. My own method is to complicate the issue rather than to clarify. You will never find me resting on one side or the other. To make a judgment, you see, is to stop feeling.

These days—besides the mulish protesters who have vowed never to go away—only the odd, lingering foreign correspondents remain, those who haven't quite given up on the possibility of a miraculous reappearance of our departed dear. What gets me most is the cruel stupidity of it all. And it *is* funny, yes. That's what's so horrible about it. I was laughing, with some anxiety though, to be sure, right up until the last few seconds. Now, I, like a whore, unpack my heart with words.

It was just a few hours after the second edition of *Inside Story* aired that Trixie was killed. The reporter, Simone Lambat, is now a great penitent. So much so that I feel guilty that I haven't told her that it wasn't all her fault. But, at the risk of sounding worse than I am, I must say, I enjoy seeing Simone pay.

It was actually Simone who suggested that I inform the public in general and the media in particular as to the true facts of the case. She feels I might rectify her misrepresentation of Trixie. Believe me, I'm not as interested in making Simone feel better as I am in making Trixie look better, but as Simone's interests happen to be served by my own, I will oblige her. And so it is that I have decided to speak to you at Channel 9, to you feminist journalists at the *Newgate Say*, and even to you, Gideon Angels.

Naturally, my version disputes *Inside Story*'s. Trix was not merely a tramp who trapped gullible husbands, but it's a little too difficult to say exactly what she was. Life is really lived at the crossroads: that's where you feel moral distinctions most; that's where you come to know. And I—I have sampled, as it were, both the moral and the immoral often enough to guess at the difference. That's more than most could say. So, you see there's reason to give one pause. The Girlie Playhouse deserves a fair accounting too, one that sees into the dressing room. And how far does one have to go? Not so far—be not alarmed—just far enough to touch the hem of the garment. That will do. It *must* do. No one who hasn't lived a dubious life can imagine what it means, finally, to decide what's right and what's wrong, for her, for him, for now, for then.

But then, you've anticipated such denials. Indulge me a moment. I loved Trixie—all the girls, the whole business—well enough to look intently and long. I know. My entire life has been an expression of my peculiar love for girls with meretricious charms. The mere clicking of pave-worn high heels down an empty corridor gives me a thrill.

But whence came my special fondness for topless dancers? From out of my past, that's where, straight out of my past. Let me explain.

Yes, I was wholly enamored of Trixie; that's indisputable. Never let it be said that I admired merely the idea of her or the symbol for which she stood. I loved *her*. I loved her thin arms, her automatic laugh, and her brutal temerity. I loved her more thoroughly and intimately than anyone before or since. But she wasn't the first.

When I was very young, I loved another famous stripper who met a bad end for her terrible pride. So when Trix came along, I was equipped with a kind of horrible hindsight. This precursor of Trixie's, this slain starlet, was my own mother.

2

Though Mother was murdered when I was only four, within that important brief span, she instilled in me the happy predilection for nudity. In my infancy, being naked in general was largely approved. Once, when a neighbor objected to my being diaperless in a sprinkler, my mother said the body was nothing to be ashamed of. But the neighbor was. There is no creature so denuded as an obese person. My mother taught me that most people had unsophisticated views about nudity. I learned to revere her body, as she dressed and bathed. I envied her and her stripper friends because their bodies were so attentively loved by everyone.

Later, my mother's death and the rumors about her life led to my obsession. For years, unwittingly, I sought her among "floozies," "strumpets," and others known by various such endearing euphemisms. Then I met Trixie. *Dea certe*. They both were so beautifully calm. Weirdly oblivious to others around them. Neither would listen to the wide groan of public opinion.

While Trixie was a potent reminder of Mom, I was also especially attracted to the plain fact of her. And I felt a closeness because of our rhyming names. (The memory of the DJ's "Showtime. Trixie on the front stage, Pixie on the back," haunts me even now.) Trixie was her real name, short for Beatrice.

My own name is adopted. I was first called "Pixie" in grade school because my aunt kept me in a pixie haircut, an economical home bowl cut that made me look like a boy. (I've considered switching to "Trixie," but I've developed a small but loyal following under "Pixie" and think it best to stick with it. Business is rough these days: protesters are out there with their dirty Theories and their fear.) The "Mad" part of my name is a more recent edition. I am so called by customers because of the artless way I dance.

I'm best when I'm naked, without script, without anyone trying to tell me what to do. I have this in common with most Playhouse dancers. For reasons that should be obvious, strippers have a lot in common. It takes a special kind of girl to do that kind of thing, you know.

So, I'm sympathetic to the plight of my peers, attuned to their feelings, wants, fears, and so on, even if such things don't come up in discussion per se. Shyness is a pretty common affliction. I've a terrible time making friends. Most of the time I sit around watching other people going about their lives. This, however, makes me a pretty good reporter. Lucky for you.

Being shy, in case you don't understand this condition, doesn't prevent one from being brave. The more shy the girl, the more courageous are her acts. Being timid and apprehensive has made me find other avenues of expression. I think I've found the one that requires more courage and is, in the end, most effective.

So much for the unique architecture of my mind for now. Doubtless, you want simple facts. I'm five-foot four barefoot and five-foot ten in four-inch heels. I have very long, white-blonde hair (actually it's peculiarly clear, like silken strands of fiber optics), and spooky dark brown eyes and brows like my mother. My features are delicate and bright, somewhat on the juvenile side. I'm usually described as "cute." I would have much preferred "good-looking" or even "interesting" such as my mother was called. Customers usually guess I'm about nineteen. I'm in excellent shape—a Playhouse dancer has to be—and my breasts are a B cup. (I think it's okay to mention that, given my profession and all.) I'm not the most attractive dancer at the Playhouse. Some of the girls are inhumanly beautiful, you know, and sometimes we have to share a stage, but I have my own special charisma, which gets me through the day. I like being naked, and I think it shows (everything shows up there).

When I do wear clothes, I wear shortish A-line dresses with Empire waists and high collars. I've never worn pantyhose in my life, only stockings. I don't wear jewelry of any kind and never much makeup. I've been told not to. My nails are unpainted. I tend to smile a lot at nothing.

Ever since the day Mother died, I have been dancing, always naked, usually alone, even on the days I don't go into the cabaret. Barefoot in the late morning, I switch on the kitchen radio. Then I stand on the porch in my short white nightie, sipping coffee, and thoughtfully explore my navel with my finger. Beyond my porch, there is always some blackbird in the man-sized red maple to scrutinize me. Any pair of eyes will do.

Shaking out my bed-rumpled hair, I begin to hum and dance, and I watch my reflection swaying prettily in the window glass. I recall a certain (yawning) feeling that I'd once forgotten—along with others in that murky chronicle of my life called "fond memories." Dancing works on me like a favorite perfume: when I smell the Iris 99 Mother wore on that day—so vivid, so compelling—the whole episode is replayed. I think about all that frustrated hope, all that unused future, as I struggle out of my nightie and step from the warm folded cotton that has just fallen to the floor.

I dance as if no one were watching, as if I were completely alone and nothing mattered, nothing at all. Have you ever seen yourself naked? Really naked? Without those unfortunate experiences? Those uncomfortable lovers? Can you throw them off, like a damp wool coat? Who are you without them? When the night has no moon and no one has picked you up at the bus station and you're walking home alone? Can you describe yourself in detail without faltering, overshooting, or flinching? And if you could—so few of us can—would you feel untroubled about it? And guileless too? I do. I can. I know that moment, marked by the slight rise in body temperature, when I'm dancing and the audience begins to take a harder look. They look with quiet wonder and recognition. They peep each out of their private little holes, hooded in darkness, without letting on to the others that they are perceiving this thing, this creature, this naked something, dancing without music, without applause, without motive, without sense, merely dancing, for her life, it seems, quietly, maniacally for her life.

You ask yourselves, Why? Well, look at this thorny crown:

I was born in a small town actually named Gunsmoke City. But for the thin photo album labeled "Gunsmoke Years" and Mom's incomplete diary, I would have few dim, balmy memories of her. With the help of these dear photos and notes, I have nursed the half-forgotten past into a very real, complex recollection, featuring Mom in an Easter hat and sunshades holding infant me. The camera clicks; she gives me another feathery kiss on my powdered belly. My feet fidget in helpless joy. My father is the broad-shouldered shadow who snapped the shutter with the sun behind him. He owned a lake resort in the middle of nowhere, near Gunsmoke, called Runaway Stay.

In the summer before I was born, Mother had received a personalized letter that grandly announced she was the winner of a secret prize. She only had to drive to Runaway Stay to claim it, and if she did, she would be reimbursed in five silver dollars for the spent gas. While she was claiming her imitation diamond necklace, sly Dad sold her a time-share condominium for a week in August. That August

I was conceived. Mother, who never married Dad, ended up renting a cabin year-round in Gunsmoke on East River Lake. She was shot in the stomach on a Sunday as we walked home from the general store. She bled to death under the noonday sun on dusty, lime-coated Farm Road 7 while mad swarms of cicadas screamed in the old gnarled oaks.

Well after midnight I was found naked on a dirt driveway, about a mile from the scene, with a grimy face, a blood-smeared belly, and a half-eaten package of sugar taffy in my hand. I was dancing frantically and deliberately to some distant music. The sheriff's headlights turned on me and were reflected in my eyes. I froze like an ill-fated deer.

Mother, who was a smart woman despite the one or two mistakes that led to my existence, had provided for me. She had saved money from dancing and with eerie foresight had purchased a sizable sudden-death policy. I was taken in by an impoverished, jealous aunt, but when it became evident that I would look exactly like my mother, with her inexplicably clear hair, dark brows, bobbed nose, and impish grin, I was shipped off to an expensive girls' school upstate, whose stately buildings perched upon a weathered hill I have since, in the process of remembering, castellated and swathed in mists.

Given my case history, I was rigorously tested at the Old Hill Girls School, but I disappointed each and every psychiatrist and was reluctantly but finally given a clean bill of mental health. Though clinically sane, I am, admittedly, very sensitive, not personally, but sensitive to others. When the Rorschach test was administered *I* could only see a semi-symmetrical inkblot, but I was able to tell the stale doctor what my classmates would see. Little Peau Corne would see a moonrise reflected in water (you had to turn the card sideways). I guessed Rose Mallow would see a pair of hibiscus flowers, and Olive Greene would imagine two bulls locking horns. I was right. They had. The excitable doctor, with caterpillar brows on alert, ushered me out of his office, and held it was some kind of prank. However, it was only that I had loved all of them, who had been at various times my bedmates, now tucked in for eternity in the mind's cold, stiff linen.

Shortly after graduating from boarding school, I inherited a garden cottage. I have lived here since, quite alone, quite happy. The house is small, but the garden is large, and I am cultivating it. It's a wildflower garden, so it needs more love than time. It isn't neat; it is not orderly. It has accidental structure amid the strewn bluets and scattered bird's foot violets. It was planted years ago by my great-grandmother, a mad Central Eastern immigrant who was seven inches taller than her husband and never wore "gotchees" under her skirt. Her perennial pyrotechnics still explode and fade within predetermined weeks. All one has to do is tend a bit. Pluck a weed here. Extinguish a mite life there. Ebony spleenwort, leaky hoses, logs, snowmelt, and pale skin; flora, peach nipples, and callused feet.

There's a resemblance between flowers and dancers. Sammy, for instance. A miniature variety, known as Red-lipped Lily, Star-lily, or simply Samantha Star. Audrey was a kind of whorled loosestrife in garden terms. Jesse was so like a daisy—completely unsuspecting of her sex appeal—that when she disrobed, she wore the same smile she wore to an audition or to thankfully receive her change at a ticket window. Andie would be a red poppy with prickly fuzz on her twisted stem. Sidney was a black-eyed Susan, doleful, wide-eyed, open.

One left the stage; another mounted. And when one was in bloom, I thought she was the best I had ever seen. And then a girl like Trixie pushes her way through; all others are diminished. She was all flora, all seasons, all.

Milksop I am not. My deliberate preciousness is but a veneer to cover knotty-pine irony. Given the choice to look back with bitterness or insane optimism, I elected the latter.

As to me, well, *I* am a dormant bulb, asleep in clayish, pitch-black earth. I'm still six years old, in my aunt's hallway, wearing a full red skirt with blue piping and matching bloomers; I am pirouetting, and my skirt is straight as a saucer. I know I am beautiful. I know my skinny immature legs are nimble and look lovely. I know Uncle Romeo (not really an uncle but a family friend) can see my bloomers. This is perfectly acceptable because they match my dress. Uncle Romeo nods politely, and an appreciative smile curls within his goatee. He pats his lap. I give him the kiss he demands—and wish I were older.

But then someone told me to stop. "Stop it," Auntie said, "Stop that prancing around like a little harlot, you Gypsy girl. Where is your modesty?" Romeo was embarrassed. How dare she think such things?

I stamped my tiny foot and demanded, "What was I doing wrong?"

"It's not what you're doing. It's what everyone'll think."

"I don't care what they think."

At twenty-one I completed an undergraduate degree—"Honors Liberal Arts," which included "life experience" credit for some poetry I'd composed at age ten. I could take any subject I could claim to be able to write poetry about, sing or dance to. Included were: Music Appreciation, Linguistics (a favorite), Astronomy I & II, Anthropology (Physical and Cultural), and Squash, among others. After graduation, I immediately sought employment as a topless dancer.

I called an old friend of Mom's, Candy Bar, now residing east of Capitol on a sweet red onion farm (in that part of the country you eat them like apples). In 1959, she'd been jailed for possession of marijuana. Story goes she was set up. A sheriff stopped her as she entered an unfriendly town where she was to have performed for one week. Her two-year stint at the state correctional facility pretty much ruined her. But she says she's happy hoeing onions. Candy still has her friends in the business, who had paid all her court costs, and she put me on to an agent, the son of her former agent.

Dick Peters's office was in a high-rise apartment. An old woman leered as I danced down the narrow hall in search of apartment 30B (my size, incidentally). I pushed the bell, *bing*; I released it, *bong*. When he buzzed me in, I found him cradling the phone receiver against his fat shoulder and meaty red ear. "Sit down," he gestured. I chose a folding chair in the center of the nearly empty room. "Not there," he said. "Here." By him. He shouted at a poker buddy on the other end of the line as if he were a cabaret owner or a Mafia boss. "We're straight then, pal? Good. See ya at eight." Mr. Peters slammed down the phone and looked me straight in the eye. "So you wanna to be a dancer, hey?" It was not the first time he had so delivered that line. "Exotic dancer, topless dancer, striptease dancer, nude dancer, go-go dancer?"

I told him I thought people might confuse "erotic" with "exotic"; "topless" sounded too negative; I didn't want to "tease" anyone; "nude" seemed dull like the color, and "go-go" sounded silly but might be fun. He stared at me like the boarding school psychiatrist used to do, then after a dramatic pause, he convulsed into action and scribbled down the addresses of three cabarets.

"You're a fine-looking gal," he said as I was leaving. "Got your mother's looks."

I spun around, in a borrowed pair of her pointy leather pumps—tobacco brown. "You knew my mom?"

He had seen her once, he said and threw a pointed finger at the wall, and following the trajectory, I saw a grainy black-and-white photo of a nude creature with brilliantly light hair, standing tiptoe in a pure, white world.

The first place Mr. Peters sent me was Some Chorus Line, a swanky private club. From beyond the red velvet rope and plush carpet foyer, I overheard a weary, "One and two and three and . . ." A team of dancers, arranged according to height, kicked and turned with inhuman precision. It was an undressing rehearsal. Velcro ripped and twelve sequined gowns split down the back and were flung outward, gliding stingray-like to the floor. I was on the avenue before the dancing master could command another kick.

The second place, Le Mirage, proved to be nonexistent. The telephone number, which Mr. Peters had copied out in demonically tiny scrawl, was answered by a fax. The third place, Happy's, was a dingy hole of unequaled despair and degradation. The stench of stale beer in the foyer prevented me from even entering.

I walked all the way downtown, and as I happened to turn the corner of a pacific street, I came upon a charming converted house with gabled roof and bright red doors. The sign said, "The Girlie Playhouse" in neat white script. A large man came out and clasped the door open. He had quick jerky movements and hollow cheeks—like my mental picture of Dad. I went in.

The sound system was impressive, and I was told I could choose my own music. On the long runway a dancer could perform with the audience surrounding her hard by on three sides, so she was, in one sense, thrown into the thick of it with them, and, in another sense, not. An attractive bouncer hovered about. That was reassuring. There was a "warm-up" stage near the bar. Two charming older bartenders, Salvatore and Carmine, each with a hang-eye on the left side.

Incidentally, I never saw the shadowy man again. The owner, Umberto, told me later that I'd probably seen the napkin supplier's brother who'd taken over his route that day.

So, there I was surrounded by Mom's dim floral cousins. She, by the way, is the crushed bloom bookmark that conjures up what was your shining future and became your bungled past. In my own peculiar case, the treasured flower is a purple thistle, found in the "Gunsmoke Years" scrapbook, placed there so that Mom could recall the special hour of its plucking. But a man with a black shoe or pipe, no, *gun!* wanted to stop her.

But never mind. I hate to dwell on that particular man on Farm Road 7 who let an aching tentacle squeeze his trigger. The trivia of his personality muddies the waters of my thinking. What interests me is Mother, the tiptoed dancer, naked in a white room staring—with black eyes—right into your soul. Something about her makes me ache—something about all dancers.

Paradoxically, a Playhouse dancer doesn't belong unless she seems out of place. She is like the graceful creature who operates the backhoe on a construction site. She's the lovely with the preposterously green eyes who makes change at the QuickMart. She serves hot dogs at Swanky Franks. (Men think: Why is she here? There must be something wrong with her. Hey, maybe I've got a chance!) You want to take her pretty pointed shoulders and demand, "What is a splendid thing like you doing here? Stop that, you; come princess, this is no place for you."

Trixie didn't listen, and she flatly refused to stop dancing. She was frustrating. Like my mom, she assumed no responsibility for her effect on people. And Trixie had a lot of the fey charm that bewitched, bewildered, and finally bothered a repulsed lover until he squeezed the trigger, so to speak.

3

Trixie first arrived one morning, to the fulfillment of all my prodigious wishes, about three months ago, when most of the regular shift of waitresses and sleepy dancers, hauling enormous bags stuffed with costumes and cosmetics, had, as usual, packed the small dressing room. It was eleven thirty, a maddening half hour before the eight-hour day shift would begin. Down the hall came a hollow step. I turned from the mirror. Trixie dropped her big duffel bag.

"This the dressing room?" she asked in a husky voice.

"This is it!" yelled Audrey with sarcastic cheerfulness.

Trixie doffed her bowtie tap shoes, faded black cutoffs, and black halter—with fascinating speed—and revealed a boyish figure. With my lipstick cocked and poised, I watched. She rummaged through her bag with her pink tongue thoughtfully pressed upon her lip. I realized, feeling my face redden, how like my mother she was. My eyes traveled up and down her long sinewy arms and legs and lingered on her wonderfully fleshy, perfectly formed butt. She had a tight, compact little torso, like chiseled ivory, a shallow navel—a mere dent—the breasts of an athletic boy. Her hair, deep black, not shiny, fell to her waist. Her skin was very pale, thin, almost bluish. Her eyes, a strange dark blue. Her nose long and straight. She held herself like a real dancer, swayed back and head high. No comparison to the slighter joys of my past.

The regular day shift—of Jesse, Andie, Audrey, Sammy, Sidney, and myself—had been working at the cabaret together for a long time. Some brief descriptions will do. Jesse had plump breasts, which hung just low enough to be natural. She had dark-circled eyes, child-just-napping eyes, and uniformly white teeth, the better to smile with, my dove. She was unquestionably the prettiest dancer. She didn't dance much; she posed and greeted and smiled; she tossed her hair and, eyes glancing down, watched her own pretty body move calmly and elegantly to and fro. The last time I saw her she was putting on a pair of lace panties, and she said she would see me tomorrow, but did not.

Umberto had shown a streak of the avant-garde when he hired Andie. She looked out of her mask of eyeliner like a raccoon. A wise-cracking, gum-smacking brat, she had stringy, dirty-blonde hair the ends of which just brushed her prominent shoulders. She had gray eyes, a drooping nose, a wicked smile. Her rear end was so round her skirt always lifted up in the back and showed the bottom halves of twin full moons.

Audrey was Audrey.

Sammy was less than five feet, danced in platform heels, had absolutely the largest breasts I have ever seen on so small a human, and smiled constantly. It was as if she couldn't believe her luck, her breasts were so big. Sam looked seventeen, was twenty-one, had a south-of-the-border accent and a wide mouth, and was married to a mild accountant named Sol.

Sooty, voluptuous Sidney started at the Playhouse when she was eighteen. She must be twenty-five by now. She'd learned patience, grew womanly and calm. Once she let me touch her breasts. "Oh, go ahead! They're just boobs, for God's sake." They were firm and cold implants. "You get used to it." Once a talk show host had thrown cold water on her—as part of some gag—she had not flinched, just batted her dense eyelashes. Nothing shocked her. (Sidney is, by the by, the only one left here with me now, in our defamed cabaret.)

We were bound by mere spatial proximity and intimate knowledge of each other's bodies. I knew the swirls of every girl's navel; I knew the hairs that escaped bikini lines and the scars that marred otherwise flawless skin, but before we were put through this trial together, I hadn't known much about their lives outside of the Playhouse, their clothed existences, their cloaked concerns. Generally tight-lipped over matters of the heart, in our dressing-room conversation we favored a combination of false bravado, reserve, and denial. We seldom mentioned real lovers, who had to be forgotten for all practical purposes between noon and eight p.m. We talked enthusiastically about costumes and shoes—and other things that meant nothing, really. We were fiercely righteous. (Ah, but the secrets we kept from each other we blurted freely onstage.) It was in the dressing room that we did the performing for each other. It was in the dressing room that we were shy and hid things. It was under these hard fluorescent lights that we lied.

I had kept my own distance, protected behind my anthropology textbook, with a voyeur's watchful silence. Then Trixie came declaring that she hadn't danced in weeks and couldn't wait to get back onstage. "How is it up there?" Until then none of the girls had actually admitted that she liked dancing. Trixie brought a tyrannical kind of honesty, glaring, accusative. Audrey stepped back. But the others, including me, eventually began to let down our guards.

Before anyone else could answer Audrey replied, "The customers are decent"—it was just like her to elect herself our representative. Audrey was the "comic stripper": she did handstands and other tricks (for instance, she could make her breasts move on their own, together or separately). "Except," she went on, "when someone makes a disgusting comment, but most of the time the music is too loud to notice.

Not that many drunks or bachelor parties during the day shift. You get a hundred dollars salary."

"Aren't we allowed to accept tips?" asked Trixie.

"Yeah," said Audrey. "Like if you sit at a table or sometimes they send down a waitress with something."

"Make any money that way?" asked the brazen girl. Our earnings were a taboo topic; to date, no one had ever named exact figures.

"Two hundred dollars a day is pretty much average," said Sammy. We were all taken aback by this personal disclosure and silently compared our own averages favorably or unfavorably.

"Speak for yourself," barked Audrey.

Then I watched Trixie as she carefully covered, with thick stage makeup, a scar that stretched around her ankle.

She was so lovely that at first I didn't want to be put on the same stage with her, but Umberto, who had overbooked for that day and needed to double up, put us up together on the half hour. She was slighter than I, which made her lovely legs fawnlike. The vertical line of her calf continued down her instep and met her toes at a sharp angle in a very high-heel shoe. After an initial orangey tang of jealousy, I learned to love to dance with her. Everyone fell in love.

Trixie, Trixie, smiter of hearts. Pretty little Trixie. And dear, dear it *is* true that men were smitten in the Girlie Playhouse. It happened to better men than the one we called Mr. Rosamund, and lesser women than Trix did the smiting. A cabaret encouraged that kind of thing, you see. The stirring music. The pretty gestures. The inward smiles. The lights.

4

MAX WAS SO STRUCK by Trixie that his semester of Classical Mythology (which fulfilled the humanities requirement of his business degree) made him compare her to a river nymph. He just couldn't help himself, no matter how much he loved his wife. His real name was Maximilian Roquefort Price, but we called him "Mr. Rosamund" because he had mentioned, at least once to each girl, that he had a wife every bit as pretty as any dancer, and her name was Rosamund. A truly indulgent, patient wife.

To hear him talk, Rosamund was indeed an extraordinary woman. She bravely fought for the rights of the homeless to remain so and for terminally ill people to take their own lives. Her charity work kept her busy and often away from home, but that was a pleasant arrangement because her husband was often at the Playhouse.

"My wife knows exactly where I spend my time," he said to me once, proudly. "I don't have anything to hide from her." Max explained that, in her entirely liberal, understanding way, Rosamund approved of his pastime. She had read somewhere that all men were essentially voyeurs. Thus, she let him "look" because, as she said, "he was a man."

Rosamund had also been a cocktail waitress herself once, back in the eighties, before she married, when cocktail waitresses still dressed up as small animals. Thus, she could appreciate "a woman's having to work for a living." She gave Max the A-OK to go and give those poor working girls a dollar; they deserved it.

"It's a perfect marriage," said Max, fingering his elegantly dented chin. We never questioned why, if he were so happily married, he came in so often. We assumed he had his reasons. To give him credit, he never did flirt seriously with any one of us, nor we with him. Until he saw Trixie.

Max was a slow-moving, thick-bodied man about six-foot two. A corkscrew curl sprang from his widow's peak, and he interminably replaced it amid his brown waves (and is probably doing so now, wherever he is). He had an agreeable aloofness about him, an enviable easiness with the world. Morbidly attractive. Other than praise for his wife, initially he disclosed very little about his personal life. He was keeping some secret, or at least pretending to. He seemed wealthy. He referred to his southern family, the de Roqueforts, as if they were some venerable institution.

He had spent his earliest days in a Georgian home that, as he described it, might have been a statesman's or a pirate's. By the time he was five, it had been made clear to him that he would never be asked to work a day in his life and should chose a hobby to pass the time. His mother suggested horses, but he preferred books, philosophy. But then the family fortune collapsed and this event was quickly followed by his father's death. Max was the eldest with four younger sisters. He never read another book that wasn't required reading for his business degree.

Regrettably, it seemed, he now owned a Mazda car dealership. What little was left of the family fortune had been invested in a dealership largely owned by Rosamund's father. When Max was fifteen, he went to work at the dealership detailing used cars. Later, he moved up to sales. Finally, at age twenty-five, he married Rosamund, whom he had dated faithfully for three years and loved for ten. She was eighteen, and the only truly pretty thing he had ever known. The sign above the dealership was changed to Price Mazdatown. Our friend had always had a sinking feeling that his father-in-law had wanted the marriage so that he could advertise the slogan, "best price in town." In addition to having contributed the name "Price" to Rosamund's family business, he had also brought to the table the de Roquefort connection, allowing the upper-middle-class doting father to purchase old-money distinction for her. Rosamund herself was not to blame for the maneuvers of her father. How could he blame the man for wanting the best for his child of such rare beauty and generous heart?

Max accepted his life, such as it was, and he told himself and us—oh, how he kept telling us—that he was happy.

He may have been fated to work at Price Mazdatown, but he did not dedicate much of his time to car sales. He had other more pressing matters to look to, to mull over, and which made him dash out suddenly. He often stared ahead in space for minutes, then shaking off his trance, scribbled on a memo pad. We would eventually find out that Max had lately resumed his bookish interests, and he was preparing, unknown to his wife who disapproved of such things, a treatise on aesthetics. Rosamund was capable of understanding (or at least allowing for) his "masculine" desire, but never his desire for philosophy.

Twice a week Max appeared in the afternoon. He placed his gloves, dove gray, on the table and stayed about an hour.

Max had first entered the Playhouse doors about two months prior to Trixie's arrival. He had been attracted, as I had been, by the quaint style of the red wooden doors that made him pause and look up at the sign, "The Girlie Playhouse." He suddenly realized that he had never been in "that kind of place" before.

When he walked in, he was stunned momentarily by the change from sunlit street to dark cabaret. He felt like a foolish trespasser, but a pretty girl (Jesse) sitting alone at a table glanced up and smiled. On the back stage was a dancing girl (Audrey), seminude, he noted with more than a little shock and excitement. He panicked and was about to retreat, but he noticed an aged Italian bartender who was busily screwing a white towel into a glass. To him he would know what to say. Max touched the worn mahogany bar, and it woke a memory that shouldn't have stirred in a strip club.

He loved old wood, he realized. What a funny thought. Rosamund's taste went entirely against the grain of his early tastes. Her (their) house was all plastic, harshly lit with recessed bulbs from above, which cast ghastly shadows on her face as she sat across from him at dinner, at their Formica table—on his face too, probably, he mused now, wondering how, indeed, he had looked to her all these years.

"What can I get you?"

"Beer," Max said out of habit from drinking with his father-in-law. "No, make that wine, red." The bartender gave him a glass of decent house wine. Max made a friend with Salvatore by identifying it. Sal had worked at the Grand, and Max recognized some of the names that Sal tossed out. His father had spent much of his time there and had probably been served by Sal himself.

"If he don't remember me," said Sal. "He'll know my partner for sure. I used to be Carmine's barback."

"He's dead," Max admitted.

"That's too bad," said Sal with straight-faced sincerity. Max liked him.

I had been watching Max from the moment he came in. Now he noticed me at the bar.

"Max," said Sal. Sal was always quick to get a man's name. "This is Pixie. Pixie, this is Max."

Then Sal, having made a match, left to tend another customer.

"I, uh, own a car dealership. You know Price Mazdatown?"

I didn't, but then I didn't drive. "I take the train. I live in the country," I explained.

"That must be nice," he said, then he added, "This is a nice club," to be polite. We sat in silence. Then, with a sudden burst, he went on to tell me that he had been reminded by the antique mirror behind the bar of his childhood home. He suddenly felt like himself again, a self that he hadn't felt since before his father died, and he was amazed that one touch of a smooth, polished bar could have brought such a change in him. It was odd, so odd—in a place like this!

I felt at home at the Playhouse, too. It was the only place where I could talk. Strangers made it easy on each other at the Playhouse. "Yeah, I like it here a lot, too."

"But it's just a job; I understand."

"No, I actually like it," I said.

"Oh sure," he said. "The money's got to be good."

"It's okay, but really it's just that I like it."

Nervously, he began to talk about his wife. "I don't usually come to places like this. I'm married, happily married. Name's Rosamund. She could be a dancer. Got the legs for it."

I didn't know what to say, so I said, "Oh?"

"Yeah." He was encouraged by my response. "She's really pretty." He emphasized the "really" in a way that bespoke artlessness. "We've been married for ten years," and he added, as he was wont to do, "I knew her for ten before that."

"Oh sure," I said, to make him feel better.

He started to come in regularly, after, of course, he had cleared it with his wife and she had so magnanimously bestowed her magazine psychologist's endorsement upon the Playhouse.

But now that I've singled Max out, let me replace his wax figurine in the Playhouse audience. That was, after all, where he belonged in the beginning, before we came to know him. In those early days, before he got Trixie in his sights, he was just one of the men who came so often that they almost became like one of the employees. We called them the beta males.

I read somewhere, probably in one of Rosamund's kind of magazines left in the dressing room by one of the nightshift girls, that the success of strip clubs could be explained (and theoretically justified) by studying other primates. A male gorilla, you see, needs many females with whom to entrust his genetics. Darwin, according to the article, explained why men liked to go to the Playhouse, where so many women appeared one after the other. The article, which was written by a man, also declared that all women, in turn, wanted to be possessed by the one and only alpha male. In other words, men are naturally polygamous and women naturally monogamous.

This, however, contradicts life as I understand it at the Playhouse. I suppose every man who agrees with the above theory thinks he's an alpha male (the writer obviously hoped he was). Though I admit alpha males are attractive, I happen to like lots of Beta males every bit as much. The more the better.

Not having inherited a belief system along with my cottage, in college I was very interested in finding out some natural-scientific basis for right and wrong, particularly where sexual matters are concerned. Enrolling in anthropology hoping to find answers, I ultimately got none. Humans may be primates, but we're also something more. That is, we're idealistic and perverse. There is no one explanation for why we are all here at the Playhouse.

The other regulars besides Max, our dear beta males, knew the girls by their real names. They tipped less than the "amateurs." They had faithfully memorized our moves and costumes and could make informed requests. Coming every day out of habitual loneliness, they, unlike the others, often seemed to have forgotten the underlying premise of the place. The familiar Dan, for instance, openly admitted that he had grown used to our breasts, of so many shapes and sizes, and talked about the weather or local news as we lay naked at his feet, but I suppose he was hiding his real thoughts under a trench coat of indifference.

There were, however, two men, Bartholomew and Percival, who were, I seriously suspected, true eunuchs. Bartholomew, a sound technician, had installed the stereo system and continued to hang around long after he completed the job. He played billiards and played well because, he said, "It was all math." According to the DJ, "He's a genius, a fucking genius, but fucking weird."

Percival, the other Playhouse pet, was anorexic, pale with a five-o'clock shadow. His earmuff headphones blasted opera arias. He had the emotional personality of a loving three-year-old, and when he smiled, his neck tendons tightened. "Hey Percival. How ya doin', buddy?" asked Bartholomew. Percival plucked up an earphone and Wagner triumphantly escaped.

"So, how'd you end up stripping?" asked Percival.

"Have a boyfriend?" asked Bart.

"No," answered Trix. "What's the bouncer's name?"

"Calvin?" asked Bart.

Calvin was gorgeous and bald and lent style to our foyer. Prior to Trixie's arrival it had been Calvin who had consumed my time and interest. He flirted in a mock sort of way that, I suspected and hoped sometimes, belied real affection.

"Umberto is very strict about contact here," Percival explained. "Calvin had to throw a guy out once for kissing Sidney's butt when she wasn't looking." Trixie said she'd keep it in mind. "Oh do!" cried Percival with strange enthusiasm.

There was also the pool player who let his tank top slip down his big black shoulder as he shot. (He caught me staring; I blushed.) The prematurely gray attorney, who was too polite to approach Trixie; like a gentleman, he waited for her signal that—oh, cruel circumstance—he never got! The tropical gardener who first came with six buddies and then returned alone making his best effort with his best bedroom eyes, to no avail, day after day. The health club owner, who gave me a lift home once, and, having gotten the address, sent flowers every Friday for two months until I told him to cut it out. The chef in checkered trousers who sacrificed his CD because Andie had to dance to "Hawkmoon 269." Coast Guard members: Larry, Alice, and Pete. The famous pyrotechnician who lost two brothers last July. The wealthy young importer, named after a baroque composer, who wrote poetry and wished he had been born in another time when he could have loved courageously and some girl would have liked it. Cito, the ex–pro ballplayer, who, Calvin once mentioned, had a false leg.

Many mute relationships had grown between the cracks. But how could it have been otherwise, with the volume at ten? Like couples in fast cars, radios blaring, we leaned into the curves together. That was enough. I didn't want to pour our discord into the silence between songs.

In a qualified way, I loved customers, a whole big bouquet of them. I gave Bartholomew a quick hug when his cat was hit by a car. But, like Mom, I loved dancing more than them. It's a madness. It's a passion. Is it possible to love two things at once? Does Pixie ever meet her Puck? And if she did, would she survive, or would she quiver and quake and forget to get out of bed?

If I fell in love, I feared he would make me stop dancing. So, in the end, however friendly we might have been with the regulars, they were kept at a distance—despite what those protesters' signs say! It had to be that way, for our own sanity and protection. I grant that this situation is perversely unfair. While we looked into many pairs of eyes, they looked back into only one. The customers were a gray flock of undistinguished, flapping souls, applauding, changing course together, revealing briefly the white undersides of wings, then disappearing against a gray backdrop.

Trixie wasn't looking for anyone in the audience any more than anyone else. Oh, but Trixie did *seem* to be interested because she stared straight at them, and that bothered people. I remember the way Dan once pointed out Trixie. He said, "That one, the one that makes freaky eye contact all the time," stabbing two fingers at his eyes, "stares at you."

But she didn't see *him*.

Explanation is perhaps warranted here. Audrey put it well, if not rudely, once when a pet customer—who was infatuated by her approachability, her good humor, her firm, uplifted bust—asked her if she wanted him too. She looked down at him while he munched on a zucchini stick. "Want who? You?" He shyly nodded. "No, of course not. Why?"

What could a customer, just another gray pigeon, do to attract his beloved? Cough? Compliment her? Customers had no peacock feathers to fan, no opportunity to beat their chests. We had the spotlight—as Calvin had once put it, expressing long-pent-up pity for his fellow male—we had the floor.

Then Max paid the price of admission, and Trixie mounted the stage. Would her eyes linger upon him more than on anyone else? He thought they did, but angles shift, and time dulls the certainty of experience. One could never remain sure about strippers who belonged to everyone and to no one.

5

The first time Max saw Trixie at the Girlie Playhouse it had been one ordinary day. I was at the corner of the boomerang-shaped bar, watching. Audrey was on the warm-up stage, and Trixie was on the main stage dancing to a favorite song, or so it seemed by the easy way she danced in a simple slip (while, over there, Audrey rolled and squatted, all frilly lace and velvet). A light above the manager's stall began to blink, indicating a deliveryman was at the back door. Umberto went to see who it was. After a few minutes he told the girls he was sorry but he had to open the side door to let the newly repaired cigarette machine (and daylight) in. There was no other way.

Audrey's makeup was very becoming in *low* lighting. Arms akimbo, she frowned at Umberto. "Shut that door," she said.

I laughed.

The light, white and clean, enveloped the pirouetting Trixie. Her skin lit up like a blue flame. She smiled at a pretty thought. Audrey tried to complain to someone at the bar, "God, I can't believe they're leaving the door open. It breaks the mood." No one was listening. We were watching Trixie dance.

Max had gotten up and was walking to the stage. He watched, with dry-mouthed awe, the swaybacked girl. Something was happening. The hair on the back of the neck bristled. She just kept dancing in a stream of light from the open door, exposed to passersby. At first,

I was slightly embarrassed for her, then I was embarrassed for myself. In darkness or in full light, she was the same girl dancing. At this realization, I was a dandelion scattered at a wish. She was by then naked, except for a navy blue thong. Max stood by in a smoky stream of daylight. Seconds passed.

I should explain something about the way Trixie looked in that little thong. Most thongs, Andie's for instance, disappear between pressed cheeks somewhere below the tailbone and don't reappear until after they've reached under to the front side. Trixie's thong did not dive in between her cheeks. Instead her full, plump buttocks lifted up and separated, and the dark strip of material was clearly visible as it ran along, covering the easy-to-imagine tender pink button, then cupping her conspicuous full, fleshy vulva underneath. And though Trixie stood with her feet together, a large triangular gap of light shone in between her thighs. As she glanced over her shoulder, her blameless swayback posture and upturned butt, gazelle-like, seem to invite the males to mate—right there in front of everybody.

Try to imagine now that thong, only a thong, a light scrap of thong, hardly concealing the target of every male ambition, as she had ceased to dance and merely stood on the edge of the stage, backside to the audience, undulating ever so slightly. Then she looked over her shoulder at Max, looked him straight in the eye. As he came nearer, gawking at her upturned butt, he bumped into a table. Wineglasses fell to the floor, and his cosmos followed.

He stooped without looking away from Trixie to pick up the mess. The porter intervened. Max, still squatting, smiled up at Trixie, and she laughed down at him. But then, mercifully, her smile faded, and she considered Max with a grave expression that implicated him, for everybody to see.

When the song ended, Trixie stood looking at him; the DJ let the silence hover, until it was shattered by a throat being cleared. Real time and place reasserted itself. In the still-bright room, she gathered her things to her breast and ran offstage. Max immediately left, shaking his head. The thongéd creature turned and murmured to his receding silhouette, "See ya."

When Max went back to his office he didn't think about Mazdas. Quite against his will, his preoccupation with Trixie began. He told me how he had sat at his desk, receiver in hand, finger on the hookswitch, considering whether he should check to see if she was listed: T. Nichols. He also thought perhaps he might follow her home after work one day. No, that was madness. Later, while on the phone with a potential lessee, he was plagued by an ache in his groin. He closed his eyes and let the receiver fall from his ear. Startled, Max decided, for the sake of his business, if nothing else, to forget about that stripper.

But when he thought of her as "that stripper," his excitement would reconstitute itself anew. All the marks he could count against her were truly part of her charm. He started to come to the cabaret more often. He stood in the back and quietly watched her dance. He rarely spoke with the other dancers. He was becoming cynical about Sammy's too-friendly greeting. Andie's tight, measured step began to make him bitter about the exorbitant price of his drink. Perhaps Trixie was just another Audrey or Sam after all. He tried to convince himself that the Playhouse was just one of the cool places that lay along the path from office to home.

From a self-imposed distance, Max was left to imagine the warmth of Trixie's cheeks, the coolness of her hands. With bright eyes and a curiously shameless grin, he anticipated her movements. He was almost sure that she looked at him in an exceptional way, that she indulged him more than any other. Indeed, everybody could see she danced for him alone, pretty much. Sometimes, when she leaned down from the stage to greet him, her bluish white face would be aureoled in sapphire light, and he could perceive a hint of her perfume mingled with perspiration. He practically loved her prominent rib cage. She laughed like his neighbor's little boy. But more than anything, he enjoyed her mercurial legs that kicked and swung and did the splits. My, she was limber. The things she could do! And then there was that free way she said hello and smiled. That was it. It was the way she managed to appear pleasant in seedy candlelight.

He would try, as I have tried, to find words for her appeal. None would be satisfactory. In the morning, the lovely phrase he composed while falling to sleep would prove to be trite or simply untrue. Welcome, Max, to the world of meretricious charms.

Trixie still insisted that she had never even spoken to the man, not really. She had his number, somewhere (tentatively glancing in her bag, pushing some loose articles left and right), but she hadn't actually found the time, or maybe it was the reason or the courage, to call him. "He's very observant," was all she would concede.

Maybe she didn't quite understand what she did to him. Ever since she was a skinny kid, she had always considered herself rather asexual. She was wrong about that, very wrong, impossibly oblivious of her hoydenish appeal. Mom, too, flaunted her looks without any regard for who might be looking and what he might feel. I remember that much.

6

AND NOW TO ASSEMBLE some version of Trixie's past, selecting facts, choosing this one, tossing that one aside, discovering a similarity in pattern here, a strange coincidence there.

All my life I have been given to this kind of ordering. At first, that psychiatrist back at Old Hill discouraged such useless musings but later realized the logic in it. Investigating *why* is like a child's game to me; it keeps me amused and has given me purpose. These two "chance" catastrophes have so indelibly marked my life that I must look for an explanation. And it is a kind of ecstasy to discover what belongs to what. In this way, I reach a philosophy, or at any rate, *a constant great idea of mine*, that there is a phenomenal pattern in the hazy chaos of events, one that cannot be explained entirely by psychological factors, neither mine, Trixie's, nor Max's; nor by sociological factors, neither that of a strip club nor of the press—though these do play a role to be sure. Even so, probability is still daringly defied. Don't you think it's strange that this should have happened to me twice? Once might have been sufficiently explained away, but twice? And it's not even the big coincidences; it's the seemingly irrelevant, superfluous details that really tease me, that remind me of a well-composed tragedy in three acts. Surely it is not I who, looking back over their histories, supplies the pattern, pins down the upturned corner of the curtain that covers chaos.

First, an ordinary coincidence: Newspaper scraps in my mother's trunk say she won a shopping mall beauty contest. Photo: pudgy age of eight months, wrapped in white feather boa, a tiny B-movie starlet.

Trixie was also a baby star. Out of millions of baby contestants she was chosen to represent Porina on every jar from apple-cinnamon to zucchini-strained. (I bought a jar of banana-strawberry the other day, just to see her smile.) She went on to play several small parts, a movie, a few commercials.

Like my mother, Trixie was survived by a much older sister from her father's previous marriage. From what my aunt has let slip, I know Mom was made to tag along on dates, and I can imagine what that must have been like.

Aware that she was not particularly wanted, did the younger sister keep never less than four paces behind, walking with hands clasped behind her back, often outdistanced by the happy couple who were walking arm in arm without a care in the world, who, she must have known, certainly never cared enough about her to turn to check if she was still in tow? I bet most times she just barely managed to keep up, without their help, and sometimes despite their attempts to give her the slip. Did the older sister and her date duck into a dark recess and laugh at the sound of the younger's tap-shoe click, going up and down the shadowy parking lot in despair and measured panic?

I'm making this all up of course, but it seems plausible that my mother and Trixie had similar experiences as unloved younger sisters.

And do you know that Trixie probably imagined it was somehow her fault that her sister never loved her? This would explain her quiet, martyr-like reserve, tinged about the edges with a tenderness and a sense of injury. (But a passive kind of revenge festered quietly behind her nervous smile, as we shall see.)

Here's another one. Though my aunt seldom spoke about my mom's early life, she did tell me one story (meant as a cautionary tale) about how she abandoned her charge one day, forcing my mother to take a local bus. There she was, my young teen mother, standing at the stop, short skirt fluttering in the wind. An off-duty policeman pulled up in an unmarked car to ask questions. Two Chinese cooks, an elderly lady, and Mom had been waiting for a bus that was at least a half hour past due. Small-town buses, they knew, sometimes failed to come at all. "Get in," he said to Mom, forgetting the cooks and the old lady, "I can't leave you standing there, not like that." (He brought her home safely, as promised. But he might not have!)

This lost-girl appearance, I should stress, most of the Playhouse dancers had in common. People have an irresistible and unnecessary temptation to get us to safety, out of the public eye, to take us in, to keep us, but mostly just to stop us—make us cut it out.

Early on, people formed obsessions over Trixie. A Max was inevitable, like the gunman waiting for my mother. According to the *Port City Watch*, T's hometown monthly, one Wednesday afternoon a lonely woman named Ann kidnapped Trixie. Photo of Ann: Well over seventy, green eyeshadow, poorly applied. Ann had been a hat-check girl in "her day." Her common-law husband had been dead for fifty years and they had lost their only infant.

Trixie's rescue was made possible by a public announcement printed on the side of milk cartons. An anthropomorphic cow on one side, a missing Trixie with her statistics on another. Trixie herself noticed the ad as she made her own cereal one morning and simply walked home that afternoon. Incidentally, toothless Ann ate Porina baby food, and the breakfast table had been set with two likenesses of Trixie. (Ann, who was a benign but serial abductor, was later hospitalized, medicated, and studied by graduate students for the rest of her life. My former psychiatrist wrote a paper on her, another strange coincidence.)

Much of this I gleaned from yellowed newspapers, but I also talked to Mrs. Nichols. I met her at the funeral—an uncomplaining sort, tall, with big feet laboriously stuffed in flat shoes, narrow shoulders and wide hips, an inversion of Trixie. She had the same limp dark hair as Trix, but cut in a bob that revealed three knobs on the back of her neck. The long nose, which made Trix look sly, was not attractive on Mamma.

Trixie's father—so one doesn't wonder at his absence and invent all sorts of ridiculous lies and print them in a national paper for the world to read and believe—was probably a good father, but a better biophysicist. He was unreachable at the time of Trixie's death.

At seventeen, Trixie became a professional ballet dancer. (I found a pair of tattered ballet shoes in my mother's trunk.) But her career with the Port City Company ended on a dramatic note. A performance at Milton Hall. At the last minute, the choreographer had decided to cut Trixie's improvised dance solo: too impassioned—"vulgar" was his word. He was replacing it with a grossly mechanical and dead number. She suspected that in some universe there was nothing wrong, exactly, with the way she danced, and would not comply. While she sat rocking in her dressing room, looking at the floor, the choreographer screamed, "Move!" But the curtain opened on an empty stage. She smiled perversely as the applause faded and turned to a rough grumble. Then she jumped up and ran to the stage, tearing off her costume. When she appeared onstage she was completely naked.

Was her father in the audience, standing against the wall with folded arms and did he finally look up, after all those years to say, "My God, is that who my daughter is?" I myself feel a little nervous and proud just thinking about it.

Then she hopped off the stage and ran down the center aisle, past arms reaching out to try to stay her, but they couldn't. Did Trixie relive this manic scene every time she went up on the Playhouse runway, as if those hands were still trying to grab her?

She wouldn't compromise her nature. I see my mother in her here. She didn't argue or beg pardon, because she suspected that she had never done anything that was really so sinful, so much as merely imprudent—as my mother silently stood her ground, facing her gunman, pushing me behind her.

Trixie left home for college immediately after this. She got a degree in the performing arts (for teaching) and minored in psychology—crazy people had fascinated her ever since that episode with Ann. (My mother never went to college. I did find a framed teaching certificate in Mom's trunk from Ermine's School of Dance.) Trixie—she told me herself—had taken the teaching degree to please her father. She liked children, but teaching smacked too much of sacrifice and service. She wanted—don't hold this against her—to be a great person, a measureless personality, whose message would be woven in the pattern of future human beings so perfectly that you could scarce tell where she ended or began. She wanted to *dance*, and to be *known* for her dancing.

At college she was the campus waif, strange and sullen, pictured in the annual at a dance wearing an outgrown dress. Her former classmates remember that she seemed unbearably shy and are surprised how she "turned out." In those days, Trixie was lonely, except for those times when she listened to music, when the bass was deep and loud enough to make the beat vibrate in her chest. She wasn't the type to try to make friends. While she was comfortable enough discussing psychology or dance, when the topic threatened to take a personal turn, she grew apprehensive. She began to wonder how to hold her arms or how to stand. She stopped following the conversation and in her head began rehearsing her contribution, lest anyone should turn to her. Most often they did not, but when they did her response came out shaky and rehearsed, false and timid.

Rather than continue in this inauthentic way she apparently accepted her separate condition. So, it really mattered very little to her what others might think when she decided to help finance her very expensive education by working in a go-go bar.

When Trixie graduated, she got a job teaching Dance Therapy at the Port City Community Center—buoyed upon a wave that had begun with a summer internship, and dedicated, to a certain degree, to the benevolent philosophy of that organization. Enrollment increased dramatically. She practiced the therapy part of her job description subtly, by befriending her students, being frank and showing her scar. She eventually got a promotion and transferred to Northwest Community Center.

Although the pay was better and the hours shorter, the rent was higher. She sought out and found the Girlie Playhouse by consulting the yellow pages. She asked the porter, who answered the phone though he had been told a hundred times not to, if he were hiring. He said sure because he thought she had said "hearing." He had just bought new batteries for his impotent hearing aid and refused to admit it didn't work. When Trix arrived with her big blue eyes, Umberto hired her despite the fact he already had enough dancers.

Trixie had been installed by the Fates at the Girlie Playhouse for about three weeks. Customers waited upstairs with offers of cool drinks as I tarried in the dressing room when Trixie was there too. Even Calvin had been abandoned in favor of this new wonder—a sin with which he was constantly charging me. Trixie reclined on the counter. She shifted her position, complained "ouch," and pulled a lipstick tube from under her back.

Umberto came in and asked, "How's Tricks?"

"Good, Um," said Trix.

"Good, Um," mimicked Um. Umberto was one of that tribe of sneakered men who wear one gold post earring. We liked him well enough.

I asked her if Max was supposed to come in. She put her front tooth on her bottom lip. “Oh, I dunno.”

I asked if she liked him.

Coy Trixie said, “I wish all my customers were like him.”

The stair door swung open with a sudden burst of music and swung shut behind Audrey, who then came into the dressing room kicking off her shoes, which performed perfect somersaults and landed on top of my bag. “Where're my slippers? Ah,” she answered herself when she spotted the heel of her purple mule. “Dan's here,” said Audrey.

Audrey, I should explain, wasn't a bona fide stripper; she was a graphic artist. She constantly threatened to quit when she had enough money to buy the computer she wanted. She was fortunate in her figure, “C” cupped, trim-waisted, but as far as I was concerned, she was otherwise unremarkable, a weak brunette (with an occasional red shimmer in the right light). She knew it too; once she had said, “If only I didn't look like the girl next door.”

“Why don't you lighten your hair some?” I tactfully agreed.

Addressing the mirror Audrey asked, “Lighten my hair? No, that's just not me.” And so, Audrey remained a field mouse. While Trixie, stunning in green, great in silk, mastered herself in high, high heels.

“Still like your job?” asked Audrey, assuming Trixie would renounce stripping on the spot. Trixie just smiled. “Hey, Trix, how much has your mating dance got you from Mr. Rosamund?” Trixie ignored her. “That much, huh?”

7

Ah, those were the days—when we could dance to the music of our own choosing. I can hardly make it through a set *these* days, as this lesser Playhouse wheezily expires, with the same old tape replaying "Wiggle It" for but a few stragglers. And it irks me to recall how *Inside Story* dubbed "Do Me" over the song Trixie had really danced to, which was, I think, "She Talks to Angels."

I, too, now am forced to dance to "Do Me." But soon this Playhouse parody will end. How I miss Mockingbird, our tall tubular DJ whose jeans button was always undone.

I can only imagine Mockingbird's glee when Umberto first outlined his job description: "In order to get to the stairs to your booth, you'll have to go through the dressing room, filled with a dozen long-legged, warm, naked girls whose happiness, by the way, will depend on you—use the power wisely—the right music and the right mood amounts to a lot around here, and they'll be appreciative. They're friendly, easy. Of course, you'll have to put up with their gossip, learning every intimate secret that women only share with other women. You'll learn things that each and every poor beggar up there would give his left leg to know."

Not only Mockingbird but even the porter had free run of the dressing room while we changed. I never minded because we had nothing to hide. Audrey would have said we had no privacy because the management had no respect for us or because we had no shame. That's what the protesters' signs say too.

Mockingbird could have easily forgotten that he was at work and not in some warm, wet paradise somewhere, but he did his job well. He came in early and stayed late, so as not to miss a single costume change. Unfortunately, he sometimes invited his buddies down.

On one occasion, moments before his friend Pete had been upstairs, like any other, getting tipsy as he stared, with maniacal deliberation, at Trixie's pelvic mound. Now here he was not a foot or two of unbarred space from Trixie's hot, damp flesh as she stripped for her next set. She, of course, was mercilessly oblivious to his presence and his gaze, bending over, stepping delicately out of her thong (still in her shoes), exposing that pink button, trotting around the dressing room, hands on hips, wondering what to wear.

"Hey, Trix. Put some clothes on. You're going to give my friend here a heart attack."

Trixie ignored him, taking an unreasonable amount of time to find the right outfit. "See what I have to put up with?" said Mockingbird.

The DJ's door was open, and Jesse was inside the booth with him, perched upon a stool. Occasionally, he surreptitiously petted her silky tan thigh. They were often in the booth together with the door closed. Not that I objected in the least. Audrey made some criticisms about Jesse's "work ethics." An internal affair, since it would be reasonably effortless to accomplish and would therefore be so distracting, had been necessarily verboten.

Not so any longer. Before we had lived in an age of stolen, animallike joy, but on Trixie's arrival we embarked upon the golden age of stripping, and began, openly, to sample the fruits until, of course, we were finally and so unfairly banished from paradise.

Jesse gave Mockingbird a warm kiss.

"Hey, cut that out," I said, brutally flipping an innocent page in the music catalog (sham annoyance).

Umberto popped his head in and waved a folded piece of paper. "Hey, Pix, welcome back. Everything okay?"

I had called in sick the day before. Actually, I hadn't exactly been sick and Umberto knew it. I'd had a pimple on an important place. Audrey had pointed it out at the end of the day before. I had been bending and bowing all day unaware, but I'd actually had a pretty good day tipwise. Sympathy dollars.

But Umberto had come to talk about his menu. This, by the way, was the first sign that Umberto was having financial troubles (according to Calvin). Umberto looked closely now at his house of cards and wondered: Could I insert this two of spades? Do I really need this Queen of Hearts?

Had we known then what we know now, we would have discouraged Umberto's plans for change, but we approved the menu and Umberto went off happy, sneakers squeaking on the linoleum. Then Calvin appeared, at Umberto's bidding no doubt. He glared at Pete, who left without argument. "No friends in the dressing room, Mockingbird," said Calvin (formal accent, deep ragged blues singer's voice). "Everyone all right?" looking specifically at me.

It was becoming clear that Calvin had a thing for me. Every day, he grabbed me and moaned "Good morning, Pixie" into my ear. I confess his bear hugs had been for a year perhaps my only warm contact with another human being.

Trixie, I knew, was troubled by this weird situation of our job, so much intimacy and no intimacy at all, so much apparent opportunity and no real opportunity at all.

She told me that at the Northwest Community Center she had intensely personal conversations with the kids. "They tell me everything, and I have to respond. It's part of my job," she said, "But they're not *my* kids—and the men out there aren't my lovers."

"They sure aren't *mine*," Audrey had characteristically added.

"It's been months since anyone actually touched me," Trixie said. "Water, water everywhere and not a drop to drink."

We weren't equipped to deal with Trixie's uninvited honesty, her revelations that materialized like icebergs in temperate seas.

8

I JUST WENT FOR a drive—as it happens, in the car that Max gave me. It's about four thirty in the morning now. There isn't a moon to speak of. I drove the back roads slowly at first, in a trance. Then, I don't know why, I sped up to sixty and turned off my lights.

I didn't go very far like that. I chickened out. When I flipped my lights back on, incredibly, I saw a deer standing knock-kneed in the middle of the road. I slammed on the brakes, stopped inches from her hoof. She looked at me maliciously for a minute or two and then leapt, like poetry, over a dry stone wall and ran into the woods.

I'd been looking over this account of mine before I picked up my car keys and walked out, leaving lights on and door ajar. I'm getting so very tired of maintaining my pose. My happy, catchy phrases are depressing when I read them over, and right now I'm experiencing post-narrative revulsion. What made me want to turn off my head-lights and accelerate was, among the other things, a song that came on the radio: "I wish I were special, but I'm a creep." Sometimes, you know, the mania wears off and depression comes crashing down. I want to be happy. I want to understand more than there is.

I'm getting a little worried that my desire to make everything fit is making me cram this square peg into that round hole. God help me if I'm mistaken about what's happened and what it all means, or if it has any meaning at all. I have half a mind to stop right here, give up, sit in my garden and wait for Calvin. I hope he's coming soon. If I do manage to turn over and start again, it's only because, I don't know, I found the missing link or something, and I'm all excited again to go on.

That space represents a very big sigh, the kind that trembles. I realize I must keep it up, this nervously polished performance of mine, because, you see, I can't bear the thought of anyone seeing me unhappy with myself. I don't want to be pathetic, nor some kind of wretched victim. I haven't yet mentioned the trials of standing naked before those who are there literally to judge you, reward or condemn you. I don't dwell upon the unreturned smiles, men who looked away. Success is usually so easy—when you understand them—that talking about failures seems a petty business. But just so you know, I have been humiliated. I have listened to assessments of my body made in the loudest frankest tones. I have been told where I am lucky and where I am not. Some days I am all round and swollen, like a Botticelli girl, starved but three months with child. When I have to share the stage with the super-busty Sidney and all the men collect down at her end, and she is radiant and superb, I keep my smile up, though I feel like crying and no one looks at me.

Onstage there is nowhere to hide. We are super-vulnerable to everyday flaws. Every morning we dancers have to check every inch and crack of our bodies for pimples and rogue hairs.

But I take a deep breath and I smile. I mount the stage and the music begins to vibrate in my chest. The lights shine everywhere. No one can get away. We are all of us defective here, some of us less ashamed of it than others. I know all about that dimple on my butt. I know my calves are too thin and my thighs are relatively full, which makes me look something like a grasshopper or a kangaroo. I know. I've glanced at the mirrors around the stage a time or two and *I have been shocked more than anyone to see myself naked in public.*

But I'm here. And while the breath of the men constantly threatens to extinguish, it actually feeds my flame.

9

I RUMMAGE ONCE MORE through Mother's trunk. Peeling labels that decorate the heavy lid inform me that she danced at cabarets from Mount Seymour to Veiled Valley, from Rococo Plains to Desert Lakes, before settling in Capitol City. Tired of flitting from place to place? Attracted to something or someone in particular in Capitol? I think so.

My father must have been a regular patron at the Capitol Cabaret. Here we have his special club member's key. Also, signed receipts for bar tabs. A '59 grand opening photo of sober-suited members and important staff. Unfortunately, Dad stands beside a waiter with an uplifted tray, and in this only photo I have of him, his features are mostly in shadow.

Here we have Mom's diary, a small leather volume of 150 pages, only the first ten of which are filled. By strange coincidence my mom began keeping a diary on the day that she received that promotion from Runaway Stay. I have in my hand the pamphlet depicting a group of log cabins nestled in an oak grove near a murky lake. The thing would have had no real significance when she opened her mail since she didn't know Dad worked there, and it's hard to see why it might have interested her, unless you figure she simply liked the name. "Runaway Stay" is moderately clever, encouraging one to seek new freedom by finding a new home. In my opinion, it addressed the same sadness that had lately prompted her to start a diary. While safeguarding her most private thoughts, I will tell you that she wrote that she was beginning to feel weary, not of dancing, but of going home alone to her fancy high-rise, ogled by the silent doorman, the elevator boy, the neighbor.

Now, I ask you, how could it be that such a vivacious wight as my mother was not properly mated? I would like to know, for I, too, am so alone.

After cataloging a short series of failed romances (interesting side note: two out of the four men's names rhymed with "fair"), she had a sudden revelation that her lover would have to be a customer, someone who would not be owed an explanation. I assume that she had not attempted to date a customer before.

She skipped a few lines then described a sullen man who tipped her generously, but who—unlike the others—had never said so much as hello. She knew only his face, his strong jaw, his crooked chipped front tooth that he often hid with the tip of his tongue.

Here, a colorized photograph of Mom and her dark green convertible Corvair. The top is down. High-heel sandals, black narrow slacks, and a cropped angora sweater, a band of apricot midriff exposed. We have that sweater still, though it's a little moth-eaten and now shrunk to doll size. Her white blonde hair dramatically covers one eye, dark brows keenly arched; her conspicuously full lips are a shade paler than her skin. She holds up a certificate of ownership for a time-share week in August at Runaway Stay. Here is the certificate itself.

The pamphlet promised to pay for her gas. What had she to lose? She packed a small suitcase, tossed it in the back of her convertible, and drove to East River Lake.

It's odd isn't it, that she began a diary just as Fate called in all bets? Funny, Dad's invitation came at such an opportune time. Curious that she happened to be musing about him as she sped, top down, toward his resort.

When she entered his log cabin office, she recognized him immediately. Tongue poised sexily on front tooth. She had never run into a customer outside of work before. (Her handwriting here is spidery and rapid.) The event was so striking that she read some kind of destiny into it and subjected herself to her fate. That's why later she did not resist Dad when they met on a path that led beyond the distant shore of the lake. Afterward, he admitted that he had sent her the invitation on purpose and that all the while he had silently watched her dance, he had been contriving a scheme to get her off that stage, out of that damned noisy cabaret.

10

MAX CAME IN AS usual at two. He raked his hair, restraightened his tie, adjusted his belt. He was tired of waiting. He had resolved to get Trixie away from the loud music and the bouncer.

Trixie was also nervous that afternoon. She changed her costumes and reapplied her never-perfect lipstick again and again. Her malicious black nightie got all twisted up on her, and she got her foot through the wrong side of her thong. She dismissed it—"bad design"—and flung it in the corner. Then she wiggled into a crimson slip, but when Audrey appeared also in red, Trixie unzipped herself in a panic. It had now been over three weeks. Had she spoken to Mr. Rosamund yet? She had not spoken to him yet.

"Oh, pliss," said Sammy throwing down her mascara in mock disgust. "Talk to heam already."

"If you don't, he'll stop coming in," said Sam. "Aren't you dating anyone, girl?" she asked. Trixie was not. "Oh, no wonder she dances like that."

Audrey said, "If you married Mr. Rosamund you wouldn't have to work another day in your life."

"I'd rather die," said Trixie.

"His wife used to be a showgirl, I think," said Audrey. "Looks like a movie star. He showed me her picture. But he has marriage troubles."

"Not Mr. Rosamund!" laughed Andie.

"Maybe they break up, hey?" suggested Sammy.

Trixie said, "He's interesting," applying her lipstick and stepping back from the mirror. "But I wouldn't go out with him." She kissed a tissue. "I don't like men who cheat."

"You're just afraid he won't like you," said Audrey.

"Trixie!" gasped Andie in mock horror. "Woodif he doesn't think you look good with your clothes on?"

I assured her she was just as sexy dressed as undressed.

"Oh, I hate this dress," she sighed. "I wish I could go up nude."

I rescued her black nightie from the corner. She put it on absent-mindedly, grabbed her bag, and started up the stairs. I called after her: "By the way, Trixie, were you aware that Maximilian Roquefort Price is a poor relation to the famous de Roqueforts, that reclusive, august southern family, famous for their philanthropy and custards, and that Mr. Rosamund once aspired to aesthetic philosophy?"

She knew he wasn't just a car salesman, she just knew it.

Max hadn't noticed before that her eyes were too large for her face, or her legs and arms too gangly. He liked her even more. From the shadowed corner where he watched, he noticed that she always wrenched her brows, and if that weren't enough to drive a man to distraction, she wrinkled up her nose a lot. An expressive face, animallike. She hadn't learned yet how to hide her busy thoughts. Transparent Trixie.

I stepped up to Max's table. "Oh, Pixie," he said in alarm. "Where did you come from?" I said that I move quietly and sometimes go unseen (to borrow one of Calvin's phrases). Max asked if I had relayed his messages to Trixie. "Not that I want anything to happen—you know I'm married. It's just that she intrigues me, and she *never* speaks. If I'm going to break this long silence it must be with something profound, or at least witty."

"You're in a bar, Max. Ask her if she wants a drink."

Trixie left the stage. She smiled at an unknown near the stage. Her search overlooked Max with his face lowered, so she fixed her attention on the men's room door. Why couldn't he just walk over? Well, for one he didn't want to seem forward or stupid.

"Just act casual. She's shy."

He laughed. "Pixie, I've seen the way she dances."

"Tell her," I said, "how much time you waste looking for her on her off-days—they hardly know you at Price Mazdatown anymore—how she has infected your speech. No doubt at dinnertime you have made some mistake like asking for the blue-eyes instead of the blue-cheese dressing."

"Or 'undressing' actually."

"And how she has invaded your dreams—your sheets are all knotted up. She wants to speak to you."

He looked doubtful. Then he recalled the way she looked at him from the stage and he started to smile.

"This is ridiculous." He was stupid for giving her his card, for not having the guts to talk to her yet, and for knocking over the table the first time he watched her dance. Every night all his errors combined into one tragicomic dream in which he was the featured clown.

"Don't be so hard on yourself," I said.

"Pix, I don't exaggerate," he said. That morning, while he checked every pore and cut never-before-discovered nose hairs, he had again practiced various looks and phrases to exhibit his charm and wit. Suddenly, Rosamund had barged in to brush her teeth, making him feel like an ass. "Frankly, though," he said, waxing irritable, "everyone knows it is ridiculous to waste so much time over a stripper. It's her job to seduce me."

I shrugged.

Now Trixie's eyes found him. She was talking with Percival—Max noted with some displeasure.

"What makes her want to do this? Is it the money, you suppose? I could use her at Mazdatown."

"It's a thrilling business, I'm sure, but I think she's more suited to this kind of work."

"It was just something to say."

"Tell you what. I'll go over to Trix, and you can join us in a minute, huh?"

I went to Trixie and then gave Max a sign. After pausing once to bump into a waitress and a second time to let Umberto shoulder past him in a heroic, but failed, effort to get the phone, Max made it to our side of the room, and Trixie said, "Hi."

"Hi. I like the way you dance."

"Yeah, I noticed," she said, laughing roughly.

He seemed embarrassed.

Trixie looked around. A nearby table was becoming available.

"Say," said Max, "would you like to sit down?"

"Oh, that would be fine," said Trixie. She glanced at the three seats and smiled faintly. Percival assessed the situation and admitted he had been on his way out. We sat down, Trixie between Max and me.

"Gorgeous girl," said Percival to Max, grinning madly. A waitress was upon us immediately. I placed my order; unofficial house rule—the customer had to buy drinks.

"Don't you need something to drink?" Max asked of Trixie, who had let the waitress go.

"What?" said Trixie.

"I was just wondering if you were thirsty. Can I get you something?"

"Oh, cranberry juice."

"You sure?" He waved at the waitress. "You don't drink?"

"Fattening."

"Oh." His eyes traveled over her slim, sinewy body. "You never called me. I gave you my card, remember?"

Trixie shrugged her shoulders. "I still have it." She opened her purse and showed him his card, which now had a lipstick print on it. "I blotted my lips," she apologized.

Poor Max. This timorous Trixie did not resemble the salient darling that lived upon the stage.

"You didn't kiss it, did you?" He asked, daringly.

She shrugged—maybe she had. Max smiled at me as if he had just won a point. "Do you mind sitting with me when I come in?"

"No," said Trixie carelessly.

He snorted—a kind of laugh or smirk. "I can't stand the crowds here sometimes," he said, too obviously leading up to a plan to meet outside the Playhouse.

"Me neither," she said, a subtle, childish note of acquiescence to his scheme.

He leaned over and held her shoulders. "I can't talk in here." The gesture was a bit too forward. Max replaced his hands in his lap, where they fumbled in shame.

She put her hand on his chest, repaying his too-forward gesture—she found a firm breast much bigger than her own. Shocked, she withdrew.

He looked at her roaming eyes. "Watcha thinking?"

She glanced at his hands; Max realized he had been tugging his wedding ring and groaned inwardly.

"Oh, nothin'," she said as noticed his huge hands. Then Mockingbird, ignorant killjoy, called her.

"Call me," he shouted after her. "Hey, you forgot your drink."

She doubled back. "Oh, yeah. I forgot."

"Here," said Max on impulse, handing her a folded twenty. "Now, you call me, now." A ghost of a southern accent.

She looked at him laughing, "Aren't you married?" and she left him standing with the rejected bill in his hand.

"Did I do something wrong?" he asked of me, throwing the bill on the table.

"If she doesn't take your money, maybe that means she likes you," I offered.

He brightened for a minute, then said sulkily, "She's taken plenty of money from me."

I said, giggling wickedly, "Well, then if she does take your money maybe that means she likes you." He did not laugh.

"I can't not tip her," he said.

"No, you can't."

"I wish I could meet her somewhere else."

"And give up watching her dance?"

"No, but who says she needs to dance here?"

"She does," I said meaningfully. "She does."

He frowned at the floor and blinked three or four times.

Trixie's favorite song began; Max glanced up. He had made an impression on her.

At the end of the day, I dared Trix one last time, "Now, you call me now," imitating Max's southern accent.

"Cut it out, Pixie. I don't know what to say to him."

Alarmed by her displeasure I said, mildly, defensively, "He'll do the talking."

Trixie panicked at the idea of making that call. If she had ever managed to make a friend or lover in her life it was only because he had pursued her with unfailing rigor. "I've never made the first call."

"If you don't try, you'll end up like me, Trixie, lonely, not just a loner anymore, but lonely."

"That's not true," she said quickly, softly. "He is, anyway, married."

"That's why it's so easy to call him. You can talk about how great his wife is. He loves to do that. It won't seem like you're interested in him that way."

"Except that I am," Trixie exhaled heavily, "and I can't pretend. I feel needy. You know, I can talk to my students just fine. You know why? because they want something from me."

"Believe me, he wants something from you, Trix."

Calvin let us use Umberto's office. Trixie sat on his empty desk, phone on her lap.

"You sure you don't need privacy?" I asked.

"No," she mouthed.

"Max Price," said her quick lover.

"Hello, this is Trixie," she said as if he hadn't been waiting for her call.

Max's voice repeated her name with an eruption of tenderness and gratitude. She asked and found he "was working late." She was "just getting off." There followed a painful pause followed by a staggered duet, "So, Pixie tells me—" (laughter).

"You first."

"Pixie tells me you might like to go out with me sometime."

She shot me an accusing look. "She did?"

"How about a weekend at the beach? I know a—"

Trixie interrupted laughing, "I can't get away"—she cleared her throat—"Excuse me, for a whole weekend."

"No? Why not?"

"I have to work; that's why not," she said hoarsely.

"Well, maybe we could work something out."

"I'm starved after work." She laughed nervously.

"Okay, I'll think of something. You dancing tomorrow?"

She was.

"I'll see you then, and we can decide what we want to do."

See ya tomorrow, they said.

"No big deal," she said to me, but she was trembling and her mouth was dry. "I sounded like an idiot, didn't I?"

"You were all right."

"Think so? I sounded more jokey than I meant to."

"He probably didn't notice."

"No?"

I imagined that later she wrapped her legs around her lucky pillow all night thinking of Max.

The next day, Max had not appeared by three, by five, or by six. Trixie asked Mockingbird to play, "Don't Tear Me Up" and "Damn, I Wish He Were My Lover."

"You wouldn't be waiting for Mr. Rosamund, would you? Ah, how cute," said sarcastic Audrey.

Later, I happened to have the warm-up stage where I could lie on the floor stretching (guys apparently like that), while on the main stage, Trixie danced in a haunted state—expecting Max to walk in at any move, at any turn. Boy, did we regret that stupid call. Then I noticed Max in the back of the cabaret, out of her view, watching her. Between songs, Trixie froze, staring vacantly, perhaps remembering something Max had said. She scanned the cabaret, noting ten customers along the runway, four in dark suits against the back wall (checking for brown curls, no), a dozen in various attitudes at the bar—none with the stature or controlled movements that defined Max. A big man at the bar let his elbow rest on his knee in perfect imitation of Max, but it wasn't he, only his stunt double whose likeness to Max quickly faded. Her anxious eye skimmed over and passed the real Max.

Max let Trixie leave the stage. In the dressing room door, she exaggerated the difficulty of taking off her panties (sighing, tugging, flinging). At last she looked up at me, blue eyes glassy, eyebrows a-twitch. She removed all obstacles from the path to excuse him: he probably forgot; he might have changed his mind; I bet he got too busy. I shouldn't have called him. It was dumb of me, all my fault.

I powdered my freshly washed throat, knowing I could alleviate her pain by mentioning, casually, "Oh, didn't you see Mr. Rosamund? He is here." I could have told her I had seen him spying on her in a haze of love and excitement, but I didn't; I savored the bittersweet way she brushed her hair with her chin raised in affected pride. I held my trembling window-struck sparrow in cupped hands. Seeing my moment, I asked, "Hey, you want to go next door for a bite?" and waited cautiously.

"Why not? I'm starved." Stoic, silly Trixie. She even flirted with Mockingbird. She pulled her dress over her head, flapping arms until her face popped through. Her ponytail wagged not unhappily as she searched for her shoes (Candie's). Finally, with our big bags, we were weaving up the dark back stair when we heard a coarse whisper.

"Trixie."

She froze.

"Trixie," Max said again.

He must have gotten through the locked door marked "Employees Only." Max moved out of the shadow. Trixie looked with a veiled stare, like a patient in recovery. Then, like the maddening dear that lived onstage, she slowly lifted her skirt. He placed his hand flatly against her navel. She sighed and his hand slipped down and traced the line of her thong between her legs. She stepped back.

"I had to work late." He put one hand on the back of her neck, his other under her chin and lifted it. (He'd apparently rehearsed this a hundred times with perfect delicacy and swiftness.) Valentino-like, he brushed her lips with his then tasted the anticipated salt on her neck. "Dinner?"

"No, it's okay. I've just made plans with Pixie," she said without thinking. He backed away and we left him standing alone in the dark stair.

11

THE PRESENT: ONE WEEK since Trixie died. Last night, I was tired of going from man to man saying, "Table dance? Table dance?" so when Percival offered a hundred dollars to take me into the infamous champagne room, I accepted. I pretended to sip champagne then pretended to drink water from an empty frosted glass, spitting it out. Percival drank his. We took turns listening to his favorite arias on his headphones.

Then Trixie's old fan offered, that prematurely gray attorney. He said I didn't have to drink the champagne. After a while he asked me to take off my top. I did. He got tipsy and talkative. He told me about his client, his daughter the basketball star, the judge (female) who manipulated him horribly. He actually asked what a nice girl like me was doing in a place like this. He talked about everything but the possibilities of our being alone together. Unfortunately, he noticed when I looked at his watch.

"Time to go?" he asked.

"Just about," I admitted.

Then he asked me, in the most startlingly matter-of-fact way, for a "peek" at a particular part of my anatomy. At first I didn't recognize the term he used. "My what?"

He repeated the word, but I'd never thought of myself in that way and left without a smile.

Next? Cito the football player. I paid Mockingbird fifty dollars to play Nirvana really loud the entire hour. All we could do was stare at each other in the dark. Big improvement. But still not what one might have suspected.

But back to my story.

12

TRIXIE HAD ONCE TOLD Percival one of her all-time favorite songs was from an opera "called—oh, what is it? Italian something. 'Baby,' no, 'oh, my Bimbo.' Oh, I can't remember."

He shook his fists. "I wish you could remember. What is it? What is it?"

Two weeks later she still hadn't remembered. It tortured him. He was stuck in a time ripple of anticipation (child running down the hallway to the glittering Christmas tree, running, running, never getting there).

Finally, she remembered to bring in the CD. When Mockingbird announced, "This one's for Percival," he jumped up, mouth open, hands on cheeks. He hugged everyone as if he had just won an Oscar.

"O mio babbino caro." I remembered the song from my Music Appreciation course; it was also, funny coincidence, the first song on a scratched vinyl platter in my mother's trunk.

Trixie was stretched out like a hood ornament, then she bounded down the runway, stumbling slightly on the would-have-been perfect spin, but who cared! She smiled.

Percival ran to the stage and kissed her shoes. The audience laughed. She glanced at Calvin, who motioned for her to step back. Percival retreated to the bar, where kind Bartholomew patted his back. "Isn't she great," he said dreamily, teeth and gums shining.

When the curtain dropped, it was significant that she had had witnesses. At least that is how I feel. In all my loneliness, while dancing down Old Road into the warm night where I live, I express certain things for which I wish—oh, how I wish—there were an audience. That is all I want, someone to hear me, see me think.

I might confess now and be done with it. No better explanation for a stripper's inclination is needed. Even without my mother's death, I would be here anyway. I need bystanders in order to feel alive (they have a word for my condition; it starts with an "e" and ends in an "ism"). Every day I look for someone to wander into the cabaret, a vicious businessman, who has no anticipation of any real talent or intensity in a place called the Girlie Playhouse; someone who probably has a few hours to kill or is lonely and will settle for the company of a stripper; someone who has previously only witnessed striptease with the glaring unloveliness of the everyday or the confounded veneer of camp. All I want to do is to show this semi-hostile customer, when he glances up from his watch, that I am real. I want him to muse and clear his throat, to come back the next afternoon, jinxed with an unreachable itch. I want him to like me, to know me, *to want to be me.*

That is my only crime—Gideon Angels—my only crime.

As Trixie left the stage, I sat down with ol' Dan, who, by the way, managed his itch well, scratching indiscreetly like a horse on the trunk of an old gnarled oak whenever he could. While he was now watching Andie in her short pleated skirt, she was doing her high-school dance, wearing a worried look, concentrating on every movement, like a crayoning preschooler. From the front row, he could see up her tartan skirt, could see what seemed to be her bare bottom. (Her thong was, as always, stuffed between her full cheeks.) Had she forgotten her panties altogether? Dan certainly hoped so. He squirmed and wiggled and tried, nonchalantly, to get a better look.

I mounted the stage after Andie and stretched as I scanned my audience, looking for a supportive pair of eyes, a curiously anxious smile. I found four electrical company employees whom I had noticed before, also a dark suit leaning against the wall, and two regulars at the bar who were promising me their attention by the way their eyes flitted but their faces remained calm.

I still blush on the first set every day. I've come to realize it has less to do with modesty than some strange chemical imbalance. I feel myself go red—first in the ears, then cheeks and chest. Then I look directly at my audience—bored but hopeful men who examine my long hair and my dark eyes, my structure and my bearing. I watch them form opinions of me, eyes traveling rapidly all over my body. I begin to see that image *they* have of Pixie. I feel a sob tangled with laughter coming on. I let that tickly fear gather. I will show them; if it kills me, I will show them.

Dancing, I have to say, has been a long unmitigated lesson in self-possession. While those inquiring eyes watched, I danced especially hard and thoughtfully, with nerves rather steadier for the excitement, finding my way through the song like the way I can find my way around my cottage in the dark. And damn me if I didn't declare what every note meant, especially the minor ones, sitting cold, yet unresolved in the basement of the song.

Dan there, soft-eyed, reflecting. Behind him Calvin stood, arms crossed, inspecting my steps, with what I at the time incorrectly imagined as purely professional concern.

Calvin occasionally left his post in the foyer to survey the situation on the floor, looking for drunks and enforcing, by his very presence, the obligatory distance between customer and dancer. I gathered up my hair, showing him my downy back and shoulders. I felt warm; my mouth watered. He stepped forward and stood up against the stage and I stood up against him. He did not move, but looked at me forever then finally closed his eyes and shook his head. I was daring, but at his expense. Then a glance at Umberto made me feel guilt for neglecting the customers. I forced myself not to look back at Calvin.

The song ended. Quiet, landing with a thud on my breast, was aggravated by a low murmur and clinking glasses. My wrinkled dress lay in a puddle on the floor. I picked up the rejected, cold thing and shook it out into life, and, during the humiliating silence, I stepped into it. Looking at Dan, I covered myself and slipped my arms through the sleeves. He smiled a transitory smile. I did the same.

Calvin took my hand and helped me negotiate the treacherous steps. Safely on terra firma, I thanked him. He bowed his head—showing me the absolute roundness of his skull. Dan called out, "Pixie, hey over here. Finish your drink." Calvin renounced his claim, out of professional courtesy. I reclaimed my seat next to Dan. Audrey had taken the stage and was shuffling in her plastic red pumps. His round eyes feigned astonishment, then he yawned and turning to me asked, "So, Pixie, you've never told me. What makes you want to be a stripper?"

13

THE NEXT MORNING UMBERTO was waiting in our dressing room. He was nervous, glum and suspiciously polite. I immediately sensed that he had bad news. This marks the point at which our cabaret began to deteriorate. Some vaguely inauspicious omens have already been indicated. But it was not until this day that the first critical fissure appeared, a fissure that would fork and spread up the walls until just a few trumpeters would be able to make it all come tumbling down.

Umberto was being forced to change the way we received our pay. This new system, innocuous in itself, would eventually facilitate the Playhouse's descent into infamy. In my opinion, the Girlie Playhouse might have survived the scandal unscathed had it not been for these changes that attracted an undesirable element to our happy camp.

The Girlie Playhouse had operated for years without much notice from the community. We had been immune from complaints and the citations from the state liquor authority that went with them. Suddenly, Umberto had been slapped with an insulting fine. What had happened (I found out later from Calvin) was that some puritan had been voted in as chief of the city's vice squad. She resurrected long-ignored restrictions on certain forms of nudity and fined violators. The Playhouse would have been okay under these conditions—we required much less control than, say, Happy's or Le Mirage—but the puritan's underlings were actually more interested in collecting fines than in controlling nudity. In sum, everything went on in much the same way it always had, only now, more so than ever, we would operate under a haze of illicitness.

"Good morning, ladies," Umberto said gravely. "I just got a notice from the state liquor authority. It's the nudity."

Trixie, who had been filing her nails, glanced up.

"There's an old law that says naked women can't be within eighteen inches of men where liquor is served."

We waited in silence. We had never heard of the rule.

"We always got around the law because we don't allow tipping onstage. But," here Umberto took an expansive pause, "Sometimes, you know how it is, the guys get a little too close. They don't know. It's not like I'd throw out a paying customer just because he gets too close."

We all claimed we had no idea.

"I'm not complaining," said Umberto. "No one is really interested in enforcing the law. What it all amounts to is, I have to pay some pretty hefty fines so the officials can look the other way."

I wondered why such a law might have ever been enacted. Eighteen inches, a foot and a half. Curious as to whether it corresponded to anything interesting, I later did some research. I wish I could say that I discovered the law was written during the plague years and that its original purpose was to protect cancan girls from tuberculosis, eighteen inches being the maximum traveling distance that a germ is willing to go to relocate to another host; however, my search produced no such rationale. The eighteen-inch rule is unapologetically arbitrary. And does not, incidentally, apply to naked male performers. But no matter; it is a strange law, like so many that we heed. We had no intention of breaking it, now that we knew of its existence. Instead, like all good citizens, we would look for the shortest route around it.

"We could put bars around the stage," offered Sam.

"Cages?" I envisioned my life as a bored orangutan in heels.

"At other clubs the girls paint flesh-colored latex on their nipples, so they're not really naked," said Sam.

We all agreed that was disgusting and insane.

"I'll pay the fine," said Um. Sam turned on her hairdryer and had to be asked to wait a minute. "That's not the end of it, Sam," Umberto continued. "What it comes down to is this. I have to cut your salaries," he paused, "in half." A chorus of offended groans.

For my part, I was comfortable enough financially. I had Mother's insurance money, owned my home, and didn't spend much. Trixie, too, had an income from the Community Center, not to mention Porina baby food. But Sidney fell into a heap of disgust on her stool, arms and legs limp. Cross-armed Audrey started explaining her budget: she wouldn't be able to get some necessary software and still pay her electric bill, Umberto, if her salary were cut.

Umberto, having given us the bad news, put in quickly—"But you can accept tips *while you're onstage*. I know you're not here for your health. You're here to make money."

"Oh, I don't care," said Sam, showing her wrist was limp, "If you gif me the money or they gif me the money."

Everyone agreed but Trixie. "I think it'll stink. What are they supposed to do? Throw money at us while we're dancing? Or maybe we won't dance anymore. We'll stand there taking money like slot machines."

I was actually of Trixie's mind, but lacked her spunk.

"What about you, Pixie?" asked Umberto chivalrously, with forbearance for the weak and meek.

"Well," I said, thinking my point quite obvious, "we could do without the liquor—since it's unthinkable to do without nudity."

Umberto flinched.

As it turned out, the puritan's efforts would have the opposite effect as she had intended (I'm sure she meant well enough). The customers effectively became our employers if not our puppeteers.

"By the way," said Umberto leaving, "I'm opening a champagne room for you. That should help."

We were doomed now, Calvin came to explain. "He means a lounge on the second floor. No stage, only booth with semitransparent curtains. And you know what that means."

None of us knew what that meant. Some of us, particularly Audrey, had a pretty good idea. Trixie was dying to know. And I was willing to find out. Champagne rooms were undiscovered country. From hearsay we had gathered that going into champagne rooms was somehow exhausting. We also knew that one had to invent ways of disposing of the cheap champagne without drinking it. It paid a lot of money. Nothing was "allowed." Nothing ever happened. And only a certain type of girl ever went in.

"Showtime," called Mockingbird.

Not a soul in the lunch crowd tried to tip while we danced: we had no tactful way of saying the rules had changed, we were being paid less and wanted their money more. Even when Bartholomew asked, "What's new?" I couldn't say, "Tips from you." By late afternoon, Umberto, out of creative desperation, thought of selling "mementos" which would "make tipping seem like a game." Paper money would be printed in pretty colors and feature Umberto's portrait. If it didn't work, he promised, we would get our regular pay until he thought of something else.

So the next day, Umberto trotted in with his play money. A cameoed Umberto's eyebrows were high on his washboard forehead and his lips seemed to be caught saying, "buck." As an introductory promotion, each customer was given five dollars' worth. A tactful card encouraged the customers to buy more: "Customers, the Girlie

Playhouse is proud to offer you the chance to show your appreciations to your favorite girls. Mementos, in two, five, and ten denominations, can be purchased and given to the dancers while they're dancing. Not legal tender. No other promotions apply. See your waitress for details." (The cards were rewritten after the first week.)

Percival gave me all his complimentary mementos with a big, mad grin. Many others did the same. A pile of mint, lemon, and aquamarine slips grew at the foot of the stage. It was kind of nice, I guess. The customers certainly liked showing their appreciation. The following set, there was a memento-throwing frenzy. The customers were lined up three deep. They threw them like confetti above my head. They had their waitresses throw them at me. At first, I couldn't fathom the spendthrifts, but then I realized that after the initial purchase, the pain of parting with one's money no longer smarted. They were able to dispose of the "worthless" mementos with happy abandon. Fun is always worth a buck or two, ten, or twenty.

"I cleaned up," bellowed Audrey who had just come down the stairs. "Did you see that guy?"

I'd seen that guy sagging, as usual, at the bar. He always tipped anonymously via the waitress—who, by the way, never failed to mention the source. That night he had thrown mementos over his shoulder onto the stage without looking at the dancer.

"How *you* doin' kiddo?" asked Audrey looking at the mementos I held in my hand. "Looky what I did," and she waved a bundle three times the size of mine.

The cash-out process was a bother. We had to wait in line outside Umberto's office in the grim hallway (cement floor, caged bulb) so long that we decided to dress there. We lined up toweled. Along midpoint we were gradually powdered, pantied, stockinged, and fastened into our bras, and at the terminal end where Umberto received us, we were completely clothed and shod, with mementos meticulously ordered and counted. Sam pattered in wearing rubber shower slippers and large cotton underwear (laughter from us) and found a place behind Sidney. Sidney, black-eyed Susan (oh, how her lashes did flutter!) asked Sam if Sol ever saw her in that underwear. "You kidding?" she answered pop-eyed. "They his." Her regular panties were at the laundry.

"Who's gonna beat Audrey's five hundred, huh?"

I handed Umberto my mementos, which proved to be six hundred and twenty-seven ("No big deal," I said later to Audrey, the next day she might make as much and I less).

Soon Umberto cut our salaries completely. And since we had all decided to buy time with our extra money, Umberto would have to place an ad for more dancers. Jesse would finish college. Sidney would go to auditions. Sammy would quit in two months to have a baby. Audrey would get that computer.

I also took several days off and decided to get out more and discover what amusements my modest hometown had to offer. I took a bouncing bus downtown. A fat, insane, and talkative driver befriended me during the short drive. When he picked me up on the weedy corner, where I waited amid four-foot phlox and wild sumac trees, he said I looked like "a woodland creature waiting in the forest primeval." All this for a fare of only fifty cents.

I read at an old-fashioned coffee shop, where Kathy (the name her tag provided) served fruit plate and cottage cheese. The decrepit town center boasted a few clinging, almost bankrupt stores: a shoe repair shop where I could still get Mom's pumps totally resoled for ten dollars by a kind, hoary-headed man; a bookseller pushing sun-faded travel guides; a salon called Debbie's or Dottie's House of Beauty, maybe even House O' Beauty.

I missed the last bus back, and with no other alternative, returned on foot. The cracked concrete streets were hot. I was the sole pedestrian. What few, rambling, rattling pickups passed by did so with contemptuous curiosity. Only drifters walked those roads. The spiritless scenery made me wonder why I never cried. I almost wished I hadn't been given the time to think. Ah, but really, you know I had to admit, as I turned on my Old Road, that I relished the distilled intensity of being alone. That's the horror mixed with joy, to realize it's not by chance but by choice that I have been left out.

In the days that followed (I'm jumping ahead a bit here, but I'll backtrack in a minute) my garden seemed to flourish due to the extra time I had to admire it. The flowers were blooming mightily, and because of Umberto's silly memento idea, I was able to enjoy them. And there was another unforeseen advantage: I became a better dancer. My favorite songs, because I hadn't heard them for a day or two, tickled and provoked me like they hadn't in a long time.

14

Now that I had so much extra time off, I decided to join the Community Center where Trixie worked. I went by bus, a long and meditative ride—how I love mass transit (you don't have to do a thing, your mind can wander down so many more streets than your own vehicle can). Kids, with damp hair and wet spots on T-shirts and shorts (bathing suits underneath), ran out the door as I went in, chirping, "thanks"—probably kids Trixie taught: carefree, imprudent, and lovable. The main lobby introduced me to a lounge with corduroy armchairs, in which starfished kids faked utter exhaustion after a swimming lesson or basketball game. Beyond the lobby, behind a glass wall, the indoor swimming pool lapped upon ceramic shores, and frisky boys were made identical by wet hair and NWCC–issue black trunks. A smiling counter clerk complimented my ID picture and cheerily wished me to "work too hard," a modest NWCC joke.

In the ladies' locker room, powder and deodorant were the prevailing scents—as opposed to the perfume and smoke of the Girlie Playhouse dressing room. There, dimple-bottomed ladies with puckered navels of childbirthing presided, but otherwise it was the same general scene.

An hour on the Keiser machines put me into a semi-mesmerized state. In my black go-go shorts and athletic halter, I worked the levers in a trance, losing count of my reps after eight or ten, sweating and gently hallucinating at the visions of rolling and pitching chrome, the manned machines around me. Then dizzily, delicately, I climbed out of one machine and onto the next. Mirrors everywhere.

Finally, a tour around the center found pretty, high-shouldered Trixie leading a gaggle of girls and boys. She sported a clingy black costume of cotton, which was beautifully faithful to the rungs on her rib cage, her delicately defined areolae, and even the dimples on each side of her coccyx. Her thong panties, which she wore over opaque back leggings, imitated, in an athletic theme, her costumes at the Playhouse. Her fine, hip-length hair was restrained by a nylon tie, though a few strands had won their freedom and hung from her temples or dangled down her nape.

I watched her class from the sidelines, on a StairMaster. Her squad had sugarplum fairy charm. The pale, gangly kids were all nervously addicted to her. There was one tomboyish blonde, younger than the rest—about ten or so—with messy, zigzag parted hair and knocked knees that reminded me of myself. The group went dutifully up and down, side to side, with the irregular grace of a flying V of geese, a different bird alternately taking the lead.

When Trixie talked to her students she looked them directly, even eerily, in the eye. I knew that look. She used it on special occasions for special people, most often from the stage, but every once in a while in person, as she did with these kids. The look was knowing and benign. It went right through you. Once when I was particularly not myself—it happened to be the eve of my birthday—Trixie put her hand on my thigh as if she knew. Though Trixie could often seem indifferent or abrupt, we know, she had her reasons. When it was important, though, she came through with comforting matter-of-fact sympathy. (*Inside Story* did not mention any of this.)

Twenty minutes into my thirty-minute session on the StairMaster, a machine from which the entire room could be buoyantly surveyed,

I was irreversibly charmed by Trixie's students, especially a girl with sagging pigtails high atop her head. She had extravagantly bow-shaped lips, which she sealed only with great effort, otherwise two very long and rough-edged front teeth completed her flop-eared rabbit appearance. What I love about children is that they are so affected. A twelve-year-old posed like a prima donna prior to mounting a balance beam. Later, she tugged on her sneaker with such flourish that I imagined she was being filmed for a footwear ad. Her mannerisms alluded to a distant maturity, and I wondered, or dreamt about, the young lady she would become. If she continued to become more of what she was then, all that pretentiousness and sophistication would turn her into a movie star. Maybe it's just more striking to note savoir faire in a twelve-year-old, or in a Playhouse dancer for that matter.

I wondered, upon my perch, now bobbing at level ten with a sweat bead on the end of my nose, why the world didn't turn out more Trixies when there were so many potential Trixies right there in the room. I supposed they realize people like me love their every move, and they get nervous and begin to feel guilty. Pity, because the naive little girls meant no more than Trixie did.

15

Max reappeared after three days of absence in a wrinkled shirt (we had not seen him since Trix and I had left him on the back stair). He found Trixie stomping around on a stage littered with pieces of paper. He elbowed Calvin's rib. "What's this?"

Calvin explained, in a slightly bitter tone, the new memento promotion, stressing, as he had for a hundred other customers that day, the interaction it promised (interaction of course meant Calvin's job would be all the more difficult). Max bought four bundles. He went to the main stage and leaned against the brass railing. Trixie was doing a complicated Latin step and didn't see him. He flung mementos at her feet. Trixie squeaked Max's name then bent over to talk to him (lucky men were they who sat behind her), knees knocking in a kind of wavering curtsy, hands tucked between her pressed thighs.

The music was loud, but she understood that he had a good day at work. What had Trixie been up to? Oh, work at the Community Center. She swiped a memento he held in his hand, tossed it over her shoulder with a coarse laugh. Trixie asked, "Think it's tacky?" Max raised an eyebrow. "Oh, gotta go. Favorite song." She resumed dancing to "Senza una donna."

Max watched, frowning proudly at her goosepimply, bluewhite skin. Then, suddenly a bit uncomfortably, he couldn't help but notice how several men, behooved by her constant smile and everything it seemed to offer, placed their mementos, like bets, on the stage.

He sat down, ordered the mandatory beer. That was his girl up there, practically. No one else seemed aware of that fact. Finally, showtime for Jesse was called, and Trixie climbed back into her gossamer nightie, getting it past her rump with great difficulty. This performance elicited several more mementos. "Have fun," she said as she passed Jesse.

Max rose and indicated her seat with a wave of his arm. Instead, she ran past, saying something about freshening up and left him waiting at the sticky table. A newly hired and overly assertive waitress accosted Max. He was made to order juice for Trixie and another beer for himself; the first had not yet been tasted. To get his money's worth, he had the waitress relight the candle. He noticed me sitting at the next table (with good ol' Dan) and raised his glass to me. I clinked it.

A beer later (the pushy waitress had come around twice), Trixie returned in a long blue dress with a slit from ankle to thigh. Her hair was in a hasty French twist. Two disobedient locks dangled down her bony back. Her opaque blue stockings had silk bows on the back of each thigh (she'd done a little shopping at an overpriced boutique the day before).

"Very sophisticated," said Max, though he thought she looked false.

She sat very upright, childishly wagging her foot. "You like it. I'm glad," she said and hugged his arm. "I missed you."

They both apologized over the mix-up about their dinner date, and he said he'd missed her too. Over those three days, every dark-haired girl that had come into Mazdatown had looked like Trixie for a second. He even thought he had seen her likeness on a baby food jar at his brother-in-law's house. He laughed at himself as they sipped their drinks.

Max looked grossly comfortable so close to Trixie. He wouldn't check in at the dealership just yet, and in fact he might take the rest of the day off. He blinked slowly and yawned, his mouth snapping shut.

Dan left, and my juice and I were invited to join them. Trixie said they had discovered that they had probably traveled by the same train from Port City. Max was sure of the date because it was just after his sister's wedding there.

Had they caught glimpses of each other, she in her mercilessly short skirt, he with his fine leather bags? Had he paid for his ticket first, with the correct change $89.95 and had she taken one of his tens and his nickel for her five twenties? Had they fought the same ridiculously heavy connecting door? Perhaps they had been in the same four-seater (he behind a newspaper) and had crossed and recrossed legs seeking that perfectly unobtrusive catty-corner angle, and had they almost, but not quite, kicked each other in the shins? (Oh, that they had! It all would have started there and then!) Had Rosamund been with Max? I wondered. And if so, had she noticed when Max watched Trixie's leggy prance down the length of the platform upon detraining?

"I guess we were just meant to meet," said Trixie.

I couldn't help but think of the unusual "coincidences" that surrounded the day my mother met my father at East River. She, too, believed that fate had intervened and so allowed herself to be swept away. It is horrible to think that their love might be entirely due to chance. Right time. Right place. Right song. That kind of thing. But given the sheer number of men whom Trixie . . . Well, it was bound to happen sooner or later that . . .

"Max," interrupted back-patting Umberto. "Hey, where ya been, how do you like the mementos, Max? Lots of new things." Umberto's new menu was jacketed in red leather held together with a gold elastic. A half dozen men were eating the salad of the day at that very minute as Umberto described his success. "There's more too. Champagne rooms," he added, looking around. "Would you like to try it?"

"I'm just fine here. Thanks, Um," said Max.

"I don't doubt it. Don't doubt it." Um looked embarrassed and fingered his earring. "Just thought you'd want to take a look at the room. I mean, I did it up real nice like. Anytime you want go up and see."

"Thanks, Um. Will do," said Max.

Umberto left but was back again in a minute. He shouted into Max's left ear so that Trixie, who was on his right, could not hear (I was on the left). "Say, Max, I don't think Trixie would mind if you went up, you know. She gets commission. The girls work hard; you know that." Max finally understood, but Umberto wanted to make it even clearer. "The waitress can set you up with a bottle and then she can disappear for an hour. Hey, sorry if the new waitresses are pushy. They work on tips, you know."

Mockingbird called showtime for Trixie.

"Can we cancel showtime if we go into the champagne room?"

Um made a sign to affirm, like an umpire indicating "safe." Max handed him his credit card.

Calvin left his post in the foyer to escort them upstairs and I followed out of curiosity. "But I liked that song," said Trixie weakly, climbing the stairs.

"There'll be music up there too," Max said gently.

"Oh?" she said agreeably.

In the champagne room there were four leather booths curtained with sheers that puddled on the floor. Only candles set the room aglow. I'd provided flower arrangements, and the air was thick with fragrance. Max tried to usher her toward the back.

"Right here's fine," she said, and they took the nearest booth instead. I sat on a stool near the door, only a few feet away from their booth. I loitered under the pretext that I intended to hang out with Calvin during my break. The sheer curtains closed behind Max. *Enfin seuls.* The wide-lipped flowers on their table bobbed as Trixie bounced her foot.

Max smiled when "Give In to Me]" started playing softly. That song was playing when he had first seen Trixie dancing, when Umberto let the light in. In a trance, he clumsily stroked her arm. "Something about this song," he said. "Very sexy."

"It was playing that first time you saw me."

"Yeah?" I heard Max say. (He had thought it was "Rape Me.")

A waitress came in and got Max's signature. The curtain remained partially open. Now I could see better. Max's tongue examined his upper lip. He crossed and recrossed his legs and adjusted himself for comfort. He probably needed to excuse himself to the men's room (all that damned beer). He fingered a lily, getting pollen on his hands. He stroked her cheek, staining her with yellow dust. "So what are we allowed to do in here?" asked Max. Trixie looked at him but didn't answer. "Anything we like?" he asked gently. He wore an automatic frown from looking down at his lap.

"I don't know," she said, giving each word equal weight.

Max ran a finger along her Roman nose, touched her sharp chin. "Have you been in here before?" he asked.

Trixie thought a minute and said carefully, "No, it's my first time."

"I see," he said. "Do you want me to tell you what goes on?"

"You've been in champagne rooms before?"

"Me?" he pointed at his chest. "I wouldn't waste the money, but I've known men who have."

"Me too," she said. "The girls usually dance at the table."

"We could do that," he said, encouraged.

Trixie stood between his knees. The music was so low I could hear her feet shuffling. She turned around and let Max help with her zipper.

Her long gown fell to the floor. She bent to pick it up, and he looked intently at her behind. She turned around again, put her hand on his shoulder.

"I think," said Max hoarsely; he cleared his throat. "They also do lap-dancing in champagne rooms."

"Do they?" said Trixie in hushed, high-pitched surprise. She got back into the booth and the sheer curtains closed.

I was still within full, albeit veiled, view. The candle on their table lit the interior of their tent. Imposing Calvin stood, arms crossed, nearby. We probably coughed at least twice between the two of us and must have made three or four other unimportant noises. I know they never forgot we were there. Did they consider all the implications of being in Umberto's champagne room? ("Yes," explained Trixie later, but "we just didn't care." My omniscience here relies partly on her retelling.) They didn't have the time, or the presence of mind, to consider what we all absolutely must consider else the world fall into complete disorder.

Mad, she was for him, I could tell, like I was for my damn pillow every night. Her hands held his head, and with childish glee for novel sensations, they, doubtless, concentrated on the textures of each other's tongue. She was sitting on his lap, facing him. His mouth was stained with her lip color. Moaning, he sunk into the luxurious dampness of her hair, and he could have lingered there forever; he might have enjoyed the cool joy of her limp locks endlessly—with no desire for anything more at all—had he not, instead, kissed her throat and gently demanded everything.

There was only a slight hesitation, having to do with a difficult button belonging to Max and with Trixie's needless caution. "What's the matter?" he whispered. She gave him a solemn look.

Past that they went on, rapidly, but at a crucial point she half-whispered, "Stop."

"What?" he asked weakly.

"Stop," she said with conviction.

He did, on a dime, to show the girl he could do it. Her arms were wrapped around Max, and he patted her back and squeezed her so tightly a puff of breath came out her nostrils. "It's okay," he said.

He supported her bottom with one hand and the back of her head as one would with an infant. She started to squirm on the verge on making a definite decision to remove herself from his lap. She wasn't going to go one slippery centimeter farther, but then suddenly she had.

"Trixie," Max croaked to the happily imprudent girl.

"Got your interest, huh?" whispered Calvin. He took my chin in his hand and made me look at him. "Aren't you interested in anyone but that girl? You are all the time watching her."

"That must mean that you are watching me."

"You're my favorite." His eyes traveled across my face. "Because you're nuts; you love it here, and you like everybody." I smiled at his comment. I liked his voice. I believed he had come, a long time ago, from Burkina Faso. His l's were exceptionally rich and liquid and his intonation always exact. "Why don't you talk to me anymore?"

"Been busy."

"Mf," he exhaled noisily and looked askance at the lovers' booth. "I'm supposed to be babysitting," and he whispered, "but I've seen enough to know when not to interfere. Soon there'll be no point to my being here at all."

I looked back at the booth. Calvin fell silent. Trixie now leaned against Max. They seemed to be both staring zombielike at the lilies. I imagined they were each rehearsing the recent play, probably stunned by their own reckless performances. How had it happened so quickly, so without ceremony?

The waitress returned, and they shook off the trance. Max suavely buttoned his coat (gentle smile at Trixie). Trixie sat up and threw her hair over her shoulders (the French twist had untwisted somewhere along the way).

Max, cool and handsome, poured the champagne with a manly finesse that Trixie noted proudly. They toasted, silently, clumsily, to the first time. What would happen now, I wondered, as they swallowed the anxiety and embarrassment that comes after one lets go?

Could anyone imagine a strip-bar seduction more simple or direct? And yet, judging from the scene as represented by the tabloids, it was a loose, gross affair, with dollars being stuffed in Trixie's thong.

Their intercourse happened, yes, before they had the opportunity to construct much of an intellectual link, but that would come. Yes, they performed the rites of coitus while Max was yet tightly fastened to the conjugal bedpost—while he was yet known by Rosamund's name, and yes, they began to copulate within the first few minutes that the opportunity presented itself, but there is a purity of the motive of lust that is overlooked by dwelling on all these matters. Theirs was quite a powerful incentive to a long-term relationship, especially since the desire was fixed upon the unique details of each other's persons. He was utterly given over to her small limber frame and narrow hips, and she was equally fascinated by his bulky shape and slowness. Nothing would bestill the thumping passion they had for each other, not time, not circumstance; it was a thing naturally sprung from the depths of their corporeal souls. And when petty disagreements might begin to agitate their relationship it would be their voracious appetites that would prevent any kind of separation—as well as, possibly, any kind of pacific union—such is the nature of this lust. Maximilian Roquefort Price had, I believe, underrated its power when he undertook his marriage to Rosamund. And on this day he, quite rightly, began to remedy a great mistake.

On this day, Trixie began to concentrate her desire on a single object. She had, I realized then, been provoking this very situation with every dance she had heretofore performed. It was only at the culmination of events that she could see that she had been leading up to this. Slightly embarrassed, she might have said to herself, "So this is what I've been suggesting. My goodness, I'd no idea." She had been dangling out her bait willy-nilly in front of a crowd, not dreaming that anyone would actually try to reel *her* in. Max had ample weight to do the honors. And she, perceiving she'd been caught, came in without a fight. So this, then, is how I judged their first episode, and mine was certainly a better view than Channel 9's.

After a half hour of purring, inaudible conversation, their lips met and made a concluding smack. They came out of the booth. When they looked at Calvin and me, they were obviously embarrassed. I hid my smile, as if I hadn't seen a thing. I said casually, "Oh I forgot you were still here. Calvin and I were just talking. Say, it's late, Trix. Better get changed."

As they went out the door, Max stumbled on the smooth carpet, and Trixie pretended not to notice.

"Pixie?" asked Calvin. "Can I drive you home tonight?"

"Drive me home? Like a date?"

Calvin laughed. "Okay, if you want."

"Well, I already bought my return ticket," I said, thinking I would rather be alone for a few hours.

"Can't you use it some other time?"

"Can't I use your invitation some other time?"

We decided on tomorrow.

Cashout time had passed; Umberto had vanished into the vast unknown of Umbertodoings, and Trixie and I would have to turn in our crumpled mementos the next day. At eight thirty, the night-shift girls had arrived, donned their sequins and silks, and left a messy dressing room in their wake. Two girls loitered behind, a pantheresque Kenyan and a pencil-thin redhead, making final adjustments to sandal straps and perfecting false lip lines. The redhead kept insisting, in a high grating voice, that someone crack her back; the Kenyan finally obliged her.

Trixie and I had to search through the jumble for Trixie's stuff. We finally found her black canvas duffel bag under a pair of cowboy boots. I was dying to bombard her with questions, but the reticent lover quietly undressed. Maybe it was the presence of strange girls.

She tried but couldn't reach her zipper, like a cat chasing its tail. She actually spun around twice and would have kept spinning if I hadn't helped her. I noticed she didn't change out of her blue panties, sentimental darling. How I envied her as she readied herself, with perfumes and powders, to rejoin her brand-new lover, who still smelt of her, who was dark-haired, dark-eyed and big. Her eyes widened, probably, at the thought of his happy name.

I suddenly told Trixie she reminded me of Mom with her pretty ways. Trixie, who knew of my mother's fame and end, said she considered that a great compliment. I told Trixie how my dad had pursued and seduced Mom on an uneven, rooty path around East River Lake. They ran into each other and, without delay, began to kiss furiously. After a while they wiped their mouths and decided, in a dazzling jolt of common sense, they'd better walk her home. Despite their mutual determination to make it to her door unfulfilled, I was conceived a few feet off the path in a patch of wild strawberries, a few of which they picked and ate afterward. Mom even brought me to the spot once for an afternoon romp and nap.

Trixie said it was a great story. "Did they marry? she asked.

No, Mom refused to stop dancing, I told her.

"Did your dad want her to?" she asked.

I said he had. Trixie's response might have been, "Men!" had she been given to such generalizations. Instead, she said under her breath, "Shame."

Outside Max was waiting. He transferred her bag to his shoulder, saying, "Gimme that." She lunged after the bag and dug out her purse, which held her money but more importantly her makeup. We parted with melodic g'nights and seeyalaters. Then Trixie and Max did a three-legged walk to the end of the block and plunged into a taxi.

As usual, I walked to the commuter train station, caught the express to the first stop outside the city, and transferred to the local. At Meadowlark station, I detrained, sluggish, blinking, and began the familiar trek along moonlit asphalt. In some spots, where the overhanging trees made a leafy tunnel, it was pitch black, and I could hear sniffling burrowing creatures to my left and right. Sometimes, a little frightened, I ran home, expecting one night to bump, comically, into a deer or a sleepwalker in dark pajamas. On the better parts of the road, a few white colonial houses with warm lights stood. A dog or two barked. In twelve hours, I would repeat the sequence in reverse.

My old road was the darkest. As it wound around the bend, it deteriorated into a path lined with Rose of Sharon, which I could smell but couldn't see. When I unlocked my door and went in, I noticed I'd left the windows open and a light burning in the bathroom. A fury of clumsy moths bounced against the walls and hung on the curtains. This was about the most exciting kind of thing that ever happened at my cottage.

My childhood psychiatrist, that pathologically impatient man with the bored sigh and tapping pencil, used to berate me for constantly describing the events of my girlfriends' lives rather than my own, which was always uneventful. To please him, I would occasionally relate an especially detailed dream that would keep him sated for a month. It became an exercise to prove to him, and myself, that I did have an existence. Actually, I *am* a worm that has eaten its way through Mother's coffin; I'm so full of her death that I have no life of my own.

There I was, in my snug cottage, with my old stove and wobbly kitchen chairs, my rag rug reality. I soon had enough of that: I phoned Trixie to get the details, since we hadn't really been able to talk with the night-shift girls around. There wasn't any answer at eleven or at twelve, and by twelve thirty I was asleep in my tiny garret, window agape and a chorus of crickets singing in my head.

I dreamt I was sitting in a dark room, in the corner, in the back. Terrifically loud jazz played relentlessly, drowning all thoughts. I was in some nightclub, not the Girlie Playhouse. At first, I could only sense the crowd of customers around me. Eventually, I began to see the faint orange outline of hard candlelit faces and the broad-shouldered ghosts of suited men.

I could see the pale shimmer of Mom's long, smooth hair, like mine, as she mingled in dead, cigar-smoky dark. Her back was to me. She sat astride, rocking. Over her shoulder, I gradually discerned the vague contours of a man's head, his slack mouth, his deep-set eyes. Her hand went to his hair and pulled his head back. Her breasts brushed his lips. He gripped her buttocks, pulled her closer. Nearby a vague sneering face was suddenly illuminated as he drew upon his cigarillo; the red-hot cherry blazed then fell pale to the table.

I noticed the curve of her spine, her shoulders drawn back (breasts still brushing his lips) toes pointed to the floor. Then she got up. The man adjusted his clothing then reached into his pocket and pushed a folded bill into her hand. With that same hand she swept a lock of hair behind her ear and moved directly to another shadow sitting nearby.

I woke with a jerk. Outside my window the crickets' cacophonous jazz played on. Mustn't think that. Mustn't think.

16

UMBERTO WANTED, AND SORT of deserved, a cut of our hefty profits. With the memento promotion, we were making far too much money for having so much fun, I admit. City rent was not cheap, so Umberto pointed out. He paid top dollar for the charming building with its quaint red double doors. He kept Calvin in fancy clothes—a doorman's appearance was crucial. The neighborhood, Newgate Cross, was up and coming; Umberto had to keep up. Why, next door had changed from "Jimmy's Barber" to "Newgate Cross Coiffure." It was rumored that a Continental Cafe was going in on the corner, and it would be even more ostentatious than the uptown one.

Umberto had renovation plans of his own. Big things in mind. An interior decorator now frequented the cabaret with samples. Mike, the air conditioner guy, wanted his money. The place had to be refrigerator-cold. That kept the men in jackets and ties and kept the girls moving. Umberto spared few expenses for our comfort. Keeping us happy was good for business, he knew. He installed new showerheads, detachable, adjustable, friendly. Wasn't that nice? (Yes, it was, Um, thanks. I enjoy sleek thighs.) He wanted to pay his waitresses and bartenders more. Along with Umberto, we wanted the Girlie Playhouse to be "the best cabaret in town," as it was advertised in the *Newgate Say*. We agreed to give him 20 percent of our tips.

(I haven't strayed from the romance, by the way. Business trouble and lovers' trouble go hand in hand. We would *all in one common ruin fall.*)

Even the 20 percent wasn't quite enough. The cabaret owner's twisted bedsheet nightmare was that no one drank heavily anymore. The day had gone when it was fashionable to light the wrong end of one's cigarette. People suddenly refused to pay good money to get stupid. In the old days—Umberto fondly mused with Carmine and Sal—a ten-dollar shot disappeared in seconds. These days the same customer dawdled a half hour with a Perrier at half the price.

As it was, Umberto already charged an insulting three dollars for six ounces of cranberry juice. He was worried that his regulars might complain if he raised his prices, and he was right; people tended to feel duped. Happily, he found customers would pay twenty at the door. But just in case the novelty wore off—music TV and nude beaches had already made nudity passé—Umberto wanted something more primary to human need. Then he hit on it. Yes, money was to be made where men wanted to look at women, but there was more where women wanted to be looked at. He decided to charge *us*. All we wanted, after all, was to dance.

That day Trixie couldn't stop grinning even to apply her lipstick. She had a cherry-sized bruise on the inside of her thigh, on the tendon that formed the ridge across those two dreamy hollows.

"To tell the truth," she began to confess, "I liked Max *before* I ever saw him. You girls mentioned 'Mr. Rosamund' all the time. I even asked Umberto about him. He said Mr. Rosamund was 'the tall one, the aristocratic-looking one, a real southern gentleman.' No kidding." Yes, indeed even unimpressionable Umberto had accurately sensed Max's sex appeal. Jeez, she hoped Max would come in today. "His height, his stiff walk, his big hands," she said. I decided then not to refer to Max as "Mr. Rosamund" anymore. Trixie leaned toward the mirror. "Oh no!" She discovered a tiny pimple that must have been blazing, unknown to her, at Max from the proud seat of her nosetip.

Could anyone guess what happened yesterday? she asked. Could I ever! But then she didn't even make me try. She told us all the sticky particulars. She divulged, with hearty realism, the miraculous synchronization, the abundance of moisture!

Trixie chattered on, stopping here to add a thing he'd said, going back to fill in a relevant fact. "Then do you know what he did?" She held the words captive behind her hands, then opening them like little doors, she whispered what he did. How rough was her voice; how shadowed her sleepy eyes: that Max had kept her up all night. She didn't spare a detail about the champagne room, that little nymph. Umberto happened to walk in and she had to mouth the last detail about her own performance ("within two minutes"). We turned and smiled stupidly.

"What? You look like kids caught playing dress-up in Mom's closet." Umberto had come in to tell us that we could keep all our new clothes in the storage room. No more hauling big bags around.

Speaking of dress-up, I recalled my mom's trunk stashed in Auntie's garage. I was permitted to open and rummage through, but only in the month of October with Halloween as my flimsy excuse. The beautiful shoes and gowns smelt permanently of East River Lake, musty and mournful. I announced that I would bring in the trunk.

"You wear a lot of your mom's stuff?" asked Trixie.

"Who was your mom? Someone famous?" asked Audrey.

"Only the most famous stripper ever," exaggerated Trixie. Truth was my mother only became known to the general public when she was shot in the stomach and died leaving a ruthless murderer at large for two years (they finally caught the moron—his name was "Ned"—working at a bait-and-tackle shop. I didn't follow the trial then—I wasn't allowed—nor did I research it later; he means nothing to me, nothing). Her picture somehow made it into the year-end issue of *LIFE*.

"She was killed?" asked Audrey with unchecked disgust.

I nodded, feeling myself blush. Sometimes, I am a character in a Jane Austen novel. Jesse looked at me with pity, as if to say, "So that's what's wrong with our poor mascot, our dear Pixie."

Trixie said my mother was her heroine and that she hoped to be as famous someday, not recognizing the tragedy she evoked.

"I can't believe you never said anything, Pixie," said Audrey. "There you are the daughter of a famous murdered stripper—a stripper yourself! What are you, nuts? Yuck, gives me the creeps. How *was* she killed? Was it very violent? Did you find her body?"

I searched for a way to explain myself, but I couldn't. I let her stare at me in disbelief. "Leave her alone, Aud," said Trixie in my defense. Miraculously, Odd obeyed.

Mockingbird called showtime. Trixie had to "throw something on real quick." Three wolfs got rid of the remaining portion of lunch, a bagel, and she had trouble keeping her lips closed over the mouthful as she pulled on a dress, any dress. The bagel wrapper was overhanded into the waste can; her face was dusted for crumbs and inspected briefly in a compact (clicked shut, thrown aside). She ran upstairs and must have swallowed the last gulp as she hopped onstage.

17

HAD WE EXPECTED MAX that day? Not really. But a little later in the afternoon he was there, briefly, wearing a slightly stupid but adorable grin. I asked about his car dealership. It's "a job." Max had always meant to sell the business, but he kept making money, you see. In the meantime, he was looking into some other more "important" way to fill his days.

"What could be more important than coming to the Playhouse?"

Max smiled. "It can't go on forever."

"I could go on forever."

"Well, for us, the men, the customers,"—Max had trouble counting himself in that group— "it can't go on indefinitely. Something has to come of it, I think. Unless you're like those two at the bar." He threw a glance at Percival and Bartholomew. "Doing the same thing over and over, expecting a different result."

"Those two," I said, "are beyond expecting. I want to do the same thing over and over again, and I hope to heaven nothing ever changes. Trixie too, that's obvious enough." Max smiled at my comment.

"Oh?" asked Max, sounding his question with doubt.

"But she'll change. When she looks back she'll see that every dance she performed before meeting you was merely a rehearsal for the day that Umberto opened the back door."

"I never saw a stripper dance like that before."

"Only a stripper could dance like that," I said under my breath. "Yesterday, you were the one persistent customer who got a different result."

"Oh, don't call me a customer."

"That's what you are, technically."

"What about nontechnically?"

"Trixie's lover."

"Oh, really?" He smiled at his success. "Of course, that's only good if she is known as 'Max's lover.'"

"Not yet," I laughed.

He looked at his feet. He thought about Rosamund. She'd been too young to marry, kept from developing interests in art or even history. She only had "housewifey" interests, charities and neighbors' lives, which bored him. By the way he phrased them, her faults seemed more his than hers. Now, Trixie, *she*'s led an interesting life. "Put herself through college. You know she was an actress as a kid?"

I hadn't heard about that yet, and I was delighted. I also learned then that Trixie was the Porina baby. I'd always loved that label, but never knew why.

"Yeah, she's different."

I laughed, "You think she's weird."

"You know, I say she has experience, but she manages to seem so out of it. It's fascinating." The waitress came by and made him suddenly feel self-conscious.

Trixie joined us, saying, "Oh, great song."

Max agreed. "We don't have music at home. Never did."

"How can you stand it?" asked Trixie.

"I haven't missed a lot of things I should have."

"I'd hate anyone who . . . Oh sorry."

But he said it was okay. He said she was right. Petty things had made him hate Rosamund. He hated her long fake nails and flat shoes. They disagreed on all the little things.

It was hard to believe that the man we had referred to as "Mr. Rosamund" might leave his wife. Rosamund was very pretty—as Max had once liked to point out. Snapshots of Trixie and Rosamund, placed side by side, would have informed us of Rosamund's finer looks. But Trixie in the flesh made Rosamund seem not to exist.

"I'd like to move out. Rosamund put wall-to-wall carpeting over maple and replaced my oak table with a Formica one." Max was a hermit crab climbing out of his shell in search of a new, larger one. "You see," he leaned toward Trixie and lowered his voice, "a man, like a work of art, is affected by his surroundings." Max and Trixie disagreed as to whether art can be affected negatively by its audience/environment or if the integrity of the artist's intent transcends the philistine and ugly thoughts of stupid viewers. Trixie took the latter position. It was only a small disagreement at the time, but, looking back at it now, I realize how ominously it foreshadowed a fundamental problem that would in time surface and do more damage than we ever might have guessed.

"You're still the same person. Formica can't change that."

Max laughed and leaned closer to her. "But I'm not, don't you see? You agree, don't you, that you can't hang a French master in a trailer home?"

"Well, yes," she paused.

Max interrupted, "Okay then. I'm right."

"I'm like your painting, hanging here. But that's the funny part," said Trixie with perverse glee, "Don't you see Max? Of course you do."

For the moment he added nothing. He still would not frame a Turner in chrome, no matter what Trixie said. Respond he would in the fullness of time.

Max had to get back to work, but before leaving he borrowed a dollar off Trixie (he'd given her all his cash) to buy a lottery ticket on his way to the office. "A ten-year habit," he said. "Rosamund won't serve dinner until I show her the ticket."

That day Calvin called "flower delivery" from the top of the stairs six times. Trixie and I got bouquets from Dan. That was nothing unusual, but then Umberto got three birds-of-paradise and a small pink pineapple, probably from the interior designer who was courting him. Cynical, ungrateful Audrey got a dozen roses. The card said, "Love, Charlie." (Charlie was alarmingly impressed with the fact that Audrey had computer skills.) "A bit presumptuous!" barked Audrey. Mockingbird went out for coffee and came back with daisies for Jesse. When Calvin called again, we thought he was goofing, but he came with a vase tucked under each arm, both for Andie, two "remember me" bouquets from two different fans with the same unimaginative florist. The sixth bouquet was from Max.

He picked her up that night in a coupe—I noted that it was not a Mazda he drove—and Trixie told him the funny thing about the flowers. He laughed at her, not the story. I waved and, like a vaudevillian clown, dogged them for a car length or two as they drove away.

"Hey, I told you I would give you a ride home"—Calvin in a blue suit, deep and dark as his skin. "This is it," he said to an old two-door sedan. We got in, slammed our long heavy doors. After we had pulled into traffic, we noticed that my door had caught imperfectly and the interior light kept itself alit. "Slam it hard this time," said Calvin. But I tried and couldn't while we were moving. "Must be something wrong with the switch," Calvin said gallantly.

As it got darker the light seemed to get brighter. Soon we were driving along the crowded parkway like a couple of goldfish in an illuminated bowl, too self-conscious to look at one another much less carry on a conversation. What's more, a fusty odor saturated my hair: smoke, perspiration and some unknown, unmistakable dressing room scent. I figured I was far enough away from him now, but I worried that he would try to kiss at the door. Calvin pulled onto the shoulder, and I opened and shut the door with better success. The light was finally extinguished.

"Whew," sighed Calvin as he reentered the roadway. Merciful darkness. Only the dashboard light's lurid glow.

During the course of ordinary small talk, Calvin brought up the fact that I had never danced anywhere but the Playhouse. He said, cryptically, "Then you don't really know." When I had asked him to clarify, he said, "What every other strip club is like."

I told him, feeling insulted, that I had an idea, that I'd been to Some Chorus Line and to Happy's.

"Happy's?" he repeated in alarm. I told him how Mr. Peters had sent me out on interviews and how I had never made it past the foyer.

When I declared that "it stank," Calvin laughed, "Yeah, I know Happy's smell well. I never told you, but I used to be the doorman. It was a little better then. After I quit Happy's, I meant to find some other kind of work. I'm a chef, you know."

I didn't know.

"Oh, so I haven't told you everything. You live out here, huh?" Empty field, decorated by telephone poles and parkway signs. We drove through a tunnel of trees that overhung the road and pulled up at my cottage. Suddenly he confessed, "I know why you do it."

This pierced me to the quick. If anyone could know me it would be Calvin, who always watched me. If he did really know then yes, I could believe that onstage I had overcome the great obstacle, *in front of lovers, friends, strangers and enemies—everyone who matters*. I had suspected as much, looking into my audience, but now here was proof, in this man who was, I was sure of it, about to say he loved me. No more anxiety about the paleness and instability of my idea of pixie, *that entity that no one has ever seen or caressed or tasted.*

He stared at me for a long time then said, "Let's go inside."

I told him I couldn't invite him in and started to get out of the car, but he hollered, "Oh no you don't," and leapt out himself. Astonished, I watched him run around to open my door. We both competed for my bag, which lay in the back seat. Calvin ended up with the prize.

"When all your promises are gone, I'll still be waiting for you," he said.

I thought, what promises?

He pinned me against his car as if I were a frightened wild thing about to squirm out of his grasp and dart into the woods. I wasn't going to struggle. I didn't struggle, but my heart was beating like a bird's.

"I have to talk to you."

"Talk to me? What about? I was only in the car with you for the past hour. Couldn't you have said it then?"

"I started to." Calvin rolled his eyes. "Never mind." He kissed me quickly on my unreadied mouth.

I watched his headlights back out of my driveway. Calvin had been, for a while, a distant whistle that I had perpetually heard but never acknowledged. Although something like this hadn't happened to me in a while, I wasn't totally innocent of the attention of an adoring male. I'd had my share of those who had chased me, had managed to get me to meet them for a dates. Sometimes the affair had even run a few months with reasonably well-exercised affection. But they had all ended in the same way, broken off irrevocably and with deep regret. The most recent era of my matelessness stretched like a desert, the horizon of which was so hazy it was indiscernible. It just went on and on and on. Calvin's appearance on this scene was so unexpected he had struck me first as an apparition, a two–palm treed, cool-pooled mirage.

Maybe a coupling with him would not end after the usual month or two when my impatience over lost liberty usually forced a retreat to my own small bed. Calvin, unlike any of my former lovers, knew me intimately upon the stage. That was *all* that he knew of me, and that had been enough, apparently. I hoped then that he might be happy to have me as I am, unlike the others who had first of all professed love and secondly demanded my resignation from dancing. Perhaps Calvin, who was part of the Playhouse and well acquainted with my activities there, would not be put off by it all, and would let me, let us, continue to do the things that gave so much satisfaction.

These were the possibilities that I let shine that night. I must admit, too, that Trixie's situation with Max lent additional illumination to my dream. Things were going better for her than they had gone for my mother with her customer cum lover. And wasn't Calvin even more suitable, in that he was already my protector and my friend?

I can't help but recall my episode with Calvin as I dredge up memories. His sonorous voice echoes in the place where I have stowed my thoughts of Trixie.

18

IMAGINE NOW. *MAX PULLS up to the house that he shares with Rosamund. It is one a.m. He sits in his car a while, listening until his favorite CD ends. What happened in the Champagne Room went beyond what he had imagined. Well, he imagined that, but he never thought. . . . He exhales noisily. He is resolved to ask her for a divorce. Can't lie to her, loves her, yes twenty years. One light on in the hallway. The bedroom dark. He starts to wipe his mouth. Lipstick. No, he thinks, don't try to hide. Oh, but that would be too cruel. He thoroughly cleans his face. He must do this without hurting.*

"Rosamund," he whispers opening the bedroom door, "You sleeping?" He walks blindly to the bed and feels for her form, which should be lying on its side in a fetal position. Nothing. "Rosamund?" He switches on the light. The bed is made. Just then he hears the front door open.

"Max?" she calls in the foyer.

"Where've you been?"

"Oh," she groans. "I'm exhausted." She throws herself on the sofa and puts her feet up. "Benefit," she says, "for the homeless."

Rosamund doesn't ask where he has been. She doesn't even suspect the affair. Hasn't she noticed his late hours? Doesn't she see it in his eyes that he doesn't love her?

"You do anything interesting today?" she asks, but before he can answer she jumps up. "God, I forgot to feed the cat."

"Rosamund, you know how I'm always saying we're so different?"

"Yes," she says, tossing back her hair. "Opposites attract."

"Well, that's not very helpful."

"Do we need help?" She looks surprised.

The phone rings. Both look at it, afraid. "Who could that be at this hour?"

I ran into Max at the Community Center, he in an NWCC–issue shirt that proclaimed his size, XXL. His photo ID was strung around his neck (left brow arched, slight snarl). Max said he had been unable to tell his wife about Trixie.

"You see, she just found out that her grandmother died and flew out for the funeral. I want to wait a week or so until she's gotten over it."

"I don't think it will do either of you any good to wait."

"That's easy for you to say, Pixie, but you're not in my position."

"I can imagine how difficult it must be."

"I've been with her for twenty years. Can you imagine that?"

Max was right. I could not imagine what it would be like to be in a relationship that had lasted twenty years.

When we walked into the fitness room, Trixie spotted us and abandoned her stationary bicycle mid-program. She took Max by a limp hand and led the way to the main equipment area where she, herself, not Kevin, ordained him in Nautilus and showed him the mysteries of Keiser with a seriousness that charmed and delighted him. She had a clipboard and chart with his name on it, a pencil behind her ear that fell out every time she leaned over him to adjust the air pressure gauge. "Oh, that was a lot," Trixie would say at the end of his reps. He was already a big guy, and the thought of a bigger, stronger Max must have subdued and pleased Trixie.

Together they made a provocative pair because of the sexy difference in their sizes; he referred to her as his better third, an endearment true to their relative weights. "Oh, that was a lot," she said again (shiver). Amorous shifty-eyed Max looked as if he might at any moment grab her and press her to his chest with a hairy forearm.

Trixie strapped Max into the butterfly press and leaned across, while he, paralyzed by desire, followed the movements of her slender arms and enjoyed a lock of heavy hair that brushed against his nose (inhaling deeply and rolling his eyes).

When he sat on one machine facing the wrong way, Trixie said without sarcasm that she had never seen anyone use it that way. With a light hand, Trixie pretended to maneuver his shoulders in the right direction (like a nurse whose patient insists he "can do it").

Later Max and Trix drove me home. I was stuffed in the back seat of his XJS. At every opportunity, his hand left the stick shift and sought her thigh. He shifted into fourth. Then, craning his neck to address me, Max told me (for the sake of idle chat) that he had moved out of his house with Rosamund and rented a hotel suite for himself.

"It's nice," said Trixie.

"It's okay," Max corrected.

Max had long-range plans. He owned and rented out a second home, a stone house, that he planned to move into. "I bought it to surprise Rosamund, but she hated it. 'Too woodsy' she'd said."

"Not far from you, Pixie." This he addressed to the road, which had produced a curve that demanded his attention.

"That'll be nice," I said.

Max kept glancing from the road to Trixie's calm profile, she every now and again replacing a strand of hair behind her ear. Max said he didn't know when he could evict the renters, probably by next month—his hand on the wheel opened and fingers splayed, a gesture of doubt—the renters were a couple, half of which had been Rose's best girlfriend in grade school. A difficult situation for Max.

We pulled up at my lichen-green cottage, with matching awning, bright white shutters, a terra-cotta pot of moss roses on the porch. Motley violet snowball bushes surrounded the lawn and completed the pretty picture, and the lovers exploded with tenderness. The house was "so cute" they didn't believe anyone really lived there. But indeed I did.

I gave a quick tour of the house—only two and a half rooms. In the living room Max seemed like a giant, easily reaching up to the cross-beams. Above was a pitched-roof alcove where I slept among photos of Old Hill girlfriends and prints of Mother and myself. There was also a cramped bathroom. Tour over, I brought them back outside as the sun was going down and an amphibian or insect half-chirped half-croaked in the nearby lowlands.

Max admired my herb area. He bent down and crushed a sage leaf, smelt it, and guessed its name. I apologized for my tiger lilies that were past their prime. I grabbed a mislaid clipper from a nearby tree stump and trimmed (an embarrassed housewife who nervously clears a cluttered table). "Now, this is a real garden," said Trixie. "It's so natural. I'm sure you work hard in it, Pixie, but it seems like it all just grew this way, you know? If I had a garden it would look like this too, not artificial, you know?" Max was smiling at her as she spoke: she was like my garden.

A fuzzy bee inspected Max's nose, and he brushed it away. We plopped down on the Adirondack chairs laughing. I brought out two potted citronella candles. Trixie had slipped her shoes off and was rubbing her long toes in the grass. They were talking about moving into Max's little stone house.

Trixie said dreamily, "The only thing I wish were different about it is that it's not by the water. I want a house on a hill, a cliff looking over the ocean."

"I can see you living in a house on a cliff," said Max gravely. "When I first saw you I thought that about you."

"Thought what?"

"Your position was precarious. All those beastly, ugly men."

"Mf, really?" said Trixie, "I never thought of myself like that at all."

"It was attractive," said Max, contradicting his earlier statement about beauty suffering in a bad environment.

"Strange," Trixie went on, "You mean 'not safe'?"

"That's what I like about you, you have no idea."

A naked girl in a room full of men feels perfectly safe. Of course, I understood this but I could see why Max might not.

"I hope I won't make you cynical."

"No! I just never looked at it from your point of view, a man's point of view, I guess." Trixie looked at her feet dejectedly. "Yep," she sighed, "strange."

Yes, it was strange, I thought, and, like Trixie, my mother had not been aware of, or perhaps intentionally disregarded, the vicious natures that prowled dirt roads. It was much more fun and emotionally satisfying to imagine instead that we were surrounded by only the benign forms of devotion and lust.

"I want to plant more trees in the back," said Max, restarting the conversation, "so that we can really hear the wind rustle the leaves at night."

I insisted that they take back a dozen furry gray four o'clocks (a sage-textured thin stalk, skinny leaves, and small bright fuchsia blooms). Trixie nodded, listening in profile, triangular nose touching the petals. "Doesn't smell."

We sat a while in painless silence.

"Getting bitten?" Max asked of Trixie, who swatted and rubbed her neck.

"Eaten up," she admitted.

I told them to "git goin' then." We slapped our faces and thighs as we said goodbye.

I went into my porch and put on the lights. I sat down and heard their car drive away and disappear. I couldn't see out, but anyone who happened to walk, drive, or crawl along the old road at night would see Pixie in her glowing glass house.

I imagined I could see Max and Trixie (mind's eye) in his convertible coupe swerving to the end of my old road and turning left at the first lighted intersection in search of the parkway.

When they find the long straight road heading due west, they cannot help remarking on the moon (it is remarkable, gibbous always is), which floats dead center above the road. They laugh at themselves for letting a thing like the moon make them so tingly.

He wants to tell her about aesthetics. He is nervous about pronouncing that word aloud. Although it is an important word in his reading vocabulary, he can't remember having ever said it lately, not since he was young, not since he met Rosamund. He wants to go back for another degree. "At my age I know that sounds impractical, but I . . ."

Trixie interrupts, "Max, I'm glad to hear it. I don't want you to sell cars for the rest of your life. Are you kidding? I mean, I don't hold it against you or anything like that, but anyone can see that you hate it. You never seemed like a salesman to me. I could just tell that there was more to you. It's the way you're so hesitant, you know. You think a lot, I think, because you're not very quick to act, you know. A salesman doesn't think. He acts. He's an actor. You're sincere, even if you are a little uncertain sometimes. Is this what you want? Going to school, I mean. I want you to do what makes you happy."

"Even if I don't make any money at it?"

"Well, you will eventually."

Her confidence is irrational, but he appreciates it. "Don't take this the wrong way, but sometimes you seem so naive."

"Optimistic," she corrects.

"Oblivious."

"I choose to be." She flashes her pretty teeth. "So it's not real innocence like you might think. I see what's there, but I look beyond it, for instance, the fact that you're a car salesman."

"You realize then that going for a degree in philosophy is not particularly sound?"

She nods.

He takes her cold hand, saying something she can't hear over the windnoise, saying that he has never felt etc.*; neither has he expected [something, something] and she, too, is, you know. Isn't it weird how it was going so fast?*

It is, she agrees, but neither wants to slow down.

I glanced at my watch. By about that time they would be coming up on the gas station.

"Stop?" asks Max who by now knows her habits and her unbelievably small bladder. He knows everything about her, loves everything about her; he wants to get her earlobe in his teeth. Trixie opens the door. Max grabs her arm. She struggles free with sham prudence (now c'mon, Max, behave), slams the door and hurries in to request the key (she really has to go).

Who is that skipping creature? he asks. And he marvels with uncomfortable delight at the speed with which their love affair is progressing. True, it has taken some time to get to know her, but how rapidly now that unbelievable first impression is being realized in her comments and ideas.

He can see Trix inside the station. He watches her take the key from the manager, a key attached to a big plastic female figure (Trixie's mimed "thanks" and bright smile). The manager leans over his counter to watch her walk out. Then, with what Max recognizes as male habit, the manager looks around to see if the pretty girl has come alone or is with a leering spouse.

Trixie instigates these situations, but she has no idea. Or maybe she does know, like she says, but feels differently about the knowledge. It all must seem so awfully petty to her sometimes, thinks Max, the way the world is about sex. She thinks she knows something we don't. It's true she doesn't seem to think like us, at all. He suddenly realizes that he must protect her.

To think Max thought he loved Rosamund! All that was a dry run compared to this. This is the one he was meant for. He envisions his role clearly now. He relaxes and turns on the radio. After a while he begins to wonder what is taking Trixie so long. Then for some strange reason he begins to worry that their affair might eventually peter out, but in this very moment of doubt, "Give In to Me," starts playing on the radio, and he feels a spasm of renewed devotion contract his gut.

In the ladies' room, as Trixie leans over the sink to peer in the mirror, she is startled by the faucet that turns on automatically by infrared sensor. Dork, she says to herself. She wipes off the crooked lipstick and tries for the second time to get it right.

She realizes that she feels nothing of that complex ambivalence that she once had for her father. Max, here was a man who knew her. She washes her hands, holds them, palms up, palms down, under the ridiculously cool and impotent blower, relieved—as she finishes them on her skirt—that she is finally talking, really talking, with another person.

She plops into the seat beside Max, rubbing her knees together. Max nods at the dashboard. "Ooh, our song," she says. They kiss until the DJ interrupts, brusquely parting, wiping their faces with their sleeves. Trixie gathers up her heavy hair and tosses it over her shoulder.

And so I imagined them as I sat on my lit porch looking, theoretically, into the blackness beyond my windows but seeing instead my own reflection in the glass.

19

I WAS WALKING DOWN Farm Road 7. At the crossroads I came to Mother's grave, marked only by a pile of white stones. The authorities had suggested her death was suicide. The deacon at the local House of God gave her a burial suited to her crime, buried on unconsecrated ground with a stake through her body. Hot, dry wind. A pile of white stones. Anthill. Sugar taffy in my hair.

I woke with a start. Slowly my bed became real to me and the dusty road a dream. *Ay, there's the rub.*

Arriving at work later that day, I opened the Playhouse door, hesitated, feeling a rush of adrenaline like I felt every time I went onstage. Calvin was as usual at his post. He was not to be avoided. "Hello," he said grabbing me, still playing unconfirmed lover, joking about his affections in case I wasn't going to take him seriously. In my mind, our situation had changed, not because of anything said the night of that mostly painfully silent journey, but rather because of my new resolutions and plans.

It was Trixie's day off. I only remember weird tidbits of that day, odd little events, all too unrelated to tell without boring; we advised Audrey on the proper concealment of scars. We helped Sammy look for her nightie. There was an absurd, unimportant, demented inside joke about Dan. Another left shoe was lost—never the right! And so the day passed.

Only Calvin's newly exaggerated presence is remarkable for that day. I danced with less spontaneity and grace than I usually managed. Calvin, I think, noticed and tried to ease the situation by not staring. The effect was positive; I began to dance with more life, confirmed in the hope that he would soon turn his eyes back to catch me. And, yes, he did, just as I had done something especially erotic and lovely—I forget what.

I do begin to remember, now, another odd event that day. The girls disagreed about what attracted more mementos. Andie insisted eye-catching costumes were the most effective. Audrey (whose orthopedic pads at the time were dangling from her second toes) thought her red bodice "worked."

"Red isn't your color," I insisted. "Clashes with your hair. Try green," I suggested. "You don't look bad in green."

"Badly," corrected Sidney. "Why are you smiling?"

Audrey was so wrong. Nothing so material could possibly gauge the charm of a stripper. I have dedicated my life to that belief. Any dancer who did not intuit this ended up like a pigeon in a Skinner box, superstitiously performing outrageous feats for erratic pellet-dropping customers. And so it is now at Happy's, Le Mirage, and the late Girlie Playhouse.

Later, Audrey decided red wasn't her color after all. I have to give the old girl credit—regardless of her impending treachery: she was rooted in her thinking. She didn't like stripping, but she understood herself and always realized—though sometimes a little too late—her own limitations. As far as her red bodice was concerned, she wore it only once more then tossed it into a corner and never took it up again. (It strangely disappeared into the black hole where left shoes lived.) Costumes weren't the thing. Ultimately the otherworldly suppleness, the slippery appeal of the Playhouse dancer was all.

It was enough certainly for Calvin, whose brim that day finally overflowed. He nabbed me in the hallway. "Come here, please," he said, his voice commanding by its low pitch alone. And this is the great incident of that otherwise fairly insignificant day, an incident, or *event* I should say rather, that, though it's not part of Trixie's story, is very much a part of mine, and I cannot omit it here—however much the exigencies of journalistic form insist. He took me by the arm and I was swept ahead of him into Umberto's office. Within minutes we were, after falling into a large easy chair and sliding to the hardwood floor, consummate lovers.

And there was a buzz from my chest to my groin. Calvin's open mouth rested heavily against my cheek. I remember looking over his shoulder, seeing that remarkable vista before me, Calvin's rashness, his sense of immediacy, his uncouth strength and intelligent eyes. I delayed that first spoken sound that would end that moment and begin the next one, the start of the long and arduous process of love. I waited, in that sparse ill-lit office, amid crated liquor, behind the locked door that muffled the voices of Audrey and Sid, for him to speak first. But we were disturbed by a rap on the door.

Calvin jumped up, righting himself. Umberto inquired, "Calvin? You in there?"

Calvin answered, opening the door a crack while I got behind the door.

"Topside quick. Trouble," Um said, and then Calvin leapt, stupendously, to do his job.

I remained behind, unnerved—at that instant the problems of patron improprieties held little fascination for me. I wondered how it could for Calvin. An important moment shattered by the likes of Umberto—it made me mad. I wish I could display the facts here more warmly, but in all honesty I can't. Our "romantic" beginning was bungled and interrupted, an awkward fledgling that flopped about and fell and never did take wing.

I waited for Calvin to return, which he did, truly, with a new lover's promptness, surrounding me, shoulder, arm, and chest. But something had happened up there that had clearly disturbed him.

In the dimly lit hallway, escorting me up the stairs and toward the back door, he made a pronouncement that produced in me a salutary chill. "The girls have started to change."

"After every set."

But Calvin wouldn't take up my joke. "What do you think you'll do?"

"I haven't any idea what you mean, Calvin."

"I mean if Umberto starts running this place like a Happy's or a Some Chorus Line, will you be happy?"

I didn't answer.

Calvin wanted to renew his offer to drive me home, but his car was in the shop. He walked me to the train, wanted to escort me all the way, but I wouldn't have it. We made plans to meet for our first proper date. He was frustrated that next Saturday was the nearest common day off.

When my train pulled out, I noticed that his dwindling black form remained on the platform until I had gone too far out of range to even imagine him still loitering there—somehow for my sake—in the cold night air.

The next morning I found Umberto sitting on Calvin's stool. "Calvin quit. Up and quit. Do you know what reason he gave?" he asked rhetorically, as if I could have guessed. "You."

20

Survivors often remember with peculiar clarity the ordinary details before a tragic event, and come to regard any and all related trivia with eerie sentimentality. The last goodbye (see ya later, yeah see ya, bye) acquires a creepy irony in the light of subsequent death. It is with this special tangy vividness that I do recall the particulars of that last Sunday swim with my mother.

The lake near Runaway Stay was artificial. It had an abbreviated shoreline of imported sand surrounded by gray-green live oaks, huge rough trees over a hundred years old with low wide-spread canopies. There was a fishing dock—about the length and width of a good strip club runway—where drowsy, beer-bellied men in floppy hats nodded at the water. Mom walked to the end with a proud, lewd swing in her hips. Knock-kneed, I waited with my inner tube and sand pail on the shore, admiring her. My soul, she was something. As I stood watching, what I felt, even at that age, was a little more than awe, something like envy. She wore a ruffled bikini, like mine, low on her hips. She had a white, straw sun hat on her pale head, hair loosely tied and trailing down her tawny back. She wore lamé sandals with high heels of stacked gold. We hadn't found any in my size (Mom had asked the useless clerk), so I went barefoot, which was every bit as sexy, Mom consoled, in its own way.

At the end of the dock, she stopped and looked at the horizon, shading her eyes with one hand, and, strangely, standing on her tiptoes.

Then she returned, twisting the soles of her feet on the wooden planks with each step; big painted mouth smiling at the sound of a half dozen cat-call whistles, and she reported back to me on the condition of the water, "A little choppy, but the wind will die down."

We decided to swim. I proudly rode Mom's hip into the water, showing her the blue-tailed dragonfly that advanced to the edge of the pier and withdrew in reverse. I pointed out a spider that ran across the water, then I returned my fat waxy finger to my ear. I was always showing her stuff, teaching her things. Mother-daughter waded deeper. When the water began lapping around our busts, our combined buoyancy made Mother's steps jerky and bouncy, kick, hop, kick hop. Then Mother and I dog-paddled—neither of us could swim—in the warm, brown lake for about twenty minutes. When we were tuckered out, when spasms started spreading my toes, we waded to shore.

I remember I had refused to wear my orange life vest because it covered my pretty bikini. She understood. Our matching swimsuits were made of blue cotton overlaid with rows of white crepe ruffles. I felt quite fancy in those pants, and the extravagant frills on the bra made the very most of the very little I had at the time.

After situating our towel and basket, we probably made a sandcastle, letting wet, muddy sand drip through our fingers into lumpy gray towers. Although there were so many sandcastle days, and I might be getting them confused, I know it was our habit to coat our castles with crushed freshwater mussel shells, in order to keep teenaged boys from stomping on them after we left. By the time the construction project was completed, the sun had dried my hair into a matted net of beige, white, and ash strands. My itchy scalp made me anxious to get home and have a bath. Before we left, Mom wanted me to change out of my damp bathing costume, but I didn't want the other bathers to see how much of my voluptuousness was actually ruffle and how little was actually me. Mom said I shouldn't be embarrassed; I had a good trim figure—she herself was not at all busty, and she would change too, if her "tiny equal" wanted.

"You first," I said. She swept her hair off her shoulders and back and asked me to tug the magic cord, and when I did her top fell off. "Ta-da," she said, laughing playfully, kicking up her bottoms and catching them with her hand, a stunt that I was anxious to copy. She was evenly tanned all over. My own bottom proved to be pasty and cold where the suit had left its mark. Mom took our white cotton wraps out of our bag and helped me into mine before putting on her own. Everyone stared and several whistled, but she didn't mind. She smiled back and waved. "Mom!" I objected. "Don't make them look over here." Then she looked at me in a way that made me feel shame for my prudishness, and quickly pulled my sundress over my head. "It's only skin, more of the same," she said. "Those old coots. They've seen it all before."

There was a fussy man, early fifties, with a pencil mustache, who had been sitting near us eating warm egg-salad sandwiches. Just the smell of a hardboiled egg makes me sick to this day. He had his lawn chair pointed in the direction of our striped towel most of that morning. I don't think Mom noticed him much at all because she didn't recognize him on the road a half an hour later. Mom often didn't recognize people. I think she was probably awfully nearsighted, which made her grope through our days in a hazy sort of sleepwalk, not really knowing for certain what lay ahead of her. I imagine she never noticed the sour expressions on some people's faces. It was either her eyes or her disposition that didn't see these things. But she always seemed to see every little glint in my greedy eye.

I know I noticed that man. I had even marked him out like a storyteller marks out a character in an early scene to prepare the audience for his big part later on. He was staring as we changed, with a beach ball in his lap. As we were leaving, the owners of the ball, two teenaged boys and their girls, came and demanded it back. He wouldn't give it up, and when the chubby boy snatched it from him, the kids burst out laughing. I understand now what was happening, but frankly I wish I didn't. It was none of our business.

Mother and I stopped at the general store before going home, and I bought, with my nickel from a found Coke bottle deposit, banana saltwater taffy wrapped in wax paper. It had already begun to melt by the time we passed the halfway-to-home mark, a fire ant mound that was right in the middle of the dirt road. I kicked the extinct volcano, and it suddenly erupted with hundreds of hot ants that trailed down the sides. I wanted to stop to watch, but Mom said fire ants would bite sticky sweet babies like me, and she reminded me of last week's *National Geographic* special about a goat that was eaten alive by army ants. Egad! I squealed, with mirth and fear, and scrambled, kicking and waving, into her arms. She patted my back to comfort me, and I patted hers to comfort me, an idiosyncrasy I continued in my Old Hill Girls School years.

Mom picked up and carried "her silly little thing," and while I looked over her shoulder, the horizon gently bounced.

Here ends the ordinary day. Used to be, the remembered facts were more fuzzy and confused; I was no real help to the authorities. But since then—with the help of news reports according to deluded psychiatrists—I have been able to recall both some significant and some absurd details. When a blurry shape blocked Mom's path, her hand was holding the back of my neck so that I couldn't turn around. "Mom?" I whined, but her long-nailed thumb was clamped behind my left ear, and her fingers gripped my right jaw. I tried to leverage myself away from her chest, but she had me there pretty tight. He said, "I know what you are trying to do . . . ," or words to that effect. Mom seemed calm and tried to pass him by quietly. I finally turned and got a glimpse: blue shirt with white stitching, white belt—Ah, the fussy man at the shore—short black pipe? She looked over her shoulder and saw what she knew to be a gun. She put me down, yanked my arm, and pushed me behind her. I didn't hear what else was said. I was shouting objections (hey, Mom, you're hurting me) that in retrospect give me a salty, foolish pang. There was a loud ugly pop. Mom fell on me. How surprisingly warm and bright her blood was. At first, I wasn't scared at all, only startled, surprised. But then I panicked when I realized our roles had been switched. She needed me to protect her. A trail of fire ants had begun to trickle toward the spot where she lay in the road. Frantic, I told her not to worry, she would be all right. Her dark eyes darted confusedly. Her plump lip curled in a kind of fascinated disgust. I collapsed on top of her and slobbered on her moist creased neck. Her Iris 99 still lingered, even after that long day on the beach. Or was it mine? Sometimes she used to put a dab on my throat too.

I don't think I ever turned away from Mother's neck to look again at her killer. Whether he stood and watched for a while or ran away immediately, I do not know. After he had performed his act, the man no longer mattered. To me he became, not an individual acting on his own urge, but the Gunsmoke City Mission's index finger. Everybody in the town knew Mom danced at a city cabaret, and they regarded her with a mixture of public scorn and private envy; mental revulsion and uncurling, stiffening, trigger-squeezing desire. According to everything Gunsmoke held dear, she should have been really depraved and gauche, but she wasn't, much to their frustration.

Mom's mouth was darkly filled. When she pushed out her tongue to lick her lips, a streak of red trickled across her downy cheek and pooled in her ear. I was holding her hand, stroking her arm, still telling her not to worry, it's gonna be all right, like she had said to me so often. She took my hand to her cheek and shook her head, as if to say she *wasn't* going to be all right, but that I would be. I would just have to be careful, that's all, and be strong and not let anyone ever do to me what they did to her. She pulled me toward her chest and held me there. I guess she didn't want me to look. She hugged me with clawing hands, but after a while she relaxed, and her chest rose erratically and slowly.

I actually fell asleep on her while she bled to death, so I don't have any recollections of her last thoughts or words. When I did finally regain a sliver of consciousness in a fully unfolded night, I was down the road a piece—dancing of all things. I certainly don't remember leaving her there on the road, but that I did.

I do vaguely remember following the music of a parked car near the lake (teenagers). I still have a tidbit of that melody rattling in my head. I hear the ironic tone; the beat was powerful, but slow. Some of the words might have been, "screaming in key." Another fragment went, "I know, but . . ." Sometimes I think I hear one precious bar of that music, but when I try to hum it, it dissolves. I remember I kept running and dancing and felt pure and loose, and I couldn't see anything but the bright lights in my eyes, and I couldn't feel anything but that music.

The sheriff's headlights probed and pierced, as he warily approached the mad little dirty night pixie dancing on a deserted road to the faraway music of some parked car.

I went further than I intended. I wanted to linger on the events of that last ordinary swim, but the recollection of particulars led to the inexorable climax. I couldn't help it, but I've done with that now, and with Mother's ghost on my retina, I turn now toward her successor, the smaller, more willowy Trixie, and remember the last time I happened to watch her dance, and because it was the last dance for me, I can't help but corrupt the innocent description with hindsight.

21

Thursday was, I believe, the last official idyllic day of the Girlie Playhouse. The cabaret has operated unhappily since then, but I prefer to dwell upon earlier times, repeating the typical details to which I've assigned exquisite significance.

Before I go on, I would like to try to describe one dance, with Max left out of it, the last dance. Everything would change in a matter of hours. Thursday was a gloomy day: white sky, brown horizon, spritzing wind. (Calvin's absence added yet another tone of melancholy.) I was at the bend in the boomerang bar—one loose shoe dangling from my toe—observing, chin-up, the stage over the heads of two customers while Trixie climbed the stairs and stood at the back of the stage on a three-step circular platform. She was wearing a cropped top and matching black shorts, shamelessly short. The ripples of her rib cage dimly showed above low-slung pants. I looked for her bicycle-wreck scar, achieved at age ten, and found it in the remembered spot just along the fifth rib.

She asked Mockingbird to play a certain song. If she danced for the full 4.31 minutes, she would use an unfair portion of set time (Ah, c'mon, was her meek rejoinder). I heard waxing applause and was momentarily perplexed as the house was virtually empty, a few guys at the bar, two or three at the stage. Then I realized the applause was part of a live recording. Trixie smiled at the distant whistles. The lead-in was long and arduous; it was a waiting sound, and as she gazed about the room, biting the nail of her index finger, I could see her eyes darting, her mind probing a thought. She glanced at Mockingbird and threw her eyes up to the ceiling. This meant, "turn it up." He did.

Trixie kicked, then took a meaningful step down. Again. The crescendo was horribly imminent when Trixie reached the bottom of the platform and had the clear runway before her.

Then she flew to the end with the music.

Two businessmen to my immediate left at the bar were jolted by her display and jerked their heads stageward, meaning, "let's have a closer look." They were drawn in with their briefcases and tinkling glasses to a table right at the runway's edge. Trixie, staring above heads, tense hands protecting the V between her legs, smiled at thin air. For the sake of the well-meaning audience, I felt the pang of her indifference. Oblivious girl, happy girl, coveted girl; we wanted her attention but got none.

Dan folded a memento into the shape of a bird, set it on the stage and waited for her to notice his offering, he with raised brows, mouth ajar, and hands miming a "ta-da!"

She overlooked his offering and passed on. Another regular, the young attorney with silver hair, folded his arms, leaned back, and watched as she, with stiff swift legs, took the runway in three leaps. Then she—by accident or with full intention, who could tell?—landed right at the stage's brink immediately above him. He had the opportunity to assert his existence by exhaling mildly over her thigh.

Now came the part of the song that gave her a vague feeling of elation, and with an odd smile and arms in the air—"Do you, don't you want me to love you?"—Trixie came down the runway with heavy, purposeful steps. She stopped suddenly, looking our dear Dan in the eye with spooky deliberation that made him shift uncomfortably in his seat. Dan seemed about to jump up and say "Yes!" but too late; she was running away again. He shouted, "Huzzah!" in mock worship, but I'd seen it; I'd seen that prick of Trixie magic stick Dan in the throat, and yes, he did, despite his attempt to make light of it, gulp and close his eyes when she had gone away.

Sweat had collected around her downy dark temples, and damp hairs clung to her flushed face. Finally, her uncomfortable top was flung to the floor. "Happy now?" mouthed the attorney, but Trixie didn't notice him. Standing motionless on the back platform, she surveyed the room. Her eyes smiled with nearsighted softness at unrecognized faces. Here was latent disdain, animated by some sharp inspiration, some sore feeling. She was piqued, manic, uncouth, funny, playful, provocative. There could be no doubt that she was happily insane, yes it's true. It made us all a little nervous. By the depth of her concentration I could see she was dancing only for herself; she was "out there" as Dan once described it, looking lonely onstage, haloed in clear light. She glanced up and smiled into the light, into her thoughts, into her estrangement from the world. The audience provided the contrast to mark her out; she kicked against it; she pushed it away; she stood on it, on us. All I could do was watch in nervous resignation knowing that I was a part of what she fought against.

She had found for herself, there on the stage under the hot lights and in the cool profundity of her detachment, fullness and quiet. Ah, her dark blue eyes mercilessly passed over us, instead reflecting our expectations, like the eyes of a small nocturnal creature encountered on a dark road giving us back our own searching lights.

While her breastbuds under bluish light gave me a shiver of satisfaction, I have to admit that I was no more than another pair of eyes that only dimly perceived what she meant by that hand cupped over her mouth, that strange look of fear between beats, that frown that she shook off with a shudder and that way she opened her arms and made herself vulnerable before a thick-tongued audience. Despite the readily apparent and cruel fact that no one would ever feel her body the way she did, I still pretended that I felt a connection each time her eyes met mine. I, and not only I, but also every pair of slitted eyes, raised brows, and parted lips expressed a keen need to be the one for whom she danced.

Every night I still enumerate the hollows, the nooks I love: the concave beauties of the sides of her buttocks, under the arms, at the groin. I keep her dancing.

Unfortunately, Bartholomew, in his astonishing knack for bad timing, decided to tell her that joke. "Hey, Trixie." He cupped his hand to his mouth and walked up to the stage, "Hey, Trix."

She jerked into a startled stare, "Huh, what?" and went to the edge to hear what he had to say. Luckily, it was a dull spot in the song. I hoped he would hurry and be done with the joke and let her get back to dancing. (Didn't he see what I saw? Didn't he know to leave her alone?) She bent down, holding up her gathered hair with one hand; the other hand clasped a bare breast. She nodded, turned her ear to his mouth, seemed to laugh. I hoped that was it; a good part of the song was approaching. She stood upright, said a parting word and just in time for the favorite line, "but she ain't no dancer," her body went limp; her shoulders crumpled and her head hung down (Trixie, sweetie, are you okay?), and with a huge sigh she buried her face in her hands, but then the hands came away and she was smiling, more happily than ever.

That day, that last day, I felt strangely compelled. Why? I'd seen her dance so many times before, and I wonder now if she or I hadn't sensed that something was coming, something sad and dark and confusing. That Thursday she danced with fey charm that to me now is almost terrible.

Yes, that day Trixie danced with such an utter abandon that, when I think of it now, I get a metallic taste in my mouth. Her hands traveled over and gripped her body as she turned, as if she were trying to rid herself of those horrible frustrating stares. Bartholomew remembered another funny part to the story and doubled back from the bar, but she was dancing with her eyes closed and he couldn't get her attention. Don't try it, Bart. Let her go. He put up his hand twice, started to speak, but realized it was futile and returned to the bar. I shook my head at him, and he looked at his lap embarrassed.

The song ended. She was all flushed and damp. The attorney waved a memento at her, afraid she would run off before he could tell her that *he* thought she was great! He wanted to get her to stop so he could tell her he really liked her, but Trixie half curtseyed and skipped on, leaving the admirer to mutely thank her slender back. She left the stage, and it became that ordinary Thursday again.

When Trixie joined us at the bar, Sidney asked her, "Don't you ever get tired?" She never did.

Umberto had given the Italian brothers an unheard-of afternoon break and tended bar. With false obsequiousness he asked Sidney, "Would you care for another, Mith?" She accepted or rejected his efforts until the game grew dull. Soon Sidney left stagebound and was replaced at the bar by tiny Sammy, who climbed, after a darling and daring effort, onto a stool and solemnly begged for coffee.

Umberto imitated her Hispanic "pliss," and she smirked back at him. All kidding aside, Umberto, setting the full cup down and an elbow after that, asked how Sol was. Sol was fine, she said pretending still to be hurt. Sol never made fun of her accent. "Is that what I was doing?" said Umberto as if indignant, but the joke went nowhere else, and so we paused and observed the silence with different degrees of boredom. Who was up now anyway? Sam and I turned to watch shapely Sidney dance. When she caught our eyes she covered hers with a dainty hand. We turned back to the mirror behind the bar. My bright hair glimmered in the dark mirror; Sam's drowsy head was at my reflection's side cradled in her hand, and next to her Trixie's profile calmly watched the door.

"Hey, I almost forgot," said Umberto with a proud toothy grin. He produced a cardboard box, put it on top of the bar, grabbed a table knife, and proceeded to gouge it open. "Looky what I got for you." He held out a wad of multicolored garters.

"What for?"

"What for? They're to put tips in," said Umberto.

Utter disgust contorted Trixie's face.

"Do we have to?" whined Sammy.

Disappointed, Umberto said, "No, you don't *have* to. I just thought you'd like it."

"Hey Umberto," I said to cheer the tasteless man, "Next time order black, not neon."

"Yeah?" Um was perplexed. "I figured you could see it better onstage, you know, under the black lights."

"Visibility isn't beauty," scoffed Trixie.

"In the animal kingdom it is," he said, and we eyed him skeptically. "Think of fish and birds."

"You're thinking of the males," I said.

"Yeah, Umberto," said Sam laughing and tossing a bundle of garters, "You wear 'em."

Trixie left her stool, gave the door one last look and went to the dressing room.

Max had not been in at all that afternoon. "Too many things to do," said Trixie when I asked her.

Later that evening, the bad weather was canceled, and the club filled up; customers sat around the stage three rows deep. Umberto turned up the music. Mockingbird sent the strobe light rotating. "Remember" played, and I was dancing. For the heck of it I had put on one of Umberto's garters, and a frightening thing happened. Our dear Dan changed. When he put a memento in my garter, his finger brushed lightly against my thigh and floated poetically through the air and into his lap. I was embarrassed. I was about to laugh it off when, over the heads of others, I saw Max's head enter and wait in the foyer.

He was freshly groomed, but seemed to be entertaining the idea of a goatee. He kept rubbing his chin, and he was having great difficulty suppressing a smile. I told him Trixie was down in the dressing room, and I asked him what was new.

"Seven million dollars," he said.

22

THROUGH NO FAULT OF his own, Max had suddenly become a fantastic personality. He would be known for the rest of his days, not as Maximilian Roquefort Price, but as "that married guy who won the seven million dollar lottery and bought seven strippers." He would become, in history's newspaper prison, the sum of his columns, inert black marks that say nothing, really, about the man. All his accomplishments, past and future, would pale in comparison to this idle deed. Just as my mother became "that murdered stripper" to the entire world, Max's real life concluded with his winning the lottery.

I am of the opinion that his life without the lottery is remarkable enough. I trust his story so far has been worth the effort of my telling it. Now, I must proceed to the next chapter, one that, as far as I'm concerned, is only remarkable for its implausibility. I'm almost tempted to skip over this bit, but then that would be just like me to omit what everyone else considers the most exciting part.

Our original Max had been quiet and shy, a nervous lip-chewing soul who didn't seem at all as if he belonged out in the world, having to find a seat or ask for drink in a crowded cabaret. He had seemed sidetracked from his lonely walk, and before I got to know him, I even thought he was aloof, but he had gradually warmed, and had been getting into more friendly habits: a salute to the bartender, Sal, when Sal gave Max his wine free of charge, a wink for the plump waitress when she said bye Max see you next time Trixie works, but this Max, this seven-million-dollar Max, was unbelievably friendly. He bought all the mementos allotted for the night's use and asked for more. The cashier obliged. Max still wanted more. "More?" she said in high-pitched disbelief and sold him the entire stock of six boxes.

The cabaret was now crowded: two doctors' conventions—of philosophy and veterinary medicine—were in town. Half the crowd wore instant introductions, "Hello my name is" labels on their lapels, and everyone felt chummy as a result. A party of six girls from the Amazon Movers Company. A groomless bachelor party mingled with the girl movers, and the father of the bride bragged to the girls that his future son-in-law had ducked out early to be with his fiancée. Percival, Dan, and Bartholomew held their posts. The attorney had stayed for one more show. The crowd was having more fun dancing themselves than watching Audrey dance.

Max had walked in on a ready-made party. He squeezed through the crowd distributing bundles of mementos to everyone. A band of regulars, six firemen in ceremonial garb, understood the value of the mementos Max piled in front of each of them. They had thought the fifty dollars' worth they had bought was splurging. The captain slapped him on the back, shook his hand, tried to buy him a drink, tried to offer him a seat and invited him to the firehouse for a tour sometime. The captain started flinging candy-colored paper at Audrey, or any dancer who happened to walk out of the dressing room door and say in surprised joy, "What's going on?" Sidney got hit with a handful thrown directly at her face. Eyes and mouth made three equally round O's. One of the girl movers at the bar pointed at Max and asked Sal, "Who is that weird guy?" Proud Sal smiled at that weird guy, our own Max made into a madman by the chance action of seven numbered ping-pong balls.

Umberto, with his vest unbuttoned, rushed out of his office and stood pigeon-toed in the doorway, green banker's light behind him lit a bill-scattered desk. He beamed at the happy, thirsty crowd and grabbed a passing waitress. "Make sure the champagne is chilled." She nodded at the floor, acknowledging Umberto at one ear and a beer-ordering man at the other. Umberto gave his success a panoramic nod.

Audrey smiled and waved from the edge of the stage, where she picked up mementos one after the other. "Don't grab so fast," he whispered to her. "Give them time to relax and have a drink."

"Okay, boss" (wink).

I was trying to make it to the dressing room to get Trixie—Max was somewhere in the main area; I could hear him calling for her—and, as I hurried between pressed shirts and padded shoulders, I was handed wads of mementos. "Hi Pix, here you go," said smiling Dan and handed me a hundred. Percival, whose earphones had slipped from one ear, handed me at least half as much. I was five hundred dollars richer by the time I had walked the ten steps to the dressing room door. Max suddenly scrambled out from under a huddle of well-wishers and met me at the door. "Where's Trix?" he asked breathlessly. I told him I was going to get her. "Get her, get her, get her," he said, turned me around, and launched me through the door.

"Max here yet?" she asked, rolling on a black thigh-high sock. "Oh shoot. Got a hole." Did I think Audrey would mind if she borrowed her sewing kit? I doubted it, I said, and she unspooled a three-foot length of black thread, licked it, squinted at the needle and started to darn her sock while it was still on her leg. I noticed there were one or two other repaired spots, at the heel and toe.

Above, her millionaire lover flung $395 in mementos at some vet; below, Trixie's $3.95 socks would begin their fourth life. She looked at me and repeated her first question. Her eyes darted and her slightly tea-stained teeth glistened. I let her waver between happiness and disappointment as I delayed my answer.

"Oh, what's this?" I pointed to some photos on the mirror. She had recently decorated the mirror with snapshots of Max and herself: Max in a poet's shirt and a sleepy hungry look, manhandling sun-hatted Trixie in a polka-dotted pinafore, a young Max unzipping a James Dean windbreaker, one foot resting on the floorboard of an old Ford. I told her Max had just arrived. "Good," she said, "hand me that powder. Gosh, it's loud up there. What's going on? You know that can't be Audrey who's still up. I never heard the crowd go crazy like that for her." She tossed talc over her shoulder, rubbed, and said to the mirror. "Oh, you know, I bet it's because she's doing a handstand, that goof!" Trixie searched for a blouse, eyes skimming, finger folding down bottom lip, wondering which one Max would like best, the black velvet, no she wore that last night. She would wear her hair up: Max liked to see as much of her well-toned, matte-white back as possible.

"You're not going to believe this . . ." (wary, cheerful Pixie).

Two lines above her nose bridge made a kind of wrinkled parenthesis, and she smiled and asked, "What, what is it?"

"Max won the lottery." No change in Trixie's expression. "Max won the lottery," I said again.

Her mouth remained open; her eyes looked right and down. "Huh?"

I repeated the news again, this time adding the detail that it was the seven-million-dollar lottery that he had won just in case she thought I meant he'd won a set of pots and pans from a supermarket raffle. There was a nervous tic in the left wing of her nostril. She said I'd been hanging around Dan too much. This was like something he'd do, she said.

I read dread in Trixie's look. Max's winning the lottery destroyed at a stroke the life she had planned and negated with equal devastation all her hard work, suffering, and striving.

She rapidly fastened herself into a bra (the cups were on the backside as she hooked it, then she spun it around), and she blindly groped her way into a blouse. "I'm not kidding. He really did win," I said seriously. Trixie looked at me, opened her mouth, closed it, grabbed her bag, and ran up the stairs with a coltish scramble.

When Max saw Trixie, her squirrelly hands clutching her purse in front of her breast, he wrested himself free of Umberto, waved away the tweedy philosopher who tried to take Umberto's place, and passed Audrey, who patted his forearm (he squeezed her elbow in reply without looking at her). He reached us, hatless, flushed, and took Trix by her shoulders. "Trixie," said Max. She looked at the new dark goatee, then she looked at his knees. "I've won the lottery, Trix." He took her wrists and put her arms around his waist. "Hey Trixie? Trixie? Hey? Hello?" He said, "Don't look so scared."

Trixie, still staring at his knees, said, "Jeez." She didn't know whether she should be happy with or for him.

"It is good news," he laughed.

"Who woulda thought? Huh, Max? Who woulda thought?" Umberto said, squeezing Max's shoulders with a tentacle-like arm. His face had become a clown's (huge toothy grin, triangular laugh lines under and at the corners of his eyes).

Mockingbird made an announcement, but it was muffled by the usually loud din. We couldn't tell whose of our rhyming names was called. "Isn't it my set, Um?" asked Trixie.

"Oh honey, don't worry about it. Take a break. Celebrate. Max here just won the lottery."

Two firemen surrendered their chairs. Trix and Max sat and dovetailed their knees. "Now," he said. "We've got to make plans." Trixie finally smiled and jiggled her feet in uncouth excitement. Max paused to create the illusion that he was planning it out just then, but he had actually already booked several rooms for the weekend at the Inn by the Sea.

She thought for a minute and said, "Okay," with that easy way she had.

"Great, we'll all go," said Max turning toward me. He waved his arm. "The whole gang."

He pulled out a crumpled brochure. A Victorian inn with ample parking, breakfast served between eight and ten. He showed Trixie her—their—suite, Queen Anne sofa, a balcony overlooking the breakfast garden. His broad finger tapped their bed. "And look, here's your room, Pixie." I was pleased. Attic room with single bed. Here was Audrey's room, an austere- looking chamber with a monk's box bed. Equally nice rooms for Jesse and Sam. Andie and Sidney would share a double room that had a view of the oldest pagoda tree in the Northern Hemisphere. We had reservations for the weekend. It was about a four-hour drive, plus an hour on the ferry. He would get a car for each of us. He'd obviously done a lot of planning; no wonder he'd been so late to arrive. "Hey, it'll be fun, don't you think?" The dimpled enthusiasm of his smile made me agree.

"Hey, silly, who's gonna dance while we're all at the beach?" asked Trixie who bet he hadn't thought of that, but he had. In fact, gloating Umberto over there with thumbs in front pockets had already been given the stage rental fee for each booking, day and night shifts, plus a little extra, to close down for the weekend. Umberto wanted to do some renovation anyway. "So everybody's happy." Trixie smiled dumbly and shook her head. "She still can't believe it," said Max. His hand on my knee said they were about to go. "Get your things. Let's get out of here."

"Pixie on the front stage," called Mockingbird. Max patted himself down, produced his business card and told me to call his partner, Mr. Blanc.

"Congratulations," I said.

"Thanks," they said in unison. Trixie cupped her hand over her mouth, but Max petted her hair to say it was okay.

Umberto had a few things he wanted to "iron out" with Max before they left. Trix waited, but then a favorite song started to play, and like an awakened sleepwalker, she stood up and touched Max's elbow. It was a song about the unexpected limitations of great love, which reminded me, in a sharp ice-on-the-teeth sort of way, of that song I'd heard playing on that night at East River Lake.

Trixie backed away whispering the lyrics then headed toward the stage. Vets, firemen, and mover girls stepped aside. Then reaching the steps, she stripped on her way up, as if she were about to jump into a lake to save a drowning friend (except that she left on her shoes). She was smiling, looking strangely relieved.

Glancing over at Max, I saw him groping the empty space beside him, having sensed she was gone without realizing it yet. After Um and Max shook hands, Max turned and saw that Trixie had disappeared. He walked calmly to the stage with an eye on his naked lover. One hand placed firmly on the rail brought his hulky frame up and over. He landed on the stage with a heroic thud, feet together. At first, Trixie balked like a puppy with a ball, but when Max offered his hand, she took it. Then he lifted her up. Leaving the stage and heading downstairs, Max kicked the dressing room door open before him. They disappeared by degrees down the stairs. Her face was pressed against his neck; her eyes were closed.

23

THAT NIGHT A STRAY fall breeze came in through my open window and got into bed with me. I woke shivering and thought of the warm lovers, who in their own bed probably curled around each other, Max scissoring Trixie with his long thick legs, both burrowed deep in a soft mattress and surrounded by feather pillows. I kicked off my skimpy blanket, rose from my thin mattress and my thinner pillows, pulled on a flannel robe, and closed the window. I looked through the glass at my withered phlox—would have to prune them when we got back from the beach—but I was pleased with the ever-virulent snowballs. My breath made two small round smudges on the pane. Summer would soon end, and I was glad Max had invited us all to the beach for one last swim, but oh, yes, we still had the autumnal carnations to look forward to. The petals were uncurling even now in the pots under the red-leaf maple.

Calvin! I remembered our date with a start. I could not go to the beach. Trixie and Max would be soon out of my orbit anyway. I decided to give up the trip, and I began, immediately, to dream how it could have gone.

Then the phone rang. "I was just thinking about you," I cried with disbelief. "Why did you quit?"

Calvin promised to explain in person; he was calling from the filling station. I made the bed that hadn't been made for months. Within twenty minutes I heard that sound of tires crushing fallen apples in my driveway. He got out of his car, looked around at my cottage and my garden in a better light, and he seemed satisfied. He was wearing, I noticed, an old leather car coat and jeans. His Italian suits had been returned at Umberto's request. I opened the screen door and he met me on my steps, hugging me with strange reserve. Then he peered into the doorway beyond the porch. "Can I come in?"

As I poured out coffee, he watched. "Umberto blames me for your quitting for some strange reason."

"Not so strange," he said looking over his coffee cup. "I told him I couldn't work with you there." He took a noisy sip and set down his cup.

"You always have before," I said, weakly, confusedly.

"Well, now I'm selfish."

His candor made me ache. "What can I do?" I cried helplessly.

"Quit."

"Quit? And do what? Why?"

"Quit because I ask you to," he said simply.

"I thought you liked to watch girls dance."

"That's true," he said quietly, taking another gulp of coffee. "I like you best."

"But you don't really know me," I objected, only because it seemed like the kind of thing I ought to say. Truthfully, I didn't believe that at all. If anyone knew me it was Calvin. I didn't know why I felt this; the feeling was not reasonable, but there it was, sharp and insistent, almost ringing in my ears. I clasped my coffee cup and let the steam warm my face. "So this is how I look in the morning." My remark, intended to distract, took on greater meaning in the succeeding silent span. It seemed as if I'd hinted at the prospect of marital familiarity, of vistas of mornings that stretched out before us.

"You look even better."

"Did you hear about Max?" I said to lighten the conversation.

"Mr. Price?"

"He won the lottery—seven million dollars. Can you believe it? That's why I was thinking about you when you called. Max invited all the dancers for a weekend at the beach. I had agreed to go but then I remembered our plans—"

"And you would have stood me up?"

"No, but since you're here—"

"Let me get this straight," Calvin closed his eyes and cupped his forehead in one hand and gestured with the other, "Price won seven million dollars in the lottery, and he got all of the dancers to go to the beach with him for the weekend? What does Umberto say?"

"I think Max gave him something," I stammered, "to close down for a few days."

"He paid him, in other words?"

"Yes, in other words."

"And you agreed to go?"

I nodded.

"What do you know about this guy? Can he be trusted?"

"I think so. I've known him for quite a while as a customer, but more lately as a friend."

Calvin sighed heavily and sat back in his chair, a frail antique that creaked under his weight. "Well, I can trust you, I think, to know what you're doing—except of course when it comes to me."

The comment hit its mark. "Tell me what you want, Calvin."

"Quit."

He was saying all the things he was required by decency to say, but I was still aggravated by his hasty demands. "I don't know you," I said. "Not enough."

"Do you want to be a stripper forever?"

"Is there something wrong with that?" I asked defensively although there had been nothing offensive in his tone. My reply, I realize now, was just a knee-jerk reaction; I was expecting him to denounce stripping, and I think perhaps some martyr-bent part of me even wanted him too, so that I could rightfully push him away, and return sulkily to my rumpled bed.

"I like the fact that you're a stripper," he returned, leaving me no room to hate him. "Don't think for one minute that I regret that you or I ever worked at the Playhouse, but now I want you all to myself."

I told him no, not now. Watching dimness wash over his expression, I was, even then, vaguely aware that I was only defending some small, symbolic patch of ground that I held, for what purpose I no longer knew. It somehow involved my mother. My irrational act somehow avenged her, was done in her honor, though I couldn't possibly place Calvin in the same category as her gunman or my father.

Calvin said, upon leaving, rolling down the window and shouting at me over the clamor of his old engine, that he would see me again when the Playhouse closed down for good.

But I fear he isn't coming. I fear that my refusal had been too unjust, and that if he has any pride, and I know he has, he'll realize I blew it. But then again he said he would come back, and I do think his word is good.

Before he left he'd taken two bags of groceries out of his car. I unpacked them when he was gone. They were filled with exotic items that he was going to use to make our dinner. Calvin, who was out of a job, had been shopping at the pricey Gourmet Grocers. I looked at the jars of spiced nuts, ginger sauce, and cranberry shrub, and I cried.

24

Trixie and Max, Millionaires! Aye, me. I took a sip of cool coffee, and used the corners of Max's business card to clean my nails. This was a wrinkle that no one had foreseen.

"Mr. Blanc, please," I said into the receiver.

"Sorry, not in yet. Can I help you?" I asked after Max, but he was reportedly at the gym. I gave my name and explained that Max had arranged for me to have any car I wanted. Oh yeah, yeah, yeah, he knew all about it. Mr. Blanc would fix me right up. Noon okay?

"Yes. Wait—was that Pixie or Trixie?"

It was Pixie, I told him.

"You're not the . . . ?"

No, I was the . . . I was her friend. Oh right—right, right—he knew that. That's where Max was; he was with Trixie. "Hey," he said, "Did you hear about Max's luck?" I told him that indeedy I had.

On my way to Price Mazdatown, I stopped off at the Community Center, since Trixie'd forgotten to call. Max was there. Life for him wouldn't change simply because he'd become a millionaire—he was from a once-wealthy family; the experience wasn't new—he said to me breathlessly. Life would change in other ways, though. He had finally confronted Rosamund about Trixie.

I was surprised that Max had not broken off with his wife sooner. One wonders how they got on together when they did meet up—what sort of hints were dropped or sharp comments made? I wondered then what kind of obtuse mortal this Rosamund could be that she hadn't sooner realized that her husband had long since stopped kissing her on the mouth much less making love to her, that for weeks now large portions of her time had been strictly her own, and that he had stopped asking for small favors or that errands be performed for him. But these speculations would go unanswered: I never met Rosamund in person, and never learned anything more than what Max told me. Nevertheless, I think it is fair for me to surmise, by the little information that I do have, that Rosamund wasn't that attentive, that she wasn't sensitive to her own problems any more than Max's, and it is on that account, and that account only, that we can forgive Max for his great sin of not telling her about his failure as a husband straight away.

A more complicated explanation is necessary to absolve Max of his other crime of silence. "You didn't tell Rosamund about the lottery?" I cried in disbelief.

"Not yet," he said hastily. "I wanted her to get used to the idea that we are splitting up first, then I'll…" he faltered.

"Oh dear," I said.

"I only had the heart to tell her half of it."

Max told me about Rosamund, red-eyed, smearing her hot tears on his cheeks and how he had been moved to confess. At first though, he said, he didn't mention the details of Trixie that devastated him; he left out the who, what, when, and how.

Rosamund said at thirty-five (Max's age) she expected that kind of thing to happen. It was normal, and she had married him for better or worse, and she would stick with him through this. Who was it, by the way? Jackie the neighbor's wife? Was it that new salesgirl, Madeline? Because if it was she had been expecting it, and, in fact—Rosamund had said, taking his hand—she forgave him in advance. She loved him no matter what.

Max had just sat there, on their pearl green sofa (which I would see later when *Inside Story* interviewed Rosamund at home), feeling a wave of helplessness and disgust. Finally, Max told her everything about Trixie.

"A stripper?" screeched Rosamund. Then, in an attack of calmness, she said they would see someone, a counselor—and get checkups. Max had listened in frank horror to her plans for an "interview" with a Dr. Instaget. Then they would go to the islands to attempt reconciliation. Rosamund didn't think she could be intimate with him before that; he'd have to understand. Max could only gape at her.

Then Rose had started to make fun of Trixie's name. "What is she? Some kind of poodle?" Max had said he thought that people with peculiar names tended to have more character. His own name had an "x" in it. Rosamund then made a vulgar remark about someone who "calls herself" Trixie.

"Oh, shut up Rosamund," he had finally said in hate, stressing the flat character of her name. He explained how he happened to like the name Trixie, demonstrating the fun-sounding name of his girlfriend.

"Don't be stupid," Rosamund said in reply.

However, Max couldn't help it.

Max told me it was true that when they were young he had gazed at Rosamund's bouncing breasts as she two-stepped in his arms, and at the time he'd thought, "So this is what true love is like," but on a vague, never fully admitted second thought, he had sighed, "What a disappointment."

He was through with that life. After the trip to the beach, Rosamund and Mr. Blanc, his partner, could have everything for all he cared.

We knew a sticky divorce was ahead of Max, but he preferred not to think about it for at least a few more days.

The summer sun had returned for an encore when I arrived at Price Mazdatown, acres of asphalt covered bumper-to-bumper with small cars. Large red letters spelled out the dealership's name on the roof, and below it was the tactless sign, BEST PRICE IN TOWN. Had Max been tempted to capitalize the 'p'? I bet he had.

I checked in at the showroom. A pewter RX-7 held the coveted position on a revolving platform. A banner exclaiming "Congratulations!" to an absent Max hung above what I took to be his office, a room with blinded windows, neglected of late. Suddenly, a young man struggled out of the RX-7—he'd been trying out the angle of the reclining seats—and asked, "Can I help ya?" brushing out the wrinkles in his oversized suit.

"Mr. Blanc?"

"Missing," said the young man. "Due in at eleven. Never been late before."

"Well," I told him, "I'll just have a look around and hope he shows."

"Okay," yawned the junior car salesman.

I wandered around and found every other four-door looked much like any other. Cupping my hand to make a visor, I applied it to several windows and squinted at the interiors. I figured that Audrey would choose the beige, or "road dust" colored, 323. The inconspicuous shade would be attractive to her because she wouldn't get as many speeding tickets, assuming she does go over fifty-five every now and again. Here was Sidney's car, the flashiest 929 with gold accents. Andie would get that pewter RX-7 in the showroom.

Then I noticed a rather large-sized red bumper car, parked with several others of the same kind. They came in fantastic candy colors: white, green, blue. I wanted one of the red toys.

The two-seater convertible reminded me of a pedal-driven car I'd had at age six. A friend had got my aunt to buy it for me when he found out about Mom's insurance money. Before this discovery, Auntie had insisted I was a penniless waif and didn't deserve toys—but never the matter. I remembered fondly my old one-seater that had been made of lightweight aluminum for maximum speed. Red with white pinstripes, it had come with a matching helmet, an option that was probably unavailable in this Mazda version—but I might check with Mr. Blanc, and I would also ask if whitewalls were available on the Miata as they had been on its prototype.

I rushed back to the sales office, through the maze of cars—some were so closely parked that my path was blocked, and twice I had to double back. Finally, I made it to the showroom, but Blanc still hadn't arrived. The younger guy gave me the key.

I waited for the missing partner in the car listening to the radio—the local hit station promised to return after the commercial with "God Part II."

Eventually, Mr. Blanc did arrive, with two black eyes, and knocked on the window. He apologized for his appearance, but failed to explain it. Amid his banditlike mask, his white and bloodshot eyes blinked fantastically. His injuries looked worse than they really were, he assured me, dabbing the corner of his eye.

I was glad, I assured him. He led the way back to the showroom where I signed several papers. Meanwhile, the younger car salesman had been sent to get my car. He reappeared after thirty minutes and asked if I wouldn't take the white one instead: it was easier to get to. No, I wanted the red one; there was a whole slew of them in the back, I said, and patiently waited. Finally, the desired car, freed, was pulled up in front.

Nervous at first, gradually I became pretty confident behind the wheel. Speed and volume do a lot for one's nerve. With car top down (not mine) and custom leather interior exposed, I headed to Newgate Cross Park to meet the others.

I was the first to arrive. Newgate Cross Park, located around the bend from the Playhouse, was a neat section of green with faux gas lanterns and extra-long oak park benches facing the river. Audrey pulled up behind me. At first I didn't realize it was she; I had looked in my rear view mirror and seen my mirror image, a red Miata with a pretty girl at the wheel. I looked again and saw the driver wore sunglasses and was Audrey. I greeted her smirk with a smirk of my own.

Then a minute later, Sidney approached in a red Miata identical to mine and Audrey's. She pulled up behind us, hopped out of her car, flung herself at me and said, with squeaky delight, "Ooh, look you got one too." Sammy arrived and parked her red Miata facing mine, and when Jesse showed up, we would have been surprised had she not been driving a red Miata. As if this weren't enough I realized we were tuned to the same station—oh, this was quite enough. What artist or madman had arranged it so that Paul Young's "I'm Gonna Tear Your Playhouse Down" would be beating in our woofers? Unsuspecting little Sammy happily tapped her platform sandal and sang along in her husky contralto. Then Andie, whom we had forgotten in our excitement, parked her red Miata in line behind Jesse's car.

It turned out that the younger car salesman, while rearranging the vehicles for me, had opened up the red Miata section, and he was too lazy to shuffle cars around all morning to get the particular one each dancer wanted. Andie said she hadn't wanted to be too demanding since the car was, after all, given free of charge. The others concurred.

We all watched as a red speck on Newgate Hill horizon slowly grew into another red Miata with Trixie at the wheel and Max folded into the passenger's seat. Max's coupe was in the shop, and it had been that joker, Mr. Blanc, who had reserved him the Miata. Trixie laughed. The lucky smack of the number seven—for there were seven red Miatas parked and poised to go. Who had dealt her this freakish hand in the mad, mad game?

Max was just pissed. It was embarrassing, he said. It looked stupid, he complained and insisted we split up, but Trix wouldn't have it. She was so pretty that day. She wore an outgrown dress and thigh-high socks, but one slightly higher than the other. When she got out of the car, she pulled them up, making a little kick each time. "That Blanc," mumbled Max.

Max was handsome that morning, wearing linen pants, light brown, cream button-down shirt, and sunglasses. His brows made perfect arches above his frames and his new, ever more compact and curly, goatee gave him a devilish aspect. He spread a map out over the hood of Sam's car, and his finger traced a bold red line down Highway 1. At Farm Road 7, we would drive east to the ferry.

Now we were all in a row. Nearby a smiling man, with a flap of hair blowing left of his bald spot like a flip top cap on toothpaste tube, asked if he could snap our picture. Trixie smiled and waved parade fashion as she drove out of the park. We all followed: I first, then Audrey, Jesse, Sam, Sidney, and last of all Andie, who'd had a false start, brought up the rear.

With my gaze fast upon the lovers, I proceeded up the ramp to the interstate. For a moment, when their car took the loop under and around the overpass, I lost sight of them and terrific longing made me downshift and speed up. They were waiting at the entrance. They found a break in the thick highway traffic—both their heads had turned to watch, both lips pronounced a silent okay—and their car lunged forward. I stamped the pedal and squeezed in behind them.

On the highway, cars and barreling semis deferred to us as if we made a parade. When we stopped at a diner in a small town for an afternoon snack, dads pointed and kids waved. At lights that were very yellow, even newly red, we were allowed to proceed ahead of anybody else.

Two road hours later, when we found the junction with 7E, Trixie's signal started palpitating, and her car swung from the far left to the far right lane. Her swerve was imitated by six others, and on the exit ramp our sequence was corrupted by a white hatchback between Sam and Sidney and a yellow rental van between Sidney and Andie. On Farm Road 7 (a different FM7, merely a coincidence) we cruised along at forty and thirty-five, the speed of the panel van, in order not to lose Andie who was, no doubt, thumping her steering wheel in contempt and boredom.

Sweet summer corn was offered for sale along the roadside. Being in convertibles, we noticed the pockets of manure fumes that drifted over the roads in certain areas. Soon signs began to speak of a ferry ahead. Trixie and Max paid the toll for all seven cars. A spiffy fellow with white gloves directed as we snaked around the cone pylons and parked. Since a ferry had recently departed, the lot was empty and our group would be first to board after a forty-five-minute wait. I got out to stretch my legs; we all did, and our red doors slammed in sync.

Looking up on the dock, I noticed a bearded dirty blonde with a video camera. After five minutes of stolen footage, he lowered the camera and waved from his roost. Max, who had been watching him too, waved back. After a slight hesitation the man came down. "Hey, how ya doin'? You part of a racing team?" he asked, eyes traveling all over Trixie. The other dancers and I, gathered in a disordered ring, looked on. Max held Trixie fast and faintly leered. Trixie said no; we were regular people who just happened to end up with the same kind of car. The man frowned because he thought Trixie was being sarcastic. He sulked off, hands in the air mimicking surrender. Imprudently perhaps, we laughed at the silly, easily offended man. He continued his taping. The direction of his lens favored Trixie, who was completely oblivious to the cameraman's attention. She laughed and nuzzled Max with her usual abandon.

The sun had long burned off the morning chill, and her socks had long since been discarded. Now her long-toed feet were perched on the driver's side mirror while her head rested in Max's lap and he petted her hair. After a while Max grew hot. "Up you go," he said and lifted her head to get out of the car for another stretch. Trixie followed and slipped her arms around his waist while he leaned on the car. (Like an anxious toddler clinging to her parent's pant leg in crowded store; a dedicated egret on a steer's back, gingerly searching for ticks; or a wren feeding her adopted changeling the giant cowbird.)

Once again Max had to shield Trixie from the long probing lens, sandwiching her between himself and the car. Trixie was never aware of any unsympathetic eyes, but her lover grew annoyed at the voyeur, now taping from the men's room door. Finally, as the sun was setting, the last ferry arrived. The big, slow-moving ship was mated with the dock. We jumped back into our cars and lumbered into the boat.

25

Our Inn by the Sea was poised upon a red clay cliff and was built by the famous Captain Cicero Adamson, a prosperous sailor whose wife, Molly Cobb Adamson, had insisted their home be built on the cliff's edge to be as close to him as possible. On top of the two-hundred-year-old house was a "widow's walk" where she is said to have stood and squinted at the horizon when her husband was away. And according to happy local legend, this captain did not drown at sea. Molly was not damned to haunt the seacliff. No, the good captain Cicero returned safely from twenty voyages to the West Indies and Japan and retired early, wealthy, and healthy, and had six children, all boys. At the trembling, gaseous age of ninety-nine, he followed his eighty-five-year old wife to the grave four days after her death.

The captain's portrait and a small brass plaque, which told his story, greeted us in the foyer.

Max had chosen the Inn by the Sea because he had gone there just before he married Rosamund to contemplate his future. The atmosphere of the Inn, which reminded him of his old family home, had made him feel so good about himself that he had found the courage to commit to Rosamund. Lately, he had begun to realize that courage would have been put to better use if he had pursued his dreams instead.

Once Max had wistfully suggested to Rosamund that they should go to the inn together. "An old inn?" she had said. "What for? I'd rather go to a nice hotel—with a pool."

When the inn had come into view, Max was that man again who had not yet married Rosamund.

The innkeeper's daughter, Victoria O'Rourke, greeted "The Max Prices" and asked if we had "come in all those red cars." Max explained that he owned a car dealership. Victoria said, looking at Max's pride of seven lovely lionesses, "Oh," two syllables, the first high the second low.

"Breakfast will be served in the garden. This is the linen closet where you'll find your beach towels, and in here is the sitting room; you'll find a television in the cabinet. It doesn't match the period furniture. This way to your rooms," she said gliding up the stair, passing a sample of driftwood art; the artist herself tapped it and mentioned that it and others like it were for sale.

The entire group stayed with the tour through all of the rooms. The dying sun bathed the western rooms in warmth. On the eastern side, which faced the sea, were the lovers' room and mine. In Max and Trixie's room, Victoria waved in the direction of the writing desk and said, "This is the writing desk." Then she walked into the bathroom and said, "Here's the bathroom." The shower curtain was pulled aside, "This is the bath." The hangers were indicated, "and you can use this closet to hang up your things." Meanwhile we had all dogged her steps, craned our necks to see where she was pointing and nodded solemnly at each bit of information.

Then she showed us my room, my Queen Anne sofa with a lace doily lovingly placed over a worn spot on the headrest, an early American highboy with eight roomy drawers that would swallow my two tops, two skirts, and ten pairs of panties. As the tour was winding down, she gave some unheeded instructions about the keys and locking doors and rules about windows and towels; we responded with a chorus of okays and thank-yous, and Victoria, because the daylight was fading, turned on the bedside light by the switch relocated for hotel use at its base. And she was gone.

She didn't exist for us that weekend beyond that little talk and tour. She vanished and left behind a bell and a card in a dish in the vestibule that said, "Ring bell for service." The vigilant bell was never called into action. The only clue I have that Victoria or her mother remained in the house during our stay was that occasionally we heard the un-Victorian sound of television beyond a back staircase marked, "private." The linen closet and invisible maid provided all the service we required.

Inside Story named Victoria as a key witness.

We all retired early that night. I slept dreamlessly and woke with the sunrise. After a leisurely coffee and fruit breakfast, we headed to the beach, where two portable CD players competed for dominance. We sat under the towering red cliffs made of clay.

I was first to visit the water, though I have never taught myself to swim. Behind me the voices of my friends were dimly heard. Near my ear buzzed an inquisitive dragonfly that drowned thoughts of Trixie and Max, Audrey and the rest. The sun glanced the water and hit my eyes.

Around my feet the sand was swept away, leaving me on the island of my own footprint with each step. I realized, suddenly, that my friends did not know my birth name. I was just called Pixie and did not come into existence unless I had some quirky girl to admire, someone else's dreams to expound and explain. What little I do own, my poor prose, is, damn me, so jittery and anxious-to-please.

Ah, Calvin. He was present in my mind now that he wasn't standing by, in a not-too-distant corner, guarding me, watching me, enjoying me, ready to spring. I missed him. Every time I looked at Trixie and Max coupling like eagles (for life), I thought of him. I wondered what he would think of me, doing this, doing that, driving my new car, laughing over Victoria's officious tour, applying sunblock to my nipples that had never seen the sun. Would he object? Would he have made some half-mocking remark to make me doubt my decency, to make me cry? Or would he have smiled at this or that?

Buoyed by the warm salt water, I didn't want to move. Was I wrong to come out here like this? leaving Calvin back there, living who knew where, in some small but clean apartment, eating his own gourmet dinners—dinners that were made, doubtless, with my theoretical enjoyment in mind. It would be unfair of me, I decided, to imagine him as a petty judge. No, he was indulgent and generous. In fact, he would have had fun here on the sand with us. But I didn't invite him, did I? No, for some reason, I had not. I had long since been in the habit of holding the world at arm's length, of stiffening under the threat of embrace. I had tried to squirm my way out of my mother's arms that day as she tried to keep me safe. Even then, I vehemently defended my independence. And, good God, that was before it happened. Maybe it's my own true kernel of self then, and not my history that makes me the way I am. I felt cold and thin and lonely.

A stray bit of laughter arrested my attention and made me resume my place among my friends.

When I returned to my towel, I found Audrey had placed it near hers for matters of convenience. "Can you get my back?" she asked showing me a bottle of oil. I knelt smiling. Prone on her belly, arms behind like one handcuffed, she untied her bikini top, especially careful to keep it from falling from her breasts.

Except for the fact that we had left our shoes behind, the other girls, including myself, were dressed, or rather undressed, as we would be during the last minutes of a set. Everyone, that is, except Audrey, had opted to go topless, unsightly tan lines being a grave concern for exotic dancers. "We've all seen your breasts, Audrey."

"That's different. That's work," she said. I rubbed oil evenly on her light skin, noticing for the first time the hundreds of tiny brown moles that defaced her fairness. She also wore a regular bikini bottom while the rest of us wore the customary thongs. "Tan lines'll look bad onstage," I warned her.

"There're kids here."

There was also, incidentally, a sign posted as we entered the beach which read, "No nude sunbathing allowed," but almost no one was fully suited. The kids Audrey referred to belonged to a totally nude French family nearby. "Audrey," I said, "even the kids are naked." She turned from her towel, while covering her breasts. "That's disgusting," she said.

"I think you're in the wrong business," laughed Max.

Our host lay on his white towel, enjoying a back massage from Sidney while Andie looked after his feet. Trixie had opened an umbrella and was reading in semi-shade. As Sidney kneaded the loose skin on Max's shoulders, he groaned a little, "Not so hard. Not so hard."

For all the world, Max certainly looked like a fortunate man. He surveyed his harem, chin on crossed arms, with an air of confident possession. "Not so hard. Not so hard," he groaned again.

"Who me?" asked Andie.

"No, Andie, you're fine. It's Sidney. I didn't know you were so strong. Whoa."

"You'll spoil him. When this weekend's over, I'll have to perform the work of seven girls."

"You do, Trix. You do," said Max, stroking her leg with his toe.

As the sun had gone behind a cloud, Trixie collapsed her umbrella and joined Max on his towel. Sammy woke from her tan, stunned and weak. Now we reclined on elbows, facing one another, feet making ruts in the sand. Jesse's brown limbs were lightly dusted with sand. Her blonde hair and her pale blue eyes had brightened.

We had been taken from our common sphere and deposited here, denuded of all things familiar that held us together as friends: Mockingbird's showtime, talk of mementos, the correct alignment of one's thong. We didn't know what to say now. We seemed to be avoiding personal reflections, although the beautifully setting sun invited them.

I decided to tell my friends a story that had happened a few years before. It related, I felt, to Audrey's strange sudden prudishness. I had been running late one morning, and, in an attempt to make my café filtre machine work faster, I caused it to explode all over me. I was naked at the time.

The coffee badly scalded my left breast. The irony of it hit me immediately. I stood screaming under a cold shower for fifteen minutes and finally decided I should get myself to the emergency clinic. An ambulance seemed like the wrong idea, too much waiting time, and I didn't want to go to a hospital. I phoned the old lady next door from the shower.

When her old Pontificate station wagon rattled down the drive, I dumped some ice in a towel, threw on a robe, and ran barefoot to the car. The kind old lady, dwarfed behind the wheel, whose sneakered toe barely reached the gas, drove to the clinic like a demon. She even stayed in the examination room with me while the young intern gave me shot after shot of painkillers and dressed the burn.

I lay on the table, robe thrown open, panting with pain and then nausea from the overdose of drugs, while the old woman beautifully held my hand. She said my breasts were so young-looking and firm, it would be a shame if . . .

Of course, I didn't want to think about that. The intern and the old lady had no idea how much of a tragedy a scalded breast could be to me. Part of me kept suggesting that I had somehow done it on purpose. It was just too ironic. Freud would have his say. That was for certain.

But that was not the end of my story. I returned the next day—Grammy again as my companion and friend—so that the progress of healing could be ascertained. The young intern came into the examination room to announce that the real doctor was now on duty, and he—since he was not actually licensed to practice yet and had only treated me because it was an emergency—would not stay for the examination. The real doctor would have a look all to himself. "In most burn cases," he explained, "I would examine you myself again along with the doctor. One ought to be able to compare yesterday's condition to today's, but since the burn is on your," he faltered a moment, "breast," he coughed, "I think it would be better to preserve your dignity if I did not"—cough—"examine you again."

"He's just worried he can't control himself," said Grammy.

Damn right, Grammy. I show my breasts to hundreds of unlicensed men every day. My dignity remains intact.

"Can you imagine," I posed to my friends, "that intern thought he had power to damage my dignity?"

"The nerve," said Trixie.

"He shouldn't be a doctor if he can't treat a breast as well as an elbow," I said.

"Well," Audrey said, "he was obviously trying to do the right thing."

"Grammy was in the room with us," I argued. "The point is, they're only breasts. When is it wrong to show them in public?"

"I'm going to breastfeed in public," said Sammy.

"Tsk," observed Audrey. "I think that's awful. Go to the ladies' room."

At this remark we collectively groaned and threw sand at Audrey.

"I don't see any scars," said Max.

There was none that you could see. Everything healed over but the smart of that man's comment.

Later that day, we went riding on hot, bored, tail-switching horses that moseyed along at an implausibly slow pace. Trixie's mare bonded with Max. He sucked his teeth and she, with woeful eyes, plodded after him, never mind that her rider kicked her sides in protest. Max led her off into the scrub.

When the stables reappeared on the other end of the loop trail, our horses broke into brisk canter. The overalled stable master (only the left strap was utilized), wondered why two horses hadn't returned with the rest of the group, but those in question suddenly sprang out of the brush, Trixie bouncing, one dangling foot freed of its stirrup.

We returned to the inn to freshen up before dinner. I won't forget my vision of Trixie in the bath. I'd looked into their bathroom for the toothpaste, about which I'd neighborly rapped on the door. In the center of the bathroom, a porcelain tub squatted on a watermarked wooden floor. The slippery maiden had obviously splashed a lot and turned in soapy water. She was now hard at toe-cleaning, leg awkwardly but dexterously bent so that her toes were very near her face, eyes squinted, a frown. Glancing up, she squealed at the intrusion, unbent her leg, and kicked the oaken door shut with a bang. And long afterward did the brass knob rattle.

During the weekend, we tried five different restaurants, the Harbor View, the Old Salts, the Pelican, Barney's, and finally Cafe de la Plage, where we met a hostess in the foyer hugging a stack of menus. She first looked with amazement, counting seven silky heads and Max's, which presided so handsomely over the group. Then she put us at the centermost table, so that diners would have an eyeful.

Jesse led the group after the hostess. She was wearing a white tennis skirt with panties that matched; this was an important detail, too, because they were often on display, as when she bent to drop her white handbag on the carpet before taking her place at the table. Her shoes were tan, matching almost perfectly the golden color of her legs. Her top was cropped showing her toned stomach and navel. I followed Jesse, watching men's mouths open and women's mouths close. I was wearing navy, a short dress with a high waist, my mother's sandals also navy, which had the ever-so-important distinction of being the highest heels of all. One after the other we snaked around the tables and seated ourselves. Who was that lucky man?

Although I enjoyed being part of a flamboyant group, at the same time I felt the pang of shame. Who could concentrate on the flavor of the sauce when Sidney was there, delicately fingering the stem of her water glass? Who could think about the aroma of the wine when Sammy brazenly smiled, with her wide hot mouth, at every passing waiter? It's little wonder, really, that we ended up in the tabloids the way we did, properly positioned among other tales of the fantastic like the woman who married her dead fiancée and the gerbil that had two heads.

Meanwhile, T and M were seated opposite each other. Max slipped off his loafer to stroke her instep with his toe while she was ordering her entrée. (There is a certain blind species of shrimp that keeps in constant contact with a small fish, his symbiotic partner, with whom he shares the house he built.)

On the second day, we flew to a neighboring island in a propeller plane. On the windy runway, the hem of Trixie's skirt waved, so childishly short and uneven. The air traffic boys with orange batons leered at her hungrily. Trixie was seated in the rear of the plane, while her heavyweight lover had to sit fore. We bounced on the runway smoothly and safely, but on the way back Max insisted that Trixie sit up front with him even if she had to hold a piece of luggage in her lap because, if we went down, he wanted to be holding her hand.

When I went to my room the last night of our stay, I didn't sleep at first. Around midnight I decided to go out onto my balcony, which I shared with Trixie and Max. When I banged through the screen door onto the terrace, I almost disturbed the coiled lovers. I hadn't noticed them in the wicker chair that was swiveled toward the sea. Trixie's legs were wrapped around his waist, arms loosely thrown over his shoulders. Her face was smashed against his chest, mouth open and a tiny spot of drool marked his shirt.

I had held onto Mom like that, my legs wrapped around her. I still remember the comfort of her body against my oblique, where our souls would be if we had them.

While I watched, Max woke, and after an especially orgasmic round of eye rubbing, he smacked his lips and said good morning Pix. "It's midnight, silly," yawned Trix, buffing the wet smudge on his shirt.

I apologized for disturbing them. They begged me to stay, but I returned to my room. Later, I overheard Trixie and Max talking softly. "She doesn't have anybody," she said. "No," said he.

In all, it was a pleasant stay. Being outdoors a lot never fails to inspire and tease. I stood upon the widow's walk looking out toward the endless end, imagining Calvin's ship, at first a dark speck, growing rapidly. As Mrs. Woolf says, "It was impossible to resist the strange intimation which every gull, flower, tree, man and woman, and the white earth itself seemed to declare (but if questioned at once to withdraw) that good triumphs, happiness prevails, order rules."

We were now poised to leave. The inn had been very good, and upon inspecting the guest book, I found that most of the previous guests agreed. "Nice place," said the Inchiquins of 86 Spies Lane, and the Messiahs, 149 Damns End, "loved it." We certainly had nothing to complain about. There was no noisy, much-visited ice machine outside my door, no neighbor with whooping cough behind a thin wall, no curly black hair in the clean tub, no unfamiliar shade of lipstick on the pillow, and no indecent quarter-eating gadgets attached to the bed.

The housekeeping had been performed with lightning speed. I'd been across the hall for a minute and came back to find wrapped soap on the bathroom countertop. The glasses had been reordered on the tea table. The sherry decanter had been refilled, and a pair of silk panties I'd searched everywhere for had reappeared and were folded and waiting on a taut bedspread.

Max would remember, though, one item about the Inn that ruined this pretty picture. When he and Trixie were lying in bed he glanced at the alarm clock and noticed a chain attached to its back that dangled down behind the nightstand.

A final note: Audrey and I happened to burst in on T and M (I did notice a "Do not disturb" sign on the doorknob but ignored it). A lovely scene presented itself to *my* view; I don't speak for Audrey. In the dim room was Max's naked figure, standing turned toward the wall. His broad, rippled back was dappled in bluish light from the TV and Trixie legs were fastened around his waist. His head hung forward so that from our point of view he might have been a headless ancient statue. His knees were bent and he leaned forward at the waist as if he were sitting on a stool. Limber Trixie was arched backward, counterbalancing his weight. This time I did not turn my eyes away as I had done in the Champagne Room. This time I watched as Max resolutely possessed the coquette, avenged himself of all the long hours of waiting and pleasant torture. I don't know how many seconds Audrey and I stood there, watching, but I do know I had enough time to take all this in. Finally, Trixie peeked around his back and shrieked, unhooking her ankles and falling to the floor. Max, with a knock-kneed Neanderthal posture—that he fell into out of feelings of shame and absurdity—frantically searched the room for his pants. Not finding these, he held a throw pillow in front of his groin. Trixie had sprung up, found his boxers and tossed them to him. When he caught them he dropped his protective cushion and Audrey and I saw more of Max than he had ever seen of us. "Oh my," I said respectfully.

Audrey said, "That's disgusting."

Now Max had turned toward the window and was hopping on one foot getting into his boxers. Trixie had managed to get on her heels (she'd looked so naked without them).

"Why don't you two do that kind of thing in your own room?"

"We wanted to watch TV," whined Trixie.

Hearing its cue, the television drew our attention. A Channel 9 reporter announced that she had the lottery winner.

"I didn't give any interview," said Max, straightening and looking at the set. "I haven't even turned in my ticket yet. It's in a safe-deposit box."

The reporter stood outside a deli. In the window a sign read, "We have a winner."

"It was here," said the reporter, "that the seven-million-dollar winning ticket was purchased, and so far the winner has not come forward to claim his prize. We asked the deli owner if he knew who it could be."

Suddenly a large man dressed in a white smock, with short clipped gray hair, very round jowls appeared on the screen. His fat tongue seemed to crowd his mouth.

"George," laughed Max. "My buddy George."

George wore the title, "Winning deli owner: George," in yellow letters below his image. The microphone was pointed at his face. He frowned at it and shiftily eyed the camera. "Yeah, I know who it is." Then obviously cued by the reporter, he turned to face her. "Max

Price, that's who it is. He come in here every day for ten years now. You think I'd know his number by now, huh? Yeah, he's got the ticket. Nice guy Max." Here George smiled straight into the camera, presumably at Max.

"Have you got a lucky store?" the reporter asked, wielding her pendulum-like microphone.

George's grin revealed the absence of an eyetooth.

The camera, having had its fill of George, followed the reporter as she walked across a street. "When we asked the deli owner where we could find Max now, he told us that we could find him right here" (long pause) "right across the street." The camera followed her raised arm. "The winner is said to own this dealership, but when we called the dealership, we were told he had no comment." The camera panned from the Price Mazdatown sign back to the reporter, who had positioned herself directly under it. "Well that's it; the mystery's solved. We now know the winner's name, but he has yet to collect his prize, and everyone is wondering why he is hiding. According to the man who sold Mr. Price the winning ticket, he's probably gone away on a second honeymoon with his loving wife, Rosamund, to whom he's been married ten years. They're probably enjoying a few more days of the simple life. Back to you, Jake."

"Thank you, Belinda. It'll be interesting to find out why Price is hiding and what he plans to do with the money."

"Yes, it would be," agreed Susan with a quick nod, and she restacked her papers.

"But we'll have to wait for that, because right now it's time for the sports report. How are those Coyotes doing, Mike?" asked the stiff-neck anchor, rotating toward Mike.

26

I HAD ALWAYS BEEN a punctual employee of the Playhouse. Mighty Northern Lines often got me in ahead of schedule, at a station one block from the cabaret. Now I was late because I couldn't find a parking place. Seven blocks from the Playhouse, I spotted a small opportunity; a Jeep had given up on a space and let my Miata have a go. I described eight different Z's parallel parking between a panel van with a forgiving bumper and a chromium motorcycle with a precarious lean. A pea-pod-snapping clerk sitting on an upturned bucket said, "Good job." I think he meant it as a joke.

As I was getting my bag out of my trunk, I noticed a young woman passing in the street. She was obviously a stripper, on her way to the Playhouse for an audition, who had gotten a little lost, having taken a wrong turn somewhere. She was as startled and as startling as a pink flamingo would be if it suddenly found itself on Main Street in the middle of a busy afternoon. She had a perfect body, tall very thin, small shapely breasts and long legs. This I can say with authority because I could see most of it. She was wearing a tiny bikini top and minuscule stretch cotton hot pants with a pack of cigarettes bulging at the hip. Very high heels. The fair flesh of her legs, arms, and stomach was totally exposed. Men on the street were too confused and alarmed to whistle. The deli clerk staggered a little when he saw her and seemed to be deliberating whether or not he should throw a coat over her or call the police. Then, I noticed behind her a shortish man carrying a duffel bag, greasy hair, gray skin. That was when I decided on the pink flamingo figure for her. She was lovely, out-of-place, and a little tacky. I felt an immediate connection, one of envy, curiosity, and desire. But most of all I was laughing to myself. Yes, yes. That's how *we* look.

She rushed down the street and became one of the many new girls added to the Playhouse lineup. I don't even know her name yet.

It was a nice trot to the Playhouse through Newgate Cross. Recently, several small dress boutiques had opened in the ground floors of some brownstones. Two new cafés had opened. Both sat less than thirty customers. One was especially famous for its complimentary plum torte. The other was known for its large selection of international magazines and newspapers. Most of the diners came alone and stayed long (I was often among them).

Newgate Cross was saved from becoming a high-traffic shopping district by its meandering cobblestone streets. Newgate Cross *Avenue* formed the lower and left arms of a cross; Newgate Cross *Drive* formed the right and upper arms of the same cross. Way back in history the Drive and the Avenue had intersected an enormous square: but now a garden wall divided the center and the separated ways veered off from each other. The Girlie Playhouse was located in the corner of the Avenue. There was a twin building on the Drive directly behind the Playhouse, ironically a children's playschool.

When I turned on the Avenue, I was offered a strange sight. A blue and white police car was parked on the sidewalk. Its doors were agape, and whirling red lights lent the scene a festive look. Behind the patrol car stood a policeman—young, feathered black hair (his hat was on the dash). He was taking dictation from a pretty, middle-aged woman, dressed in jeans and a T-shirt pulled over a denim button-down. She had a red cap on her head. Her head was lowered. She made a two-handed visor with her hands to hide her face, and she was shaking.

When the policeman said something to her, she looked at the roof of the opposite building and did not answer. The policeman shrugged and went on writing. The other policeman, older, with less gear, guns, and sticks attached to his belt than the younger one had, stood at the entrance talking to Umberto. For a weird second, the sergeant's familiar face belonged to George the deli owner, then the mirage faded. But I knew him from somewhere.

I actually noticed these details rather quickly, because something else really caught my eye. Affixed to the front of the cabaret was a new glittering sign. Hundreds of little plastic silver discs spelled out "The Girlie Playhouse." The neat scripted sign had been replaced. In the window was a newly installed neon light in the shape of a shapely woman. Was Umberto being arrested for bad taste? I wondered. Then I noticed (funny how you miss something like that at first) one of the neon lady's legs was missing. Glass was scattered on the pavement and next to the glass a stick, which the older policeman now picked up with a gloved hand and introduced into a sack. As I drew closer, I heard the steady thud of music (the doors were open) and also heard the crackling of police handheld radios. Some of our neighbors were assembled on the sidewalk across from the scene. The restaurant owner rubbed his chin, pointed, shrugged.

I then noticed a picket poster propped against the patrol car. Upside down but it read, "Not in Our Neighborhood." I wondered what new person or business had moved in. I noticed too that she wasn't alone. I recognized two or three of her friends by their red caps. They were "Gideon Angels," according to their matching T-shirts. Some others had signs, but theirs were on the pavement, probably abandoned when the brunette did whatever it was she did to get the police to drive up on the curb and interview her.

It might be necessary to add at this point that the "Gideon Angels" had lately been in the news. Their leader, a tall, good-looking brunette, who had given up an engineering career to become a freelance activist, had been brutally assaulted in Newgate Cross Park, but at the time it didn't occur to me that there could be any connection between that incident and the broken neon leg of Umberto's female sign. The woman on the sidewalk I guessed (correctly) was the leader, very pretty, but rather too tall. Because I knew about her ordeal I was sympathetic to her cause, although I wasn't quite sure what it was. My own mother, after all, had been a victim of a violent crime. And when I passed her, I decided I would give her and her group an affirmative nod. As I approached, Umberto glanced up at me and began waving. Pix c'mon, c'mon get in here.

As I replied defensively that I'd never been late before, something warm and soft thumped me on the shoulder, and I turned, ready with a grin for whomever was trying to get my attention, when another tomato, a big vine-ripened beefsteak one, hit my face. My smile instantly disappeared. There was laughter in the direction of the red missile's trajectory. It had been delivered of one of the "angels." The three women clustered and performed a guilty shuffle, and then a brazen blonde in tightish leggings held up another tomato and showed it to me from across the street. "Want another?"

I felt my cheeks turn red. The younger officer jogged noisily toward the mischievous group. Finally, I understood Umberto's frantic antics, followed his advice and got myself inside. "Good log, Umberto. What is going on?"

"They don't like the sign," he said feebly.

I didn't either, I told him, wiping my face with his hanky. "You probably ought to take it down."

Um said he would take it down if it was that ugly. On second thought he might keep it up on principle. "I have a right to put up any kind of sign I want."

"Umberto, why defend your right to be tacky?"

A red glob fell splat on the tile. "What a waste of a perfectly good tomato," said Umberto. I agreed; tomatoes were my favorite fruit.

"My dad used to have this tomato patch. Summers I'd sit out there with a saltshaker."

We both stared at the mess.

"Excuse me, Miss," said the older police officer. Now I recognized him as a customer. White eyelashes. Startling light blue eyes that some lucky people, mostly Gaelic, get when they grow old. He explained that the one woman was being charged with disorderly conduct. His caricature-like facial features truly worked when he spoke. A square of hard flesh formed over his nose between colliding and concerned brows. Assault could be added to the perpetrator's charges, if I wanted. Her friend was already going downtown for destruction of private property, i.e. Umberto's neon leg. He held up the bagged evidence and rattled it.

I remembered having seen the sergeant eyeing my overheated darling as she perched upon a stool, sucking a cranberry cocktail with pursed cranberry lips. Then he added, "I like that skinny girl a lot, the one with the long black hair down to her butt." He winked; his radio crackled.

"Trixie?"

"I don't know her name. She's a little weird, a lot of energy, always smiles." As he spoke he represented the description facially: widened his eyes, wagged his head, and showed his teeth.

Um and I recognized Trixie. "That's her. She studied dance."

The sergeant said he thought Trixie was trained, "Even so she's still got that roughness."

I agreed, yes, yes, our proud, unrehearsed pet. The younger officer stuck his head in the door to say that he was ready to take the ladies downtown. He asked again, very matter-of-factly, if I wanted to press charges. He had his pencil and pad ready.

I told him it was all probably a misunderstanding (the tomato had been mistaken; surely I was not its target). I thought we could resolve things without "going downtown." The younger officer rolled his eyes and slapped the doorframe. "Up to you sweetie" (false smile).

The nice sergeant made himself comfortable on the doorman's stool like he might shoot the breeze all afternoon. I asked him what the Gideon Angels were upset about.

"Well, one of them must've seen the new sign and thought the place had recently opened." He shifted his gearbelt and replaced a pencil slipping from his ear. "You know I'd like to avoid an arrest," he said, finger leisurely scratching his neck. "If we told them the Playhouse was practically a neighborhood institution . . ."

"I think that lady's new to the neighborhood herself," interrupted Umberto. (In fact true: she had recently moved from the East Side to Newgate. It had been in all the papers: "ANGELS ABANDON CRIME-INFESTED NEIGHBORHOOD.")

Eager to protect, serve, and please, the sergeant devised a plan. He would talk to the ladies, tell them how long the Girlie Playhouse had been around, how good it was for the neighborhood to have established businesses, particularly one that was open late and kept a doorman. He took off his hat and dreamily rubbed his head. "We" could invite the ladies in for a show. "Get that Trixie girl to dance for them." It was a hopeful, Pixielike scheme.

The younger officer intruded again, "They still want to protest, and they'll have to get a permit, but they promise to be back this evening." A little too anxious to generate paperwork, he was. The younger was officious, hard-nosed, while his partner was a lackadaisical beat cop, obviously more interested in chatting about Trixie's "great legs" than he was in arresting anyone. After he spoke with Um and me, he would probably chat with the leading Angel in the same avuncular tone.

"Well, if they do come back, invite them in old pal, hey?" said the blue-eyed sergeant.

Umberto said, "I already asked them to come in and see the show. That's when she broke the sign."

"And I thank her for that." I patted Um's shoulder. "We should have never let you decorate on your own."

"We'll be going now," said the young officer (we were wasting the taxpayers' money). The sergeant frowned, pointed to his chest and beyond the door: he'd be able to appease the ladies.

Umberto unplugged the blue and pink-lighted lady and gingerly drew her out of the window. His thin lips quivered. "Pah, I'll take the big one down tomorrow."

Then he remembered something and smiled. With all the commotion he'd forgotten to welcome me back. "Just wait until you meet the new girls!"

27

It is now time to describe the inauspicious change in the lineup of Playhouse dancers, and I will proceed like the sympathetic pixie that I am, a pixie whose optimism has been wrecked twice and rebuilt with better, more elastic, more plastic materials. I liked the new girls, despite their obvious flaws. They both were highly motivated, a condition that comes from dancing for tips, and sometimes they made tiny—insignificant really—personal compromises. They went out of their way to be nice to people they didn't really like. They turned the other cheek when a dollar was the reward. But, you see, they hadn't had the advantages we'd had. The Playhouse had a long-standing, unambiguous reputation as a quiet place where the sane, polite patron could admire talented dancers who, it was rumored, had certain erotic charms. At the Girlie Playhouse we'd had the opportunity to perform solo on a large stage to whatever music we wanted, and we'd had a good salary that, for a while anyway, precluded any need to accept tips.

I have often wondered what happened to dancers who didn't find a Playhouse. What was a trixie runner-up to do, say, if she didn't notice the understated Playhouse sign, or took the shorter route instead of the meandering Newgate Cross Avenue? She might have joined the company at Some Chorus Line or Happy's. True, her special light might have shined more brightly in those grim places, but there is also the chance that her spark might have fizzled in the damp dank kindling, in a place where her own audience pitied her.

Of all the Playhouse dancers, Audrey was the one exception. She never liked exotic dancing and had done it only for the money, but she was gone now. She quit the day we returned from the beach. She'd never been much of a dancer. She had no sex appeal. She burlesqued sexiness, yes, but only as a goof. She was no phony, I grant her that. She may not have loved dancing, but she was clever and sometimes a good sport, and I was sad to see the comic stripper go.

"Won't she miss dancing? Isn't she afraid of gaining weight?" Trixie wondered when she heard the news.

Audrey wasn't the only dancer out. Sammy retired that Tuesday; the baby was due in six months.

Umberto had thought of running an ad in the local paper ever since we cut back bookings, and over the weekend he'd finally gotten around to placing one. He'd called the *Newgate Say*, and after a maze of recorded directions (push one for general information, two for rates etc.), he reached a live person in the help wanted section, and by some weird stroke of fate she happened to be a Gideon Angel (there were a lot of them on that indulgent publication). He gave the information for the ad as follows: "Wanted Dancer—no better make it, Dancer Wanted—for well-established, elegant cabaret in Newgate Cross. We prefer girls with some professional training but will consider applicants who have only natural ability and a lot of charisma. Must be able to work two eight-hour shifts per week and provide own costumes. A fee will be charged for stage rental, but talented dancers can expect to earn at least four hundred dollars a day. Audition at the Girlie Playhouse—g, i, r, l, i, e. That's right. 7 Newgate Cross Avenue."

"My goodness," said the *Newgate Say* employee. "That's a lot of money."

"It's hard work," he said.

"Are you sure about the term 'girls'?" she asked professionally. "Would it perhaps be more appropriate to use the term, 'women'?"

Umberto was confused. "No," he said slowly. "Put girls. It goes with the name, you know."

"The Girlie Playhouse wouldn't be a topless club, would it?"

"Uh well, yes, it is."

"Oh well, that's another department," she said. "Hold while I transfer you." Umberto held for a few bars of "O mio babbino caro," and suddenly a new voice said, "May I take your ad?"

Umberto started to reread his notes, but the man advised him that in that section of the classified the rate was considerably higher per word. "Isn't this still Help Wanted?" asked Umberto. It was, the man said, "Help Wanted Adult Entertainment."

"Oh, oh sure," said meek Umberto, and together they wrote a new ad. It was more concise and would attract more attention: "Need quick cash? Dance at the Girlie Playhouse. Up to $800 a day. No exp nec. Audition 7 NGC Ave."

Two actresses answered the ad, Stacey Smart and Katie Cook—who cheerfully suggested that we call her "Cookie," and despite the narrow odds that a sensitive human might respond to such a classified, it seemed to me a ghost of trixieness existed in one of these rather numb topless dancers.

Cookie had formerly been at Le Mirage. She had fine translucent skin, a greedy smile, an extraordinary snubbed nose with freckles painted across it; pert torpedo breasts, small and fair areolae, and she had a golden ring in her perfectly round and quite deep navel (I had to look twice). I happened to be in the dressing room when she showed up for her audition. She was sheathed in a silver gown and plumped with womanliness and silicone, but she still had a trace of girlish charm hidden in the matter-of-fact-whore tone of her greeting, "How is it here, make any money?"

I asked her how it had been working at Le Mirage, and she promptly replied with a special "ugh," that recalled a kid's love/hate toward school. She said we were lucky to have Mockingbird. The DJ at Le Mirage constantly yelled, "Come on folks tip those girls working hard for ya." The low music was a mere background to his carnival-like announcements.

"You used to work on salary? I knew there was a reason why I didn't want to work here before," said my mercenary with a tap-gun laugh. Still she had a snide way of eyeing her profile in the mirror that held me in thrall, albeit a qualified thrall.

She said at Le Mirage the management had catered to fantasies and changed the themes of its rooms weekly. They were equipped with a fog machine, bubble maker, laser lights, and giant champagne-glass whirlpool. There was a safari room, a sports bar, a sheik's tent. From Le Mirage basement any dancer could borrow feather boas, silk sheets, whips, or platform shoes. The safari room was second home to an aging lioness with viscous saliva, a foul-smelling spider monkey whose cage she'd been required to clean, and a boa constrictor. I asked her why she left the club. "Oh, I got bored; same ol' thing."

I watched her audition. She clomped onto the stage, bent knees knocking. Immediately, she unfastened and shivered out of her blouse because—I assume her reasoning—the customer downstage might only stay the duration of a single beer and would want her to do her thing as soon, and as without fanfare, as possible.

Squinting at the customer who had shown the most promise (biggest pile of mementos, longest hand-in-pocket stare), she fluttered her hand and chirped, "Hi," tugged her bikini top loose and removed it with preposterously slow speed. The customer responded with sham anticipation (eyes wide, mouth same). Her top lay on his head like strange earflaps; she waited for her reward, lips puckered and pouting. Frisky and indiscriminate as a puppy.

Umberto hired her on the spot.

Each time she was asked her name, she said, "Katie Cook, but you can call me Cookie;" there followed a three-noted laugh, big eager smile—slippery teeth parted, tongue bathed in saliva. Kid-like, she could repeat a joke fifty times and derive the same jittery pleasure each time. She was not worried that a customer might guess she'd delivered her clever line before nor did she care if he overheard while she delighted his left-side neighbor with the same play.

Unlike the regular Playhouse dancers, she made mementos part of her performance. After some trouble, she got a customer to slide his limp memento into her cleavage. He was encouraged and wanted to try it again. Once she had all his mementos tucked decoratively in her thong, etc., she snatched her bikini top off his head, held it loosely over her breasts and went to the next guy, who watched Cookie slowly remove her top again, pucker and pout again, and giggle again.

Her routine became so familiar that if I had not been captivated by some of her other qualities, I might have scorned the Cookie Show. She had a coarse, noisy, obvious love for herself that I liked. A remarkable giggle punctuated her every other word, and while a lesser pixie might have thought this Cookie was all pretense, I heard a clean peal of real laughter and saw a truly gluttonous grin as she captured those mementos. She really enjoyed herself. She flagrantly admired her breasts, chin to chest, and her eyes often lingered in the glass above the bar, but her favorite mirror was a customer's eye in which her fishbowl image was adored memento after memento.

Her fellow, Stacey Smart, alas, was only a poor mimicker of Cookie's already semi-fraudulent performances. The tragic starlet,

Miss Smart, had warm-toned, biscuity skin, brown eyes and golden hair, dark eyebrows and full red lips outlined in brown. She had a slow southern accent and a narcotic stare and had danced at the now-defunct Happy's. Sitting on the counter, crossing her fat thighs, she went on and on about how most Happy dancers were students or actresses like herself. They also had the occasional Russian exile who lacked back teeth but had a daughter with a terminal disease. "Girls like that tended to bring down the classiness of a place, you know?"

I had been completely silent through her tirade. Smart was at the mirror, head tilted back, nostrils flaring an inch from the glass, mouth opened wide, and brows raised. As she applied her liner, she spoke without moving her lips much at all. "Don't you hate it," her lip brush filled in the Cupid's bow and dashed across her lower lip, "when they don't tip you? We work so hard."

"Who?"

"Those *pre*verts up there. God, I'm tired. Do you have a tampon? No? Well, we're not on the same cycle yet. In a month or two we will be, that's a promise. We girls stick together in more ways than one."

A shrugging confused Pixie.

"Hard work, what we do."

I said dancing was physically demanding, but then we might be paying for aerobics classes instead.

"Well," she said. "It's frigging hard work, dancing naked in front of people."

Though the dressing room Smart was indignant, onstage she was a vision of compliance and cheap surrender. Her fake ecstatic facial expressions had earned her a disgusting, alliterative name at Happy's, and despite that she was an unbelievably hardworking performer, she barely earned a hundred dollars a day. Her method: she squared off in front of a pigeon, this time poor polite Dan, did a faulty half-backbend, slowly lowering to her knees. Then later, stuck in an uncomfortable, tendon-damaging split, she massaged her breasts and contorted her features; brows screwed up; lids fluttered; mouth seemed to moan. Dan probably noticed the resemblance to Munch's *The Scream*. He coughed, nodded, handed her a memento and longed to be left alone. Smart, transformed out of her ecstatic state by the offered memento, yelled "Thanks," and hurried to the next customer to repeat the process. Dan left a glass wobbling on the table as he slipped out the door.

Oh my goodness. What a bore. I chuckled with Percival and Dave, the pyrotechnician, at the bar. Despite her disastrous audition, Umberto hired her anyway, hoping she would "loosen up a little." We laughed. Umberto's mouth opened to defend her, but snapped shut (molars clicking), when the memento Miss Smart had been tugging was let go and she tumbled onto her back.

Another would-be dancer—backpack, blue jeans, high heels—stumbled in with a rolled *Newgate Say* in her pocket. Fuming of gin and pineapple juice, she messily inquired after the position, but Umberto had the sagacity to send the intoxicated child on her way. A woman of 250 pounds squeezed through the door with a snot-nose child in tow, but Umberto told her the uniform wouldn't fit (there was no uniform), and she properly departed. A young man showed up dressed in tight slacks and black turtleneck. He had all the credentials required of an excellent dancer, and he demonstrated some interesting moves, but Umberto couldn't help but think he might not be right for the *Girlie* Playhouse. To be polite, Umberto took his résumé.

Smart was onstage again, allowing a customer to make change from her garter. She made that strange face of hers and staggered away. Umberto decided to put a sign in the dressing room: "Attention Girls: Dancers cannot make change. Mementos can only be accepted by hand. Feet must be kept no more than eighteen inches apart." Um explained the restrictions were industry standard. Andie protested loudly, "We never had rules before." Jesse looked blankly at the sign, at Miss Smart, and sighed.

When Umberto left, Cookie said that at Le Mirage, rules vigorously enforced by the management had been as enthusiastically disregarded by the girls. In fact, she said, her customers used to consult the list of restrictions (posted above the bar), when they wanted to make special requests. Cookie could get ten dollars for slapping her bottom, twelve for touching her breasts, seven for sticking out her tongue, and five for touching a customer's hand. Once as a goof, she had penciled in "No thumb sucking" and had been able to demand twenty dollars for the illicit act.

It hadn't been a day of quality entertainment at the Girlie Playhouse. We had seen one of its worst days attendance-wise. Outside, the Gideon Angels had returned in greater numbers with ruder signs, and though we were safe inside, updates of their discontent leaked in with customers newly arrived. The beat of the winged doors let in muffled shouts.

Luckily, we dancers had a dressing-room exit. I wouldn't have to dodge vegetables on my way out. When closing time finally arrived, I looked for Cookie and Smart, but they'd already left together. I learned from Umberto that they had, unfortunately, left by the front door.

28

THE TWO BIGGEST NEWS items of the next week were Max's winning the lottery and the Gideon Angels' demonstration outside the Girlie Playhouse. Then came the combined news coverage when it was found, incredibly, that the stories overlapped. The tabloids feed on coincidence and hardly had to invent a thing.

We were featured on three local and two network programs, reduced to comically simple, albeit true, versions of ourselves. Trixie's appearances were brief and paraphrased, but she managed to convey her poignant charm. My appearance was less successful. My face looked curiously muscular. My brows were more arched than I know them to be. But most disconcerting of all, below my babbling image, my name was framed in ironic quotes as if I weren't really a pixie at all.

We all struggled with unfamiliar views of ourselves. Max was first to make local news. I'd seen several other lottery winners accept the four-by-two-foot check. They all had absurd similarities, disheveled hair, some new pretentious accessory, like a cane or an ascot. They embraced their spouses—who, by the way, seemed a wee bit insecure—and thanked God in a speech that was shamefully overworked.

It was the evening after the Cookie/Smart premiere that I drove over to Trixie's studio. Max answered my knock. Several pairs of his shoes, strewn in a corner, mapped out intricate dance steps.

Max sat on the sofa. Trixie coiled in his lap. I sat at their feet. When Max returned from the beach, the lottery authorities had called a press conference. He'd agreed and immediately regretted it. Belinda, the reporter who had interviewed George, was front-row-center with her friend and journalism-school companion, Simone Lambat, a reporter from *Inside Story*—who would be the one to later break the story about Trixie, Max, and the Playhouse.

Simone's blondish, kinky hair had a carroty tint. Her nose was straight but long, and her close-set eyes narrowed strangely on the inside corners, giving her a sneaky, cynical look. She had a slight but chilly foreign accent. Immediately, he did not trust her.

I should say that Simone has performed her penance during these last few terrible days, looking in on me while I have lain numb in bed. She has watered my plants and washed my dishes. As insensitive as she had been about Trixie in the beginning, she is remorseful later. In both instances, she was unjustifiably extreme, obviously one of those people who gets a kick out of being alternately beastly and contrite. I suffered her good deeds for her sake, but I have not forgiven her for her small but nasty part. But I'm jumping ahead here.

At the interview, Max noticed Belinda was obviously peeved that her scoop was fair game to her peers, and she eyed Max possessively as if he were her own discovery, *Maximilian belindarius*. She introduced him to Simone only to establish her claim to him. Simone, however, was not the kind of friend who would honor such flimsy claims, neither professional nor personal.

During the interview, the lights had been astonishingly hot. He'd been asked unexpected questions—for example, Simone Lambat had asked about his de Roquefort connection. This made him nervous. What else did these strangers know about him? He sweated, and—he told us—he was worried his forehead would look shiny. The interview had dragged on an hour, and the reporters seemed to repeat many of the same questions as if they hadn't been satisfied by his earlier responses. When someone asked, for the third time, what he planned to do with the money, he repeated exactly as he had before, "Try to live a reasonably happy life." Fortunately, Max'd had the presence of mind to advise the press of his recent split with Rosamund, and they had refrained from mentioning her during the interview.

We taped the three-minute piece and watched it several times. We noticed that he paused after each question, peering over his reading glasses, eyes wandering around the room. Most of his stutters and blinks were not that noticeable. There was one funny thing he did with his lips when asked if he would live up to the de Roquefort reputation for philanthropy. Simone's question. Finally, Max ejected the tape. He turned to the twelve o'clock news. While still blocking the set, he exclaimed, "Look, it's Belinda again."

He moved away. Belinda, the now familiar reporter, stood outside the Girlie Playhouse explaining why demonstrators were picketing the cabaret. She aimed the mike at Stacey Smart, who said, rather dramatically, "I'm Stacey Smart, actress."

"But you're working as a stripper, right?"

"Yes, that's right." Although Smart sounded like an idiot, I have to admit that she did look rather glamorous on camera, sexy, sleepy, southern, and ten pounds lighter.

"What do you say to the Gideon Angels' allegations that strip clubs encourage violent crimes against women?"

Smart, who had been rehearsing her answer, forgot to listen to the question and replied, "It's a free country. I have a right to do what I choose." Cookie was grinning stupidly over Smart's shoulder.

"Where'd they get those girls?" demanded Trixie. I explained, and she gave an aggravated, "Ugh."

"While that may be true," said Belinda, walking away from Smart. "There are those in the neighborhood who believe they have a right to protest against the cabaret. I asked Karen here what she thought."

Karen was ready: "If they'll do *that* for money, what's to stop them from becoming prostitutes?"

"So you don't think an erotic cabaret belongs in Newgate?" asked Belinda.

No, Karen did not.

Belinda recapped that recently Tully, Gideon Angel leader, had been assaulted in Newgate Cross Park not two blocks from the Girlie Playhouse.

Max looked at the screen gloomily. He had long since lost the ability to see the Playhouse with an outsider's eye, but now he saw it with Karen's, and he was shocked. He decided that even though it might be unfair, Karen's opinion deserved consideration. The character of any place was determined, after all, not by facts but by people's perception of those facts. In this sense, Karen was right, he said.

I didn't realize it then, but his conception of strippers was narrowing and hardening itself until it had no relationship with any living dancer that he knew personally.

It all reminds me now of my father. Two months after I was conceived, Dad, who had worshipped my mother's salacious nudity for months in the smoke-filled cabaret, suddenly, madly, wanted her to quit because exotic dancing was wrong: it had led to their great transgression (me). Mother might have quit for Dad, for love, or for marriage, but she wouldn't just quit. She left Dad's log cabin in disgust. (Dad, by the way, eventually relapsed and ended up with another stripper called "Barb.")

Trixie switched off the television set in disgust. "How come the biggest weirdos wind up on TV? I'm going to call that reporter,

Belinda. Max, you have her number, don't you?" Max fished a card out of his pocket and handed it to Trixie. She grabbed and examined it. "I'm going to call her." Trixie in her peevishness elbowed Max, who wobbled without suspending his stare into an empty corner.

"Why do you need to call that reporter, dear?"

Trixie replaced the phone and looked at him with astonishment. "Why, to set her straight. Why else?"

"Straight about what?"

I folded myself up on the couch. Trixie noticed my discomfort and softened her tone. "The Playhouse doesn't need bad press. It won't be good for business."

"I don't think you have to worry about business anymore, about money I mean," said Max.

"I like having to work."

Max was obviously irritated by this revelation. He sat, eyes on the blank screen, uneasily fingering the corner of a pillow. He was once again in the position of having to persuade her to accept his gifts, a ridiculous predicament. "There's no reason why you would have to stop working—at the Community Center."

"Oh, teaching gives me something, but it's not like dancing."

"So dance," Max said abruptly. "But do it somewhere else. There are plenty of places to dance."

"Name some," she dared. "Where we won't have to share the stage, where we can do exactly what we want, where we won't have to learn someone else's steps or dance to music we don't like."

"Oh, there must be theaters, companies."

Trixie rested her forehead in her palm. After a long pause she said, "It's not the same."

Max jumped. "Exactly. Don't tell me you want to be a stripper. I thought it was just the money."

Trixie looked at him with bitterness. "You're not making sense."

"You're the one who's not making sense. You don't have to strip anymore."

"I never *had to* before," she said.

"What do you get, Trixie, what do you get out of being at a strip club that you couldn't get dancing somewhere else?"

"I like it."

Max looked at me to verify the insane simplicity of her statement.

"Is that so hard to imagine, Max?" I asked.

"Yes," he said.

"You don't have to imagine it!" Trixie cried. "You were there! You've seen me dance. You should know."

Max had to concede, "Yes, but you don't need to do it in a strip club. That's my point. The place shouldn't matter if dancing is the thing you really care about."

"Personally," I said, taking the chance that I was treading where I might not be welcome, "I couldn't imagine stripping anywhere else but a strip club."

"Do you need all those men watching you? Dreaming God knows what about you? Like, for instance, Dan? Does he inspire you?"

"Frankly, he does. I like a challenge."

"I'm totally indifferent to Dan," said Trixie coldly.

"Then why, for heaven's sake, do you need to dance for him?"

"It's not *for* him," replied Trixie, groping for her point. "It's *at* him."

"Oh, I see, *at* him. Well, that makes perfect sense." Max laughed, tickled with the idea that her argument was weak. "Pixie, now you tell me, do you dance *at* or *for* your customers?"

I hesitated for a few minutes, biting my thumbnail, considering this delicate point. "Through," I said finally. "Through."

Max threw his arms in the air.

"Oh, I don't want to fight," said Trixie with affected cheerfulness. "Let's forget it until later. In the meantime, however," Trixie glanced at

Belinda's card, "I can't stand to see them misrepresent the Playhouse." Trixie thought a while. "I won't mention your name, Max, if you don't want me to."

"It's not that," barked Max. "You can mention my name."

"I won't."

"I said you could—I just don't see why you would need to."

"I won't, I said."

"I'm not concerned about *my* reputation. I don't want you to come off sounding like those girls they interviewed. What was her name? Stacey Smack?"

His irritation had no sooner provoked this remark than he realized that Trixie was not like those tawdry girls (was she?). His face softened, but too late. Trixie gasped. Whereupon Max relapsed. "You damn well might."

There was, wasn't there, a little tawdriness in Trixie too, in all dancers? It went along with the territory of sequins, boas, and thigh-high stockings. But no, she wasn't like those other girls. I explained to Max that Stacey and Cookie were as crass as they seemed; TV hadn't lied.

The next morning, Trixie missed Belinda at the station because they had overslept. Flanneled Max gulped coffee in groggy silence. He was unable to locate the inflamed core that had upset him so the night before. What about Trixie's contacting the reporter had made him angry? Whatever it had been, he remembered he had been right about it. Perhaps Trixie wouldn't bring it up again. For the moment, it seemed she had forgotten about it.

But lo! at noon, Belinda, camera, and two-man crew waited outside the Playhouse. It was my day off so I missed the surprisingly friendly reporter and her crew who chatted while the girls dressed in between sets. I was told that Belinda herself confessed that she had been a go-go girl in her slim college days. So saying, she won the confidence of Jesse and Andie. Everyone was interviewed briefly, and Trixie was interviewed at length.

Trixie didn't think it was necessary to mention Max—their news items were unrelated, but she talked freely about dancing and her work at the Community Center. When Jesse called to tell me to watch the news, she described the day in detail. Trixie had talked for a long time. They had asked a lot of questions and she gave very good answers.

"Did they interview you?"

"Only for a few minutes," said Jesse. "I basically just said that the Playhouse wasn't a bad place to work."

It was on at five. Hours of footage had been compressed into three minutes. I lay in bed in front of my small color portable. Belinda appeared in front of the cabaret, dressed like a private eye. "Residents of Newgate Cross Park are in an uproar over the existence of a topless bar in their neighborhood. Protesters have been picketing for two days, and they say that they intend to remain outside the Girlie Playhouse until city officials hear their case"—meaningful pause— "They are demanding that the place be closed down." She spoke over film clips of the protest from the day before. "For those of you who may not be familiar with the Girlie Playhouse—a business that has been located in this community for over ten years, according to its owners—Channel Nine's investigatory team decided to get the inside scoop." Belinda entered the cabaret.

Jesse posed in a bikini while the camera settled on her chest. A smiling waitress counted her cash. Strobe lights flashed. It was all pretty confusing. I could just discern Andie's arms and thighs. In the dressing room, Jesse and Sidney counted their tips. Belinda asked them how much they made. "On a good day," said Jesse. "About a thousand."

"What's a bad day?" asked Belinda.

Sidney squinted as if she couldn't remember a bad day. "Oh, about three hundred."

Belinda pointed out that all kinds were to be found working in cabarets. Then Trixie was shown dancing. While the camera traversed her body it skipped from shiny calves to the tiny dent that was her navel to her powdered shoulders, missing certain parts which the station considered not airable during prime time (Trixie had insisted that no censor blocks be used on her body). The cabaret had been eliminated through a close-up lens: Trixie seemed to be performing at the foot of my bed. Trixie stared straight into the camera (Nicky the cameraman had kept saying, "Looky over here, over here"). She never seemed so brazen before, and I was excited like all the other citizens supine under taut floral bedspreads watching in private delight.

Belinda appeared again to explain that Trixie was not only a dancer but also a teacher at the Northwest Community Center. "So," Belinda added, winking, "you can't say she doesn't have class."

Then I saw what had survived of Trixie's interview. She was perched upon a barstool in the dressing room, smiling zealously. The reporter asked the burning question, "Why do you find yourself working as a stripper?"

Trixie said, "I like dancing; it's fun."

Back to Jake in the studio who said, "I guess she likes that kinda thing, huh, Susan?"

"Guess she does." (squeamish smile).

29

I HAD MISSED THAT day at work in order to see a gynecologist (Sammy's, coincidentally). My mind and my body are obviously one at the Playhouse. At the doctor's, we discuss me as if my personality had nothing to do with my body.

I was late, but that was nothing unusual. But that one time with Calvin was unusual.

I was told to arrive a half hour early to answer questions about my life history and the histories of everyone genetically similar. I was pretty confident about all the "no's" I was ticking off, but then my pen hesitated in my Psychological Illness/Depression column. If I checked "yes," there would be some embarrassing questions to follow during the examination. Should I confess? And to what, exactly?

"What sort of depression?"

"I sleep ten to twelve hours a night. If I don't I'm in trouble. I'm delicate. I need sleep, exercise, oatmeal in the morning, or else I cry a lot and I look like hell."

"What brings it on?" (Would I detect concern mingled with professionalism?)

I checked the "no" column.

She examined me thoroughly. It seemed like she had both hands inside me the whole time. At one point, she announced cheerily, "rectum!" and inserted her latexed finger in that location. 'You're going to hate this, but it's good for you.' She took several samples but I knew she wouldn't find out from that what is really wrong with me:

I'm terrified—and that has affected my ability to procreate.

As I expected, she says that I am not pregnant, but something else is wrong. I was scheduled for several elaborate tests. Results: It's nothing life threatening to me as an individual (though it would be a problem for the species if everyone were like me). It's only a concern with my personal fertility.

The problem with me is that my estrogen levels always remain constant because my glands "never send the right messages" and never "ordered any eggs."

No wonder I shirked at the prospect of nesting. No wonder I chased Calvin away. It was the wrong hormones talking. Could I call him up and apologize for my pituitary?

Well, now anyway I have my explanation, such as it is, for why I won't leave the Playhouse, why I never have attached myself to a male for the purposes of controlled breeding. But what would Trixie say to Max?

She liked that kind of thing.

30

Trixie and Max had watched the program together at home. Max had, like me, seen her for the first time in a lurid light. Although she had danced no differently than usual, the program showed none of the peculiar moves that expressed her iridescent charm. The editors favored the frames that showed her taking something off, and they also preferred her pout to her more usual smile. In short, Trixie seemed more like a stereotypical stripper than I care to grant. Max had been disturbed by this version of Trixie. It was very much the one that he had predicted the night before. He was particularly annoyed with the way she seemed to flirt with the camera. Was he wrong to think that he was special? Did she look at all her customers like that?

Trixie had not been affected by the show in the same way he had. True, she was surprised at the unfamiliar version of herself, but she recognized herself nonetheless. She was still confident that she was who she was. She only wished they had shown more; to have been more thorough would have been better.

"It's a shame they didn't really show me dancing much, huh, Max? But I think I looked okay, though. Don't you?"

"I'll be glad when you stop dancing," he said.

"I thought we settled that already."

"I never gave in. You shouldn't be doing that now that you're . . . now that you're with me. I know you don't mean to lead men on, but you can't help it. I don't want men thinking that way about you."

She looked at him incredulously.

He reminded her that men do after all, through no fault of her own, have certain physical reactions that make them imagine certain things. And since it was not unreasonable of him to not want men thinking those things about his girl then—but he was interrupted.

Trixie, who was informed on such male tendencies, nevertheless denied emphatically that such things *ever* happened and that in fact she was surprised that he could think such a thing when, after all, nudity was very common these days and meant *nothing*, literally nothing.

He raised a reprimanding eyebrow.

"Oh, of course I know," sighed Trix, exasperated. "I can't be bothered with *that*. It'll inhibit me."

Max softened, "I hate to surprise you, but you are the most uninhibited creature on this planet. When we were waiting in line at the post office the other day, I noticed you were sticking your finger in your belly-button. Most people don't do that kind of thing in public after age five."

She laughed. "Stop it. I wasn't."

"You were, my pet."

Trixie phoned me. It was quite a triumphant moment when my telephone rang, jarring my cottage night. I answered cautiously, timidly, "Hello? Who's there?" as if calling up from my abyss.

Their argument seemed to cause so much pain where none seemed wanting. He was concerned with the reputation that strip clubs had; he didn't want her to be confused with the inelegant ladies that usually worked in such places; he didn't want her associated with lecherous men who thought strippers were whores—all reasonable worries in my opinion: I'm not so blind.

It was certainly obvious to Trixie that Max's thoughts were powerfully lewd. In a way, Trixie felt that she was battling with him rather than against him, trying to work out a way of modifying the rest of the world's perceptions to fit with their own.

In the meantime, however, Max insisted that Trixie stop dancing. She was thoroughly confused about this; all logic had broken down and now only soreness directed her thoughts and words. I said that they weren't really in dispute over what, only when and why. I told her that someday she would have to quit the Playhouse.

"Why?" she asked, weakly.

I said someday she would become self-conscious about her flirtatious ways.

"I don't flirt," she said, making my point.

"Of course you don't," I said generously.

"After seeing me on TV, Max is all of a sudden concerned about what other people think." She went on rapidly, "I told him I didn't care what other people thought, and he said I'd better. I said they probably thought the same thing he thought. I don't know whether that reassured him or scared him; he said that nobody, *nobody*, saw me the way he did, and that all the customers in the Playhouse could not care less whether I was a good dancer or not. He said they only had one thing in mind." Here she drawled out an imitation of his southern accent. "Like I didn't know. Why don't you talk to Max? Soothe him?"

"I will, I promise, next time I see him."

"He says he's not coming in anymore."

"Not coming in? Why on earth?"

"I know. It's ridiculous. Will you call him?" she pleaded.

"On the phone?"

"Yes, 'on the phone.' You can't just *call* him."

I laughed. I was not used to having phone friends.

When I called Max, I found he had other things on his mind than whether or not Trixie should stop dancing (he had already made up his mind that she would). Max had finally paid an overdue visit to his office. Countless charities were molesting his secretary. To ease her day, Max had given her permission to disconnect any caller who wanted "Mr. Price" instead of a Mazda. Inadvertently snubbed along with the charities was Rosamund's lawyer. Every time he called Price Mazdatown, politely asking for Mr. Price, the line mysteriously went dead. However, indefatigable coincidence relayed Max's wife's plans to him just the same. When he went out at lunch, he noticed the *Newgate Say* headline: "ESTRANGED WIFE OF LOTTERY WINNER WANTS HALF."

He closed and locked his office door, spread the paper on his desk. A bad photo of Rosamund on the steps of the courthouse greeted him below the headline. She wore a matronly beige business suit, a white blouse he'd bought for her, and low-heel shoes. Max shuddered. He quickly scanned the text: The wife of the city's most recent lottery winner has filed for divorce. Price publicly accepted the winnings without his wife. Price's business partner and wife both had "no comment." The Prices' neighbors, names withheld, reported that Price has not been home in a week. Wife is distraught. Wife's lawyer had no comment other than to say that his client is entitled to standard compensation.

Max sighed heavily and reread the article. It seemed less offensive the second time. He had intended to give her a lot. He had unconsciously left the business, house, cars, and savings to her already. But the lottery winnings? The lottery had come at a time when Rosamund seemed halfway around the world of his existence. Perhaps she was simply bitter. Perhaps she only meant to scare him. It had been unreasonable of him to abandon her without a word. He hadn't thought about her much at all in the past several days. He guiltily realized that he must have been heavy on her mind. She must have seen him on the news. That must have been hard on her. He was astonished at his own insensitivity. He tried Rosamund's number and got a busy. He tried again and again, still busy. Some of his sympathy began to fade. Fatigued, he went out to his secretary's desk and told her to put all calls through. When he got back to his desk the phone was already ringing. A news show. A talk show. Another news show. He declined the offers and freed up the lines again. Another talk show host called.

As Max described his discomfiture at being suddenly so interesting to the general public, I thought about how my mother's past was subjected to scrutiny, how she was written about, reported on, and analyzed until her life seemed nothing but scrapings on a forensic lab floor. Both of them, passive players, had been acted upon by chance, suddenly made famous by the luck of the draw.

Max was, he admitted to me, flattered at first by the attention, but when he had finally realized how those TV people intended to portray him, he was insulted.

With the receiver pressed against a red ear, Max listened to "Elly's producer," who was doing a show on lottery winners in serious debt and divorce court. She already had the last three years' winners. Would he care to join the panel? Another call. Max, tapping a pencil, listened to Monty's angle: lottery winners and gambling addictions. How much had he spent on tickets before he won? Another call. Max was invited to go on a celebrity game show. Still others. The blonde on Channel 5 asked him for a date.

Max tried to phone Rosamund again. This time her line rang, but there was no answer. She was in the garden being filmed by Simone Lambat.

Meanwhile Umberto, flipping through the channels, paused on an *Inside Story* commercial and noticed immediately his girls in their red Miatas. "Max Price, recent lottery winner, pays a high price for his stripper-girlfriends." The next frame should have shown Max's real and only true girlfriend, but in place of Trixie's face was Audrey's.

31

THE MISTAKEN IDENTIFICATION WAS quickly remedied by Audrey herself, who made a call to the station. Audrey had been chosen from footage featuring seven girls driving Miatas because she, with hair highlighted red in the sun, looked the tackiest.

An amateur video operator had called Belinda when he recognized Max and Trixie on two different Channel 9 news shows. He said he had filmed the lottery winner and seven of those Playhouse strippers on the ferry to the island. Belinda stupidly mentioned this incredible coincidence to Simone.

"My mother lives on the island. What's his name?"

"Cy Candid. Isn't that a great name for a photographer!" Belinda was thinking more about the implausibility of everything than protecting her scoop.

The amateur video operator was none other than the dirty-blonde man on the ferry who had taken such an interest in Trixie. Simone asked him how much Belinda had offered and gave him three times as much for an exclusive.

Simone was delirious. The headline "seven figures for seven figures" jingled in her mind. Simone knew there had not been another story so right for tabloid news since the headless body was discovered at a topless bar. Or when that tollbooth attendant had gunned down seven motorists. The seventh driver happened to be the man's father who had abandoned him three days after his birth. A baby picture of the gunman was found in the dead man's wallet. The beauty of the story was there had been no other connection between father and son other than genetics. The boy had been adopted by parents named "Williamson" and the biological father's first name was William.

But this story was even more interesting to Simone. She had a thing against strippers. While Belinda and Simone were at journalism school together, Belinda had worked at Go-go Heavenly. This fact in itself might have remained innocuous if it weren't for the other fact that one day Simone's boyfriend, Jason, caught Belinda in the act when he accidentally (he swears) stumbled into the club on his way home from work. Belinda and Jason dated secretly and unseriously at first, but come early spring they eloped, while Simone was studying for her midterms.

Belinda never knew that Simone blamed her for the C minus nor that consequently her applications to the better graduate schools had been rejected. Indeed, I think perhaps Simone herself was unaware of the grudge she carried with her all the years of their continued friendship. As it worked out, the continued friendship ultimately made revenge more convenient.

Although she was working at *Inside Story*, Simone considered herself a serious feminist journalist. She had a long history with the movement and had even fallen in with the Gideon Angels for a brief spell after college. However, on *Inside Story* she inevitably failed to make her feminist point in the allotted six minutes. More often than not, her boss and editor, Marcel, would scrap the most important seconds of video. I should mention that Marcel, who happened to be a regular at Some Chorus Line—he had a crush on the sixth brunette from the left—hated feminists and Simone, who thought his certain desires made him a dubious species of pig. So it may seem odd that when the producers occasionally required that *Inside Story* run a piece on women's issues, Marcel never failed to assign Simone—the explanation being that Marcel thought her accent made any serious piece sound like a parody of itself. He had a secret mission to sabotage any women's issue spot in this manner. When she begged permission to do a piece on the Gideon Angels vs. strippers, he readily agreed.

Umberto rented a large-screen TV. "Coming right up: Max the playboy lottery winner takes it to the max." Photo of Max in a tuxedo. Max recognized the photo that until recently had occupied an unimportant spot on Rosamund's dressing table. "Playboy?" he complained. "That was taken at a charity dinner. The highlight was a goitery old man who spoke about the merits of euthanasia."

"You can't expect them to know everything," said Umberto.

After the commercial, instead of the promised report on Max, we were shown a segment about a woman with sixteen aliases and five husbands. The taunting anchor promised again, "Coming up next: Seven strippers sell sex by the seaside." Stolen footage focused on rascally Max and Trixie, her feet twitching on the dashboard. Then seven pretty girls in seven red cars drove out of the ferry through a strip of sunlight, a brunette, a blonde, a redhead in sunglasses, a sandy blonde, a black girl, a brunette, another dirty blond, all of us wearing censor blocks on our eyes.

"Was that us?" asked Sidney.

I giggled. It was ridiculous and true.

"Pixie," said Umberto. "You didn't come to a complete stop at the stop sign."

After another commercial, instead of the report on strippers, we learned about a diner that was slated for demolition because a Negro burial ground was said to exist beneath it. Booth sixteen, by the way, was haunted. Poltergeists constantly drained the water glasses and snatched the tips. Umberto bought everyone a round.

"What would you do if you won seven million dollars? Would you hire seven strippers for a weekend of wild sex at the beach? That's what lottery winner Max Price did, and Simone Lambat has the *Inside Story*."

Crowd: "Way to go Max," "That's living."

"Everyone in Newgate wondered why lottery winner Max Price waited three days before coming forward to claim his prize," said Simone.

A wedding photo of the Prices. The couple four-handedly slice through a spongy white cake. "Max and Rosamund Price were the perfect couple. At the wedding friends said they belong on top of the cake. But when Max won the lottery, their happy life together ended." Video imaging tore the photo in twain. "Rosamund Price still lives in their modest three-bedroom home." Rosamund trudging across a lawn.

She was indeed pretty, just as Max had said so many months before. She was lithe, clever-looking, clear-eyed. She was wearing blue jeans and an oversized sweater, perhaps Max's. Trixie noticed the electric bug killer hanging from the eaves, the mailbox mimicking the house, the plastic garbage pails that all had formerly defined Max's life.

"But Mrs. Price hasn't seen her husband since he won the lottery." A gloved Rosamund equipped with clippers cut a rose. "Abandoned, she passes her sad days working in her garden, waiting for her husband to return."

The garden, I noticed, was one of those well-manicured ones, symmetrical. Max was annoyed; those gloves weren't even hers.

Then we saw Rosamund curled on a sofa, fondling a bored gray cat. Part of Simone's leg, her profile and a section of curl were visible in the corner of the screen. "Tell us how you discovered your husband had won the lottery."

"I saw him on the news like everybody else," said Rosamund.

Simone's curl wagged in reproof. "He hasn't called you?"

"No."

"How did your husband usually choose the numbers he played?"

"Well, he always played the same combination of dates, his birthday, my birthday, and our wedding anniversary."

"09, 06, 12, 14, 10, 24, 84," read Simone from a card. "Is that the combination of dates that were special to the both of you?"

"Yes, it is."

Max said he had completely forgotten that his lucky numbers corresponded to dates. Over the years of playing the lottery they had lost all meaning. He used similar numbers for various other codes that he was required to remember. For example, he used 0906 to get cash from automatic tellers. 102484 opened his gym locker. Ironically, he tended to forget his anniversary, while he always remembered how to get to his jogging shoes.

"What would you say to Max if you knew he was listening tonight?"

Rosamund faced the camera. "Max, come home. Wherever you are, come home." Judging from the response in the Playhouse audience, Rosamund played the loving wife earnestly and well: three husbands noisily scooted their chairs and excused themselves from the rest of the show.

Footage of Trixie appropriated from the local affiliate. Strippers were generally great for ratings, but Simone had shown restraint, and never gone beyond Trix's shoulder. We did see a lot of money changing hands, and ending up mostly in Umberto's. You see, Simone preferred the issues behind the sex scandal to the sex itself. She interviewed Tully Gideon, who said the customers at cabarets exploited women. Then Dan, dear familiar Dan, said, "I love those girls."

Next edit, Simone stood by the *very* motel where the "tryst" had taken place. "Here is where it all happened," she gestured toward the cozy Inn by the Sea, its curtains drawn in shame. Simone rang the bell and "Victoria O'Rourke, Innkeeper" opened the door. "Seven of them in red sports cars. They parked them right there."

"Over there?"

The camera found an empty lot.

"Seven women driving seven red cars, and Mr. Price picked up the tab? Didn't you think that was strange?"

"Not at the time, because I didn't know who he was."

"And now?"

"They were strippers. I saw *that* immediately. I figured they probably wanted to open an escort service or something. But not in my place. The whole town was talking about them. They were parading around everywhere like they didn't care who knew what they were really up to. They went topless on the beach."

"Do you mean without their . . . ?"

"Naked! And it's illegal, you know. A lot of people don't realize that, but there are *signs*. I think he got the idea because they finally left."

And Max had chosen her inn for its privacy.

In slow motion, our cars dreamily swerved down a winding road. "Price not only paid for the hotel, but he also gave each woman her own car. What did they do for these cars? Well, we were able to get an exclusive interview with one of the strippers."

A shadow said, "I'm not proud of the fact that I was a stripper." The Playhouse audience exploded with surprised shouts at Audrey's voice.

"Sh!" hushed Umberto. "I want to hear."

"But I did what I needed to get by," said Audrey.

"Why did you decide to come forward today?"

"Because I saw the commercials you broadcasted. They implied that I was his lover."

"And you're not?" asked Simone indifferently.

"No, I'm not! I never had anything to do with customers, really. Some of the other girls, especially Trixie, were regular—well, you know what."

Our audience booed Audrey.

"Is Trixie the one who stayed in Price's room most of the time?"

"Yes."

"Were you aware that they engaged in sexual conduct?"

"Trixie bragged about it when they did it at the Playhouse."

"Did you say *at* the club?"

"Oh, yeah."

Umberto objected, "Not in my place. Where? When? That's what I want to know!" Max and Trixie looked at each other guiltily. The rest of us who knew squirmed but remained silent.

Audrey continued, "They were doing it all over the place, in the cabaret, the car, on the beach, at the inn in the sitting room."

"In public?"

"Yes."

"Did he pay her?"

"For sex?" A pause. "Mr. Rosamund, I mean Mr. Price is a real big tipper."

Audrey had always been a bit of a complainer, but we had no idea she had looked down on her job to the extent she apparently did. When Sidney declared, "How could she do that?" I suggested that Audrey had been forced into a strange position being misrepresented as some kind of seaside strumpet. Instead of defending us all from accusations, she found it easier to distinguish herself from the accused.

The *Inside Story* segment ended with a tearful plea from Rosamund, voice quavering, "I still love him." She wiped her cheek with a knuckle. "And would take him back."

I watched Max's grave profile in the flickering light. Trixie squeezed his hand, and they both stared ahead. The public obviously rooted for the wife. I knew he couldn't explain to reporters how he felt yesterday when he had pressed his hand against Trixie's breast and that he still felt her heart thumping in his fingertips. How could he make Simone Lambat understand that the way Trixie's crossed feet swung under her chair gave him soul-ache? These details meant nothing to the viewers, but they were overwhelming to him.

32

After the nationally televised publicity, Umberto correctly anticipated a crowd at his red doors, and overnight he had hired an expensive mercenary crew. Umberto had reduced the main stage; eliminated the warm-up stage; brought in portable pedestal stages; installed wall-to-wall mirrors that seemed to create endless girls dancing arm in arm.

With renewed faith in neon, he had outlined the ceiling seams in pink and blue lines. Bright cursive indicated necessaries like "Bar," "Men's Room," and "Champagne Room," and produced a dusty glow throughout. Luminous veins of red beat down what was left of the runway. The familiar bartenders, Sal and Carmine, who always remembered your drink if not your name, had been replaced, with suspicious expediency, by busty twins in tuxedo vests. The DJ booth had been demolished. A *One Hundred and One Dance Greats* recording had made Mockingbird obsolete. The record would become repetitious after four hundred and twenty minutes, yes—"But who cared?" asked Umberto rhetorically. He explained that after the *Inside Story* segment, last night's turnover had been phenomenal. Seven hundred customers in and out. He no longer wanted the regular who savored only one expensive drink; Umberto would cater to the tourist with a short attention span and disposable cash.

Trixie, Sidney, Andie, Cookie, and I hesitated by the bar. "From now on you only dance on these pedestals when the customer gives you a dance ticket." He exhibited a red coupon between forefinger and thumb (mementos, too costly, had been scrapped), "You get a ticket from the customer," he transferred the ticket from left to right hand, "You get up on the pedestal," he imitated stepping, "and you dance to one song."

"How much?" asked Cookie.

"Ten."

"What's my cut?"

"Five."

"Make it eight."

"Seven fifty."

"Deal," said Cookie and proceeded to the dressing room.

"Why can't we dance on the stage?" asked Andie.

"I'm trying something new here, give me a break. Besides, they're portable." He kicked one; it rolled and bumped a chair. "You each get your own. Plus, I hired a big star who's using the main stage. Every week, we'll have a different performer. Tracey Topps, Cleo Cleavage and her sister Kristie Kanyon, Betty Boobs, Mandy Mountains, Puss Bosoms, Tina Tits, Noelia Knockers, Brenda Beamers, Busty Heart, Topsy Curvey, Julie Juggs, and the Boobsy Twins. Yep, different girl every week of the year."

Could there really be fifty-two puns on "breasts"?

"Not that I don't have my own stars right here," continued Umberto, beaming. "Trixie, the porter has a box of fan mail addressed to you care of the ol' GP. People were asking for you all night. I told them to come back during the day. And, Sidney, a few were asking after the voluptuous one. That's you hey, hey, hey. I'm telling you. You guys are stars. Get ready for your fans!"

"A bunch of guys who think we're rentable for weekends?"

"Great," moaned Andie.

"Who cares what they think?" said Trixie.

"I care," said Sidney.

"I don't mean I don't care, I mean they'd be wrong to think that."

"Umberto," said Andie. "There is no way I'm gonna get on top of one of those barrels and dance for someone who saw me on *Inside Story*."

"You won't have time to dance. I'm telling you, we were mobbed last night after the show. You guys are stars, they'll give you dance tickets just to talk."

Umberto, as our longtime friend and boss, eventually persuaded us to give it a try. While we dressed, strange women began arriving for a mass audition Umberto was holding that afternoon. A City University student was first to arrive (major philosophy/religion, hobby ballet). She had bark-colored hair, a pallid complexion, a knobby nose, and a good figure. She timidly unpacked a black leotard. A faded blonde said she admired Trixie, keep it up. A six-foot girl named Phoenix, with unbelievably high cheekbones and pouting lips, arrived, and like so many others unzipped her bag, stripped, and silently began curling her hair.

Then the featured dancer appeared, a monumental and revolting beauty. Ma'am Mary aimed a crooked finger at a corner, and the bandy-legged porter dropped her trunk with a crash. She opened the lid and yanked a feather boa from a jumble of costumes, red wigs, and devices. She passed around some glossy magazines that depicted the star in astounding postures.

"Twixie, Twixie whom may I ask is Twixie?" I stupidly looked at my friend, and Trixie had to confess it was she. Ma'am Mary drew up a low stool companionly beside her. "Sit, sit." She patted the tuffet. "I like your act, sister. You could go all over, if you need a little diwection . . ."

"No,"

"Why not?" The huge star sat up straight.

"Showtime," shouted Umberto on cue.

The house was full upstairs. Loose groups of five or six men hallooed and hoorayed. Few independent thinkers. Cookie had made a beeline for the noisiest group, got a ticket in her teeth and climbed onto a pedestal. When she teetered, a padded shoulder came to her rescue and gallantly remained while she shimmied out of her top.

It was strange to see a dancer naked standing *among* the men in the audience. I could still be shocked after all these years of stripping. But with this shock I felt some excitement, hard to manage at the time, but something I have since accepted. Stacey was also already on a pedestal and she, too, was surrounded on all sides. Sidney too. And Andie, who, it seemed, was enjoying the table dance that she performed for a solemn man in the corner.

Behind Cookie, a man was bending to get a closer look. "Ooh," she cried, when he kissed her. I thought she would hit him, but instead she said, "Naughty, naughty. That'll cost ya."

"Cut that out, Ron," said another man tugging Cookie's thong.

"Oops," laughed Cookie. "None of that. Bottom stays on." Then she whispered, smiling, in the man's ear and he put another twenty in her thong. Cookie lurched back and stumbled from her pedestal. Someone helped her climb back on.

Trix and I were sitting at the bar and noticed the several who pointed our way mouthing, "She the one?" A labeled conventioneer was launched from his group and headed toward us jerking loose his tie. "I don't care what they say. I think you're a helluvalot better looking than that guy's wife, whatshername? Rosamund?"

"Oh?" Trixie didn't know what else to add.

He waited. "Well, I just thought I'd tell you that."

"Okay."

"I'll be going now," he raised his hand, crumpled his fingers, and retreated.

Umberto passed by. "Gonna dance?"

"Not just yet."

"Waiting for a good song," I explained.

"Don't wait too long," he said, rubbing thumb on fingers (money-making gesture).

"I wouldn't mind dancing to this one," she said. She climbed on a pedestal, and the nearest man gave her a ticket.

She uncovered her willowy nudity and started to sway. But the old man seemed more interested in talking with her than enjoying her dance. She bent to listen, brushing her hair behind her ears. He gesticulated wildly until the end of the song. Then he gave her another coupon to sit down.

Someone offered me a ticket. I looked up at Bartholomew. He sat down. I got up on the pedestal and without further ado took off my top. His eyebrows pumped suggestively and I did my best to make a "show" of it, do sort of campy funny things for my old buddy Bart, but I found that slight undulations, solemnly performed, were the only moves possible on the treacherous pedestal. Bart, with tilted head, melting smile, drooping eyes, whispered my name.

I was aware, for the first time, of Bart's particular scent, of shaving gel and deodorant mixed a little with the smell of fried foods. I saw three or four ingrown hairs on his cheek, which he had obviously picked earlier that day. "Hey you know, Pix," he said. "Let me take you away from all this. You shouldn't have to work. You want to meet somewhere else sometime? Maybe have dinner?"

Ah! I made my clumsy excuses, lying badly about having to go freshen up.

I wasn't alone for long. Before I made it to the dressing room door, I was persuaded to dance for six different men in rapid, sweaty succession. My clothes had been on and off six times in twenty minutes. I resorted to just holding my blouse up against my chest as I went from table to table.

I was like Cookie, doing the same routine over and over, but I kept producing the same positive results, namely coupons. Table dancing was simple and straightforward—if done with strangers. Old friends got the wrong idea. You wanted strangers to get the wrong idea. That was sort of the point.

Then I saw my favorite billiard player was half-sitting on a stool, half leaning against it with his feet apart and planted on the ground. His hands drummed the rim of the seat between his legs. He had already positioned the pedestal between his feet, and when I climbed up on it, he grabbed my blouse, which I had still held to my breast, and tossed it on the bar. His eyes had slight elliptical folds that made him somewhat exotic. As I writhed and wiggled for him, within inches of his face, of his hands, he watched with a grave expression. There were entire seconds when we looked each other in full in the face without flinching, and I wondered which one of us would crack a smile first. But after several minutes, I still had not and neither had he. The vague blurry forms that drank and danced around us seemed even vaguer, and were, I thought, as uninterested in us as we were in them. All we needed was a darker corner, a little screen from the noise and we might have done anything we liked. He smelt of alcohol and cologne and I had braced myself with my hands on his broad, very broad shoulders. He had always reminded me, I realized, of Calvin. He could have been his paler brother. That thought made me want to either touch his lips or look up with a start at the door to where Calvin used to sit and where he would be watching me, judging me, if he had come back to get me.

This new strange intimacy would be too much for me to resist if I kept it up. I wondered if this was the thing that Calvin tried to warn me about. Dancing this close would have its effect on me, I knew,

I didn't think I would be able, like Cookie, to just walk away. I would have to become either promiscuous or cynical, neither would be gratifying over the long haul.

But there he was, this paler brother, and Calvin was not. When I crossed my arms over my breasts, his eyes followed the crisscross pattern and then met mine. I swallowed. He swallowed. The song ended. He had no more coupons. He looked at me beseechingly. "So, what are you doing here?"

But I didn't stay!

A man I had never seen before grabbed my arm and drew me away toward his table. I suffered several noisy men to surround me and narrate vulgarly while I danced for one of them. "Look at that. Look at that. Hey, hey, hey, you know what that means." My guy, embarrassed for them, turned and said, "Behave yourselves." To me he whispered, "Can't take them anywhere." These were the guys you did stunts and jokey things for, I decided. None of them had come in to enjoy the dancing. Too bad Audrey wasn't around. She would have suited them fine.

When the song ended he said, "Hey, that was great. Have a seat." I didn't want to. He and his group didn't seem sober enough for me, but he pleaded, and I couldn't get out of it without seeming rude. This man was a common young professional who probably resented his job as much as he loved his home team. I could tell by the way he had so violently tugged his necktie loose as if it were an iron collar. "Is all that stuff they're saying true?"

"Oh, you know reporters tend to exaggerate a bit."

"I knew they did. You know what I hate? The ones who say men're somekinda ogres."

"Who?"

"The protesters. They're outside. Didn't you know? I wouldn't've even come in, but I wanted to piss them off. I hate their type. Hey, you're not one of those women who hates men are you?" I shook my head vigorously. His buddies had filed off to the bar and he became more sullen in his expression. He watched his hands fumble on the table. "Say, let me have your number and I can give you a call, all right? My name's Henry. We can get to know each other. I'm not such a bad-looking guy, am I?"

I started to answer politely in the negative, but he interrupted, throwing out his hands, "I'm sorry. I'm sorry. Didn't mean to offend you." He was as skittish and bad tempered as a severely trained dog. I got up, knocking over my freshly poured wine.

I took to a shadowed nook, safe from the intoxicating strobe, and surveyed the muggy room. Sidney's curls had started to unfold, and she was arguing unsuccessfully about the price of a dance ticket. Andie passed by, kicking her pedestal, and groaned in my direction. Trixie stood on a pedestal scribbling her autograph, with a no-doubt childish scrawl, on slips of napkin and bank receipts. Umberto had volunteered his back as a writing desk.

Suddenly, an immense Middle Easterner took the stage, dressed in fuchsia shirt opened to his hairy navel, flared black slacks. He announced, "Ma'am Mary."

The redheaded star mounted the stage, flapping red wing sleeves, but she received only one tired hooray. The rest of the pathologically inattentive audience scratched themselves and/or shifted in their warm seats. Ma'am Mary's infamous ninety-nine-inch bust got only one, "Hey, lookydat, like basketballs," and her final act, a violently explicit, not to mention acrobatic, event, involving swords, fire, and the emcee's sober assistance, only received one weak collective, "Ah."

If a circus performer couldn't hold their attention, Andie and Sidney's subtle charms, dazzling on any well-lit roomy stage, would be completely overlooked. And who would notice the way Trixie's finger twitched in this crowd? She worked and worked on her pedestal, but did anyone really watch her? Men yelled and applauded but did they really appreciate her in the way I did?

By five o'clock Trixie's dance card was still full, as Umberto had predicted. She limped with a soiled Band-Aid on her heel, looking for a free seat to slip off the pinching shoe (true fact: standing in high heels on a small pedestal is infinitely more tiring than dancing in them). When she spotted the last vacant seat on earth, its neighbor patted invitingly. She hesitated; he re-patted.

She flexed her freed toes. "My feet are killing me," she said. He absorbed this information with a smile. He had seen the news and was intrigued. He asked a few personal questions, to which she replied, "Uh huh." After a while he handed her a coupon. She refused, saying her feet needed a rest; he insisted. She was finally persuaded to dance barefoot.

Her silk top fell easily from her breasts, skidded past her hips, and fell in a rumpled circle around her pink, sweaty toes. She stretched her arms behind her back until her shoulder joints cracked juicily. He blew on her stomach. His eyes traveled over her sinewy nakedness, and her hand instinctively went to the spot where his gaze lingered, the hollow at her groin. When she moved her hand to brush away her bangs, his eyes were lured with it, and he smiled at her amazing blue eyes. Would she like him to rub her burning muscles? Before she answered, he stood and clamped her shoulders, and Trixie, subdued and soothed, let her head hang loosely. He kneaded her damp skin and watched her pupils dart under her fluttering lids, and when the song ended, she opened her eyes and smiled. He surrendered the nightie that had somehow gotten into his lap. He watched while she dressed.

How intrusive it was—that some stranger could . . . She was not some fruit that one could sniff and handle.

"Wanna sit?"

"No, better not."

"Why not?" he asked with a quiet laugh.

"I have to go change," she lied.

"Suit yourself."

Trixie smiled faintly.

"Hey," he said as she turned to walk away. "Sit."

She did.

"Why don't you forget that playboy? He'll never marry you. You'll never get that money." She didn't answer. "I'd marry you. Hey, what about that?"

What would Max think of her sitting with this stranger who shouldn't have meant any more to her than any other stranger she had sat with over the years, but he did. He *was* attractive, and he stared at her not unlike the way Max had stared.

She remained at his table, I believe, not simply because he had paid his ticket but because she was not satisfied with what she had given him. She had danced, yes, but she had only been able to show a small part of herself on that tiny pedestal. She wanted to give him the whole complete picture and *then* go her way. But she didn't have a stage to do it on anymore, only that low pedestal there, eighteen inches off the floor and twenty-four in diameter, a pedestal that wasn't high or removed enough to take her out of his parameters. She wanted her stage back, if only for one more dance, to show this new audience.

"Whew." Dan sat next to me. "They've got another camera crew out there."

"You didn't give another interview?" I hoped.

"Are you kidding? My wife loved having me explain to all her friends and family how 'I really love those girls!' No, this time I held my hat over my face." Dan thought a minute. "Damn, now they've got footage of me looking like some pervert dodging the camera."

"That seems like all we've got today." We looked around at the scratchy group of nervous men.

Dan explained how Simone had seemed so patient. When she asked him what he thought about a woman like Trixie, Dan, who was accurate with descriptions, but slow to invent them, couldn't deliver the sound bite all dim-witted citizens in the midst of crisis seem innately able to do. "She was always grinning," he'd offered, but here the cameraman had run out of film. When he reloaded, Simone asked Dan to repeat. He fumbled, sensing his inadequacy, and said, "I really love those girls." He wanted to explain, but it was a wrap. Simone was already interviewing a protester who said all Dans were scum.

Poor Dan tipped and saluted Ma'am Mary, who was leaving the stage. Then Trixie stepped up to our table.

"Hey, didn't I see you on TV?" asked Trixie.

"Hiya, Trix," said Dan, and they embraced briefly. "Have you seen this?" and he unfolded the evening edition of the *Newgate Say*. Trixie squinted at the two-page article with photos of herself that she hadn't seen in years. CHILD STAR TURNS TRIX. (Tabloid headlines and country and western songs both owe their "wit" to a very dubious species of pun.) Some loser, some trivia nut researcher, had recognized the maiden in *Despair*, as well as the chafed-nose child in the tissue ads and the messy-haired kid in the detangler spots (but not the Porina baby!). The article called Trixie's mom a "stage mother" and accused her of robbing Trixie of her childhood. The writer mentioned Trixie's brief association with the Port City Ballet Company and incorrectly suggested that she was asked to leave because she lacked the talent. Furthermore, we were informed that Miss Nichols, more recently a Northwest Community Center instructor, had been removed from the schedule pending investigation.

"They wouldn't do that. I'm going to call them." She turned to run to the phone but ran into Max instead. He threw another copy of the paper on top of Dan's.

"You've seen it," said Max.

"I've got to call the Community Center."

"I already did; it's true." Max glanced at the table-dancing girls, slithering between customers' knees. "What's this?" asked Max.

Dan cleared his throat.

"What's going on?" Max repeated.

Trixie didn't have an explanation any better than Dan's and sat biting her lip.

Cookie's giggly soprano called out, "Is this the millionaire? Oh, I want one. Trixie where'd you get him?" (Sitting.) "Can I sit?" (Shivering with pleasure.) "Move your skinny bod, Trix." She snuggled against Max's arm.

"Hi there," said Smart seizing his other arm. "Is this your boyfriend?"

"Will you excuse us ladies?" said tactful Max. "We were just going." Max whispered that Belinda was outside clamoring for another interview.

"No," said Trixie. "I don't think I want to give her another interview, maybe somebody else, but Belinda, I don't like what she did to my dancing. She cut it."

"Maybe Simone Lambat will do a better job," I suggested.

"Yeah, maybe," agreed Trixie, brightening.

"And maybe not," said Max. "I think we should get the hell away from reporters, away from this place."

Trixie agreed to go. Max looked at me with a self-satisfied smile. Her retreat would only be temporary. The Playhouse was so changed; she needed time to think. I volunteered to leave too. We said goodbye to Dan and left our coupons with Cookie who, instantly distracted, began counting like King Midas.

We took the back stairs from the dressing room. When we opened the back door, a spotlight was aimed at our faces. Blinded, we shielded our eyes from the stinging light (we weren't hiding, but it looked that way later on TV). Belinda and zealous Gideons surrounded us in the alley. Belinda told Max and Trixie that they owed her an interview. It was *her* story. When Max objected, she took him aside. “Look,” she said, “these other reporters will eat you alive. Don’t trust them. You know me. I’ll give you your fair say.”

“I haven’t got anything to say,” said Max.

“I have,” interrupted Trixie. “Why did you cut my dance scenes?”

“Excuse me?” asked Belinda genuinely confused.

“You cut my dancing. You made it look,” she searched for the word, “trite.”

“I thought you looked sexy,” said Belinda. “We could do it over, but I can’t imagine—”

“That’s right,” I said. “You can’t imagine.”

Suddenly the crowd waxed violent. One of the Gideon Angels demanded of me, “How old are you? Nineteen? Twenty? It’s not worth the money to degrade yourself. What are you going to do in another six, eight years when you start losing your looks?”

“I’m thirty,” I said calmly. Pixies don’t grow old the way you do, silly woman.

Tully accosted Trixie, trying to get her to answer questions, but Max held Trixie’s face against his chest and squeezed through the ring. Tully shouted, “Stop catering to male fantasies.” I grabbed Belinda’s mike and said, “Trixie’d dance for everyone—man or woman, schnauzer, pterodactyl, doesn’t matter.”

Max was pulling my arm. “C’mon,” he said. “Don’t argue.” But they were yelling. Everything was a mess, and they were rough-handling my dove.

Citizens of Gunsmoke! Angels of Gideon! Hold your fire! There are pixies and pucks in that club. There’s a pearl in that oyster, a needle in that haystack, a diamond in that rough. Listen, Angels, I know that when Stacey Smart bends over and reaches between her legs for that money, her fuzzy, meaty lips escape the hem of her panties. I know her upside-down face, cheeks hanging against the hollows of her eyes, is grotesque, but it does no good to try to make her stop. Just laugh at her, laugh. And Ned, oh Ned, I know it was inappropriate that your penis swelled and stiffened to the point that its cap-headed form could be distinguished through your bathing trunks and people laughed at you, but oh, Ned, my Ned, my murderer Ned, why is it so wrong that my mother aroused a moral man?

Anyway, it all doesn't matter. The Cookies and Ma'am Marys only thrive on your opinions. You're bedfellows, you are. Wake up, roll over, scratch and sniff the indolent human sharing an unfair portion of your pillow.

33

On the way to Trixie's apartment, we twisted through obscure alleys and unknown side streets in order to throw off any would-be followers. But when we arrived, the Channel 9 van was already there. "I'm listed," she sighed. Max pulled a U-turn. Trixie braced herself, hands on the dash. I was safely squeezed between bucket seats. Max drove to the parkway. "We're inviting ourselves over to your place, Pixie. Is that okay?" It was splendid by me.

After twenty minutes, Trixie asked Max to pull over at a gas station. As Trixie was getting out of the car, Max tried to grab her hand. "I gotta go."

Max and I waited under the bright island. "Help me out here," he said. "What does she want?"

"Not to run away."

Max reacted with indignant surprise. "From the Playhouse? Why not?"

"She might *move on* easily enough, but she doesn't want to *run away* as if . . ." I bravely tried to clarify the situation by highlighting these subtle shades of meaning, knowing Max would see no practical difference.

"What?"

I struggled. "She isn't sure that you really do know her."

"What? What is it?" he asked, turning red.

"Oh, Max, it's nothing so mysterious," I sighed, having given up the idea that what Trixie found—what I found—so engaging, so enlarging and enlightening about stripping was anything so fantastic at all. Wasn't it actually something basic, something really quite profound in its universal appeal?

"Well, you act like it is." He took me up. "Is it the control that you girls have over the men?"

"Control?" I screeched (the word came as such a shock to me). "What a disgusting idea! Where'd you get it, Max? from TV? Control. I never controlled a soul."

"Hah," yelled Max. He thought he had pierced a hole in the flimsy sack of my argument. "You can enjoy your control without having to admit you have it." Max pushed his face between the seats. An angry knot of flesh formed over his nose bridge.

"I don't want the responsibility. Yuck," I said waving Max's hard face away.

"Well, then what is it?"

"It's being onstage. It's the one place that I'm Pixie."

"Why does she have to be Trixie with her clothes off?"

"She's a stripper, Max." I said, giving up.

"But why at a strip club, Pixie? Couldn't she dance—or strip—somewhere else, without men inviting her for drinks or handing her money? I wonder what's taking her so long."

"Probably putting on her lipstick. Do you want her, Max, to say that the atmosphere of the Playhouse isn't a part of what she liked? Because she's not going to be able to say that."

"Ah, there's the rub," he said with a triumphant flourish. "If I'm it, she shouldn't be interested in seducing other men, right?"

"It happens."

"Then you admit it!" he cried like a prosecuting attorney.

"What's to admit?"

"Well, I don't want her to strip anymore."

"First, she wants to know from you that watching her dance has been one of the most enlightening, not to mention arousing while, yes, troubling, experiences of your life." I pretended to exaggerate for comic effect. "When you saw her onstage you recognized her, gasped, and said, 'Oh! an immortal.'"

"I wouldn't quite put it that way, but I'm here."

"There's something about the Playhouse that she needs, and you're trying to convince her that she doesn't or, failing that, that she shouldn't. I'm telling you that is never going to happen."

"I don't want her to do anything she doesn't want to do."

"So your plan is to change what she wants. I'm telling you it won't happen. I know. My mother liked frolicking nude in front of hundreds of lecherous men, and for the life of her she couldn't see the harm in it. But she would have sacrificed it for him."

"No man wants to know it's a sacrifice for his girl to stop flashing her breasts at men she doesn't know."

"Well, it is. Sorry, Max. Why don't you just accept this concession if she offers it?"

"She won't." Max rested his case with a finality that made me shiver. I had nothing to say to this.

"It's really a question of formal freedom then, isn't it? Detachment," he said, coming uncomfortably close to our truth. "But that's not real freedom."

I almost felt sorry.

Presently, he added, "Your father, he wanted your mom to stop?"

"He left her, Max."

"Pix, see that car?" A black car-service sedan at a neighboring pump had been idling there throughout our conversation and hadn't gotten gas.

"Let's see if he follows when we go," I advised calmly.

After Trixie finally returned, offering gum and beef jerky, we left the sedan behind. But soon thereafter Max spotted the black ghost in his rearview mirror keeping an even pace behind us. He cautiously mentioned it to Trixie. "Where?" she twisted in her seat. "Oh, him, yeah."

"Don't look," scolded Max.

"Change lanes and see if he follows," I suggested. We went left; the car went left. We switched back to the right lane; the black sedan followed. We slowed down to thirty, and the car mimicked our speed.

"Not very subtle, are they?"

"What are we gonna do?" cried Trixie.

Frustrated, Max threatened to stop the car, yank them out of their car, and ask them what the hell they wanted.

We were approaching my exit. "We don't want to lead them to Pixie's," said Trixie.

"Let's pull over right now." Max turned the wheel sharply and drove on the grassy shoulder; astonished grasshoppers flew from our path. The black car followed, rocking and pitching, and came to a stop behind us. Nothing happened. "Get down," ordered Max. Trixie ducked, and I got down behind the seats. We heard the thud of a heavy door. Max narrated, "A man, dark suit, coming this way, unbuttoning his jacket."

An enormous belly and tie appeared in the driver's side window. "Beatrice Nichols?" The man bent to look in the window (round face, bulging eyes, more hair in his nose and ears than on his head).

"What do you want?" demanded Max, rolling down his window.

"To talk to the Porina baby" (friendly, nonthreatening). "You don't remember me, do you, Trixie?" Trixie leaned over Max's lap, looked up at her inquisitor. "Who's been signing your paychecks for the past twenty-four years?"

"Mr. Porina?" (Meekly optimistic).

"It's Chuck, you know that. It's been what? Ten years? I had more hair back then."

"When Mom and I visited the city. I was twelve."

"Trixie?" inquired Max.

"This is Mr. Porina, Porina baby foods. Mr. Porina, this is Max Price, and that's Pixie back there" (grin, rapid wave).

"What can we do for you, Mr. Porina?" asked Max persistently suspicious.

"I'd like to talk about this media mess."

"Nobody's said anything about Porina," said Trixie.

"Not yet" (looking around). "Say, where're you folks headed? I wouldn't mind a quiet talk." Trixie looked at me for consent, and I invited the baby food magnate over to my place.

Max and Mr. Porina, who resembled a gigantic infant, squeezed into my love seat, while Trixie and I sat Indian-style on my rag rug.

"You see," Mr. Porina said, putting down the bouquet for which he'd heartily thanked me. "We could blow millions on PR costs. We don't want to change the labels. We've got too much invested in that face of yours, kid."

"Exactly what do you want her to do?" asked Max.

"Well, we've got the best PR people on this. They say give the tabloids an ending to satisfy their audience, and they'll close the chapter. If we don't, they'll keep digging and eventually some weirdo with thick glasses will discover the Porina baby's identity. Look how quickly they recognized you from that obscure film and those ancient ads."

"What do the PR people suggest?" asked Max.

"Well first, Trixie, you've got to go on TV and renounce the strip club business." Trixie protested, but Porina continued. "Now, just wait a minute. I know what you're going to say, but you've got to announce that you're quitting, retiring, giving up, whatever you want to call it. They won't be as interested in you if they can't film you naked. Then—now listen up, Max, this involves you—you can do one of two things: either announce that you and your wife are reconciled or that you and Trixie are engaged. Give them a sense of what my PR people call 'closure.' You don't have to do either. Simply say it."

Trixie sat quietly on the couch, eyes vacant. Max was notably cheered that he had found support in an unexpected quarter. "I think he's got a point, Honey. I will buy you a ring. We'll hold hands on the evening news."

"And if I were you, Max, I'd dispose of that suit with your wife. Give her half of everything. She'll take it."

"I've already got my attorneys preparing the papers."

"I'm not going to renounce dancing," said Trixie quietly.

"Well, all I can do is ask. We're depending on you. What mother is going to buy her kid baby food with a stripper on the label?"

"Change the labels."

"Besides the expense, it would be a major embarrassment for the company—we'll do it if necessary, but we'll never regain our quality image if we lose Trixie's pretty blue eyes. Well, like I said," (hands on knees rising) "all I can do is ask. Good luck, Trixie." He kissed the top of her head. "Good meeting you, Max. Hey, I don't suppose a token of gratitude would impress you millionaires?"

"No, it wouldn't," said Max.

"All right then. Much obliged, Pixie." He stopped in the doorway. "Oh, by the way, *Inside Story* is featuring Fancy Pants there at seven thirty. If I were you, I'd take a look."

34

IN THE LATEST EDITION of *Inside Story,* Simone told the sad story of a tragic child star, Hollywood offering nothing now that she was grown. Trixie had failed to live up to parental expectations, failed as an actress, failed as a ballet dancer, failed as a model, and ended up teaching aerobics at a public gym. Simone tried to explain on Trixie's behalf that being a single girl in the city is difficult. Trixie had probably answered a misleading ad in a disreputable paper. She probably didn't want to sell her naked body to anyone with the price of admission, but she did it, because she needed the money. One had to feel sorry for Trixie, said Simone. But that's only part of what made Trixie choose the life she did. For this special edition, *Inside Story* interviewed nationally renowned child psychologist, Dr. Peter Cox.

The doctor sat behind his desk, behind him leather-bound books. "While I'm not familiar with the details of Miss Nichols's case, I have treated hundreds of child stars with similar dysfunctions."

"Could you explain?"

"The typical child star has one parent, usually the mother, and often out of economic necessity, she puts her daughter to work, and in this society, modeling or acting is the only form of employment available to youngsters."

Simone nods.

"Mother and daughter, having been rejected by the father, crave male attention. In Miss Nichols's case, she may have received a lot of positive attention from strange men when she was younger. What was the actor's name in *Despair*?"

"Rodrick Timber," informed Simone.

"Oh, yes, well of course, a very domineering masculine influence there. Her condition can lead to a dysfunction known as exhibitionism."

"Exhibitionism?"

"Yes, it's the tendency to expose the parts of one's body that are conventionally concealed, especially in seeking sexual stimulation or gratification." The doctor folded his hands.

"And you think Beatrice Nichols is an exhibitionist?"

"That would be my professional opinion, yes."

Next Simone, clad in the reporter uniform, a raincoat, stood in a sunny park. "Tully Gideon, of the Gideon Angels, a well-known women's right activist and honored leader in the feminist community, had this to say."

Tully, wearing the traditional Gideon Angel cap, sat in the same park, with Simone's mike pointed at her mouth. Behind her, brightly clothed kids swung on the monkey bars. She narrowed her brows and spoke: "I feel sorry for women like Trixie. Our group's goal is to educate the people involved in the sex industry. The women often don't realize they're being abused, and the men don't think they're degrading women . . ."

Tully had more to say, but Trixie turned off the set and picked up the phone to call *Inside Story*. "I'll demand longer airtime than I got last time. I won't let them edit me. I'll take charge of the direction. I'll make them show what it's really like to dance at the Playhouse."

"Trixie, once they get you on film they can do whateverthehell they like with you. That's what the tabloids do," said Max.

Trixie, ignoring Max's plea, called *Inside Story*. Simone Lambat was out in the field, but Trixie was put through to Marcel, her boss. Marcel was anxious to speak with Trixie. He had asked Simone to interview her, but Simone was starting to let her feminist ideas ruin his show. She said she did not want to give that "trollop" any more airtime. Marcel felt obliged to exercise his power. Simone would do the interview or else lose her job.

"Anything you want," said Marcel when Trixie asked if she could have full artistic control over the final version.

"I choose the music—no voice-overs when I'm on," she added.

"You got it," he said. He had Simone on another line. "She'll do it. I'll make her."

When Trixie hung up, the phone instantly rang. "Simone Lambat is here." It was Umberto's voice. "Do another interview, Trix, please," he said. "It's such good publicity for the cabaret. Your regulars miss you. I'll let you use the stage. The big one."

"Tell her I'll be there in an hour."

35

THE LOVERS WERE SILENT on the drive back into the city. Trixie spent the forty minutes rubbing her temples. Max was silent. I, too, was quietly reflecting. I studied the dust cloud we had kicked up these past few months: Trixie's click-clackety step in the corridor, Audrey's too-loud laugh, Rosamund's hot tears. At the Playhouse, people were waiting in hate with their signs and their own troubles.

I have lived a thousand years since my mother and I met Ned that Sunday afternoon, and no, I have not grown cynical. I was born a pixie, and every morning of my life I have tried to collect the drops of goodwill that would have otherwise burned off in the noonday sun, and I—Ah, to hell with it.

I was tired. Trixie was heading back to the Playhouse. Why? Because despite its recent degradation, it was still the best place for Trixie to do what she did. Maybe it was even better now, I reflected. After all, "she liked that kind of thing," as that newscaster had so correctly, if not elegantly, put it on day one. She liked it. She could easily imagine what they were thinking, the hundreds—no, I'm sure it's thousands by now—of pondering impatient men who knew her frequently, habitually, intimately, if from afar (eighteen inches or less), who knew that her areolae were exactly the same shade of faded brick as her lips and could recognize her in the dark by the sesame-seed smell of her flesh; that is, she could easily have imagined if she had cared: for she was too busy thinking her own thoughts. *She liked that kind of thing.* The perfect opportunity had presented itself only once. But her one encounter with Max in the champagne room would have given her enough material to last her the rest of a long and pleasurable fantasy life. She liked that kind of thing. All this was finally beginning to dawn on Max, and he was feeling, I think, that glutted feeling of postcoital revulsion, as if he had found grit and gristle mixed with his rich cream and berries.

Softly now, we are treading on dangerous ground. People throw tomatoes and shoot mothers because of what I'm about to acknowledge and applaud. Yes, despite the beauty and the poetry and all that bunk, the way the Playhouse girls dance is undeniably obscene. Did I mention that the sergeant described Trixie as "the one who sometimes dances with her hand pressed between her legs like she needs to take a tinkle"? Yes, she does that, or did that rather, but her bladder was not what prompted her. And there was that way she stuck her finger in her belly button and eyed the audience with a suggestively quirky grin. Yes, I think I have mentioned that. Do you know how many people tried to grab her by the arm to inform her, as if she didn't know, that she was provocative yet innocent? Do you know how many men thought that they were the only ones that recognized her pornographic appeal? I cannot count. Of course, my darling was modestly aware, and so was I, but I have not dwelt on explicit sexuality because, well, I took it for granted. But now I think it's time to make it clear. If this sounds like an admission, it is. Yes, Gideon Angels, you were right, in your own way. Yes, Ned, you had your point. We were all, indeed, a little guilty of being obscene. I don't mind the label if one considers the etymology of the word: "offstage"—if you remember, linguistics was a favorite subject of mine in college. And so, yes, we publicly displayed private feelings. We did things in front of everybody that few people have the confidence or courage to do when absolutely alone. I confess. Nevertheless, we at the Playhouse had elected prefigleaf felicity, exempt from shame.

When we arrived at the Playhouse, Trixie and I got out, but Max remained in the car. The police had barricaded off the sidewalk immediately around the club. The protesters had been rounded up and contained one hundred feet from the entrance. The familiar blue-eyed sergeant, leaning on a sawhorse, waved. Apparently, the protesters had been blocking traffic. The *Inside Story* van was parked in front. The music was quite loud on the street although the door was closed.

Simone Lambat waddled over to our car, toting various bags and notebooks. Trixie got out and introduced herself. Simone said nothing, but her eyes traveled up and down Trixie's body while her upper lip expressed disgust.

"I'm Ken, I'm Bob," said her two-man crew, who both shook Trixie's hand at once, smiling kindly.

Simone shot them a glance that told them to keep their places. "Let's make this interview short. Just explain why you ended up working as a stripper, that sort of thing. Like, was it the money, or feelings of inadequacy, or what?"

"I'm not here to be interviewed," Trixie said defiantly. "I'm here to dance."

Simone laughed, "Sorry, I'm not filming *that*. I didn't go into journalism to add to the objectification of women."

"Why not?" she asked pitifully.

"I'm sorry you have to ask," said Simone.

"There's nothing wrong!" cried Trixie, feeling her words betray her, thinking perhaps that, in a sense, there was, particularly as far as Max was concerned—but still, she faltered. "There's nothing wrong with it." But what did she mean by "it"? Merely dancing without clothes? Or the fact that she regularly—consciously or unconsciously, it matters little—aroused forty strong men en masse?

"It's disgusting," Simone laughed and then seemed shocked when Trixie slowly knelt on the pavement, gasping into her hands. I wasn't surprised: the recent banquet of strange intimacy in the amended Playhouse, Mr. Porina's hardly concealed disapproval, the Gideon Angels' hatred in place of empathy—all of this combined must have been overwhelming.

"Shh, Trix," I whispered into her ear. There I was again, kissing a moist neck, wrapping my devotion around her shoulders like a ratty old shawl.

Simone stood with crossed arms looking down on us. "I'll be in the dressing room," she said with the confidence she would get what she wanted from Trixie.

Deserted on the curb, Trixie finally began to sob out loud. I was suddenly overcome with an image of my mother crying like that—completely baffled, furious. And, my God, they were both so beautiful.

Simone doubled back. "Say," she said to me, "aren't you the daughter of that murdered prostitute? You know you don't have to do this," Simone went on. "You could get a job anywhere, these days. Why?"

I began to shake. We could hear the not-so-distant jeering of the protesters down the street.

"Shut up!" screamed Trixie, with such hysterics that even I was frightened. Simone took a cautious step toward Trixie. "Leave me alone!" Trixie snapped. It was as if Simone had been talking about her, not my mother. Trixie took it all on herself.

Simone retreated inside the Playhouse and never actually saw what came next. She only knew that moments later Trix was dead. I've allowed her to suffer guilt all this time. But truth be told, Simone, you set the tone with your mockery and repugnance, that's all. Go your way now; I'm done with you.

Ah, my head hurts. I feel his approach.

Gradually Trixie's spasms quieted. She looked for something to wipe her nose. I got a tissue from the car. She did nothing for a long time, except that she sighed and stared blankly at the curb. Meanwhile, Max was still in the car parked across the street. His face was turned away from me, but I could see his reflection in the rearview mirror. He was annoyed. His face told me he was irritated by Trixie's outburst. Not upset, not sad, not concerned, only annoyed, maybe even a little bored.

Faced with a little criticism about Mom's meretricious charms, my father had deserted his own feelings. So, I hated Max a little when I realized what he was about to do to Trixie. Trixie looked at him. "What is it?"

He slowly got out of the car, crossed the street, and loomed over her. "Why are you so upset?" His lips barely moved as he spoke in a tired, fixed tone.

Hiding her face under her long black hair, she said in a hoarse whisper, "It's not just the Playhouse; it's really the principle of the thing."

His dark eyes looked at her without feeling. She stood up and looked directly in his face, unashamed now of her inflamed eyes. She wanted to hate his words, but how could she hate him with his petulant lips, stiff posture, big hands? She placed an unwanted hand on his forearm. He clasped it halfheartedly then let it drop. Specks of warm rain started to mist his hair.

"Are you ashamed of me?" Her voice broke. Wet strands of hair stuck to her cheek. Max tried to remove them. She made an aggravated wave at his hand and stepped two steps left and back.

Sound of his dry lips parting, "It's an ugly place, and those are ugly people in there."

She laughed and started toward the club. "You didn't think it was ugly."

"I didn't realize. I was in a desperate situation. I wasn't thinking. Don't go in there," he warned. "If you do—" They stopped when they reached the curb.

She looked at the lapel of his coat and wanted to rest her cheek against the soft camel hair. She stroked it warily. Oh, how I saw that Max could have had her sympathy if he had only taken it. One charitable word, a faint knowing smile, would have done it, but he didn't comprehend his effect. If he had he wouldn't have stupidly tried instead to be stern. He stooped, conclusively, to that now. He received her gesture with absolute coldness, blinking rapidly three times like an automaton. She withdrew her hand. "If I do," she said, "I'll do what I do. I'll show you what they think of me." It was awkward; it was so awkward that she did not put her arms around him. "You seem to have forgotten, Max, what you know. C'mon, let's go inside."

"It's not like stripping is art or anything," he called after her. "I fell in love with you *after* I got to know you. Honestly, I didn't think you were really that great at first. I thought the strip club scene was offensive, if you want to know what I truly think."

Trixie, pausing, articulated her confusion by hesitating there on the curb, by raising her hand to push back her hair from her eyes. I know that she might have quit stripping easily enough, gone off to live happily ever after with Max, but only on the one condition that she be allowed to *have been* a beautiful lost thing, a lonely sad little stripper, peculiarly erotic and fey. But he took that away from her. She died humiliated.

I have had a lot of time to think about what happened next. I've done little else in that past—what is it?—ten days or so, and I think I do know what happened to her as she stood there thinking, not thinking. She fell out of love. You see, she had always needed the Playhouse like a faith needs a doubt, as the song says. She'd thought Max understood.

I could see that, at a stroke, he had obliterated the basis on which she had constructed their happiness. The recognition had all seemed so real. She had thought, we all had thought, that her high-heeled soul had convinced Max, the only audience who really mattered. Max's love had been proof that she was sound. But now he claimed her dancing meant nothing to him. He was disgusted and bored.

She was shaking. Was she wrong? Was she insane? The way she felt when dancing, as if all the king's hounds had been let loose. Was stripping really only absurd and ugly? In front of everybody? If Max had not understood, then no one had and there was simply no point to anything. Maybe she wasn't special, after all; maybe she was merely common.

Suddenly it started to pour. "Let's get out of the rain," Max suggested. Trixie turned toward the XJS, an unthinking reflex. I could see she didn't want to go with him. As I remember this scene now I am reminded of the other time, the night—she had been only seventeen—of the canceled performance. Was she wrong? No, they were, and she hated them.

I saw Max sigh with relief at her choice of direction. He touched her back as if feeling her would confirm her loyalty (she winced). But yes, she was going back to the car, back to the car. He closed his eyes, thankful, calmed. I realized his heartlessness hid mere jealously. He had been scared, that's all. For a moment I thought we might get through this mess.

But Trixie did not see all this in Max's face. Her back was turned. She was about to cross the street, but a bus pulled up to let passengers off. She stepped off the curb. Max held her elbow to pull her back. She resisted. She looked at her silk blouse as if vaguely concerned that the rain would ruin it if she waited—an irrelevant detail that I'm sure added to her frustration and confusion. It was becoming even more transparent in the rain, sticking to her skin. She started again for to the car. Max grabbed her, "Would you just wait for the bus to go?"

"My shirt," she yelled. "It's raining."

"Damn that shirt. I'll buy you real clothes."

She struggled out of her blouse and threw it at him. She stood there in the rain, damp hair clinging like black vines to her chest and arms. She seemed especially thin and wasted on the street like that. Then she bolted around the bus down Newgate Avenue. At the rear of the XJS, her feet slipped and she landed on her hip. Awful comedy, my dear.

"Move!" cried Max from the curb, starting. Trixie looked at a speeding red car, and cried in the negative, not at the driver but, I think, at herself for not moving.

My mother didn't move; she could have run or left town or repented or married, but she didn't. And I always suspected that she felt a little satisfaction, as she lay dying in the bright, hot dust, knowing that my dad's stomach would contract when he got the news. Trixie left us impenitent like the thief on the third cross, recalcitrant and embittered. I'd always had a reluctant admiration for that man; now I knew why.

After impact, the red car skidded against the curb and stopped. The driver's door was flung open by a red-elbowed arm, and flopped shut again. Again the hairy arm propped the door open. A man unfolded himself from behind the wheel. The driver of the Miata was an avuncular, red-eared, stout tourist from the Southeast. He had no connection with Price Mazdatown; the car had been purchased back home.

Now the driver, joining Max next to Trixie's body, scratched the back of his meaty neck and waited, turning this way and that, for the authorities to come (the blue-eyed sergeant was already jogging toward us in slow motion). Inside the cabaret, *One Hundred and One Dance Greats* had stopped. Umberto stood on the damp pavement shivering.

The record had stopped, but I heard music. I heard the song that had eluded me for twenty-six years, as clearly as on that night, a voice screaming in key. It got louder and made me prickly as I walked toward the cabaret where my audience waited—Oh Simone, you brought out your cameras and your lights? That's right, make them brighter. Onstage, naked, I am myself. This is what I am, shedding my panties and shoes, dancing; I am a mad, bad, bad pixie. The audience recognizes me, you know. They can tell.

36

THE GIRLIE PLAYHOUSE HAS closed. The sign has been removed and the stage dismantled, and the real estate agent doesn't tell prospective buyers, who might possibly like to open an insurance firm or art school, what had gone on in there before.

Calvin has not come yet, but I believe he is on his way. He's probably sitting astride a Jersey barrier by his old disabled car as it violently spews steam. The girls have all scattered. Rosamund strokes Max's arm as they walk from the grave.

I am still dancing down the center of a long winding dark country road, headlights rushing by on either side; speeding cars streak past, one after the other. Frustrated, I dance on the double yellow lines trying desperately to ignore those cars. They mean nothing to me, nothing. With my eyes on the blueblack horizon, with a faraway smile I dance, damn it. And I will dance all the days of my life unless, finally, one hard-driving pair of lights is reflected in my eyes.

Other Heresy Press Titles

Fiction:

Nothing Sacred: Outspoken Voices in Contemporary Fiction edited by Bernard Schweizer and James Morrow

Deadpan by Richard Walter

Animal by Alan Fishbone

Unsettled States by Tom Casey

Devil Take It by Daniel Debs Nossiter

Alice, or The Wild Girl by Michael R. Liska

The Hermit by Katerina Grishakova

Tomorrow, the War by Max Watman

Nonfiction:

The War on Words: 10Arguments Against Free Speech—And Why They Fail by Greg Lukianoff and Nadine Strossen

Half-Jew—Full Life: The Unlikely Journey of a Voluntary Jew from Nazi Persecution to the American Dream by Georgette Bennett

Viewpoint Diversity: What It Is, Why We Need It, and How to Get It edited by John Tomasi and Bernard Schweizer

Mission Statement

Heresy Press Promotes freedom, honesty, openness, dissent, and real diversity in all of its manifestations. We discourage authors from descending into self-censorship, we don't blink at alleged acts of cultural appropriation, and we won't pander to the presumed sensitivities of hypothetical readers. We also don't judge works based on the author's age, gender identity, racial affiliation, political orientation, culture, religion, non-religion, or cancellation status. Heresy Press's ultimate commitment is to enduring quality standards, i.e., literary merit, originality, relevance, courage, humor, and aesthetic appeal.

Newsletter

Don't miss the Heresy Press Newsletter:
https://heresy-press.com/newsletter